Bride of Promise

V. J. Shaw

PublishAmerica
Baltimore

© 2007 by V. J. Shaw.
All rights reserved. No part of this book may be reproduced, stored in a retrieval system or transmitted in any form or by any means without the prior written permission of the publishers, except by a reviewer who may quote brief passages in a review to be printed in a newspaper, magazine or journal.

First printing

All characters appearing in this work are fictitious. Any resemblance to real persons, living or dead, is purely coincidental.

ISBN: 1-4137-8079-2
PUBLISHED BY PUBLISHAMERICA, LLLP
www.publishamerica.com
Baltimore

Printed in the United States of America

Dedicated to my two wonderfully productive girls,
lovely reasons for believing in romance!

Table of Contents

CHAPTER 1: Fire and Fury 7
CHAPTER 2: Secrecy and Seclusion 23
CHAPTER 3: Mansion Management 30
CHAPTER 4: The Church Soloist 45
CHAPTER 5: Sacrifice of Life and Limb 55
CHAPTER 6: To Shoot or Not to Shoot 66
CHAPTER 7: A Captain's Wishes 74
CHAPTER 8: Alone Together 84
CHAPTER 9: Men, Machinery and Manure 101
CHAPTER 10: Nepotism in Charge 111
CHAPTER 11: The Tummy Tilts East 128
CHAPTER 12: Three Weddings to Go 149
CHAPTER 13: Arrive, Celebrate, Leave 161
CHAPTER 14: Detectives to the Rescue 169
CHAPTER 15: Confrontation or Duel? 178
CHAPTER 16: Olive Branch Picnic 193

CHAPTER 1:
Fire and Fury

If soft fluffy evenings were graded, then this one drifting down on Boston's lantern hazy streets could vie for valedictorian. Smiling blue-eyed, twenty-one-year-old Bethany, batting long thick lashes, delighted in a game of toss-back with voluminous snowflakes. Quickly accumulating beneath pointed toes and slippery heels, she hurried through the shadowy night to her now presumed sleeping household. Although marveling over a wondrously magical Christmas Eve, the huge moisture laden snowflakes also numbed the nose and extremities. Thinly shod was hardly a vanity prerequisite to her dainty footsteps. Mostly it indicated her family's ill preparation for a long Northeastern winter.

At the last moment she'd impulsively decided to attend prayer service. So her five-month-old baby's wash still sat soaking on the hearth. *I must finish up tonight even if Jacob scolds me for coming to bed after midnight, there weren't enough diapers for tomorrow.* And *never* would she deliberately desecrate the Lord's own birthday. Tomorrow might be just another day to him, but it loomed sacred to her.

They would, however, enjoy the holiday from work and a special meal. Lord willing, maybe her thin wiry husband would even inquire about "other" Christmas celebrations? Since marrying Jacob Clark, with his luxuriant brown curly hair and mustache, she cherished her faith more devoutly than she ever imagined possible. Every moment spent in the well-appointed church, stuffy and pompous or not, filled a need that resounded throughout her being.

Although she loved Jacob dearly, felt cherished in return, and had no desire to change that happy situation, her past sin, of knowingly marrying an unbeliever, remained unchanged. God's mercy and forgiveness were always available she knew firsthand, but Jacob's parents' lack of religious devotion gave her no quarter. Shoved to the brink of hatred when they'd eloped, an unbridgeable chasm widened daily between themselves and the newlyweds.

Smiling with pure joy that she should still consider herself a newlywed, she hastened her now lagging pace so she'd the sooner be snuggled warmly beside Jacob in bed. What a vexation, to bring such torment between him and his parents! Yes, she'd deliberately chosen a rough row to hoe, but had never imagined it hurting Jacob (and certainly no one besides herself.) In retrospect, she acknowledged she'd been entirely too self-absorbed and self-centered to consider anything but her own troubles.

As hard as working in the mills had been, either emotionally or physically, it drained her more trying to valiantly make this up to him. Nothing was ever enough, maybe because she fought a spiritual battle? Or, maybe having the baby, being so tired all the time, she reasoned, made it seem more ominous than it really was? Regardless, she vowed, she'd continue to bring Christianity into their home—by action, deed, love and more visible devotion.

If only born ugly or straight figured, this wrong choice might never have happened. But, there was nothing she could do to change flawless skin, high coloring, black wavy hair that curled into attractive ringlets in the summer heat, nor womanly curves that bordered on voluptuous (and always attracted the worst sort.) Ugly may be unjust, but startling beauty that turned heads wherever she went endangered her person. As a result, Bethany practically hibernated, especially in summer, going out only when basic needs demanded. Hiding shyly behind her deep shovel bonnet, she excluded everything except church attendance (once again her regular habit as before her confinement) or the market. Lately though, tending the baby had become such a large part of her life, she thought less about it. Still, Bethany needed faith to help her cope and embrace life's challenges, including fervent prayers for Jacob.

BRIDE OF PROMISE

Her radiance, quickness to smile with naturally upturned lips, and outgoing love of life had endeared her to a few select friends, and that had to be enough for now. She slightly envied carefree Tilly and her mom. She'd just left them at the door of a party to which she wasn't invited. By now they must be comfortably warm and enjoying themselves immensely.

Enough of this penance, she scolded herself. *Pay attention!* Quickening strides were more than the slippery stuff allowed. Twice she'd skidded to a near fall, once swinging into and her full skirt swinging around a just caught lamppost. Sighting the final corner downward, before the long hill climb upward, she noticed a heavy smell of smoke. Not a new or strange odor in Boston's 1842 late December. It just was very strong, probably due to the lack of wind? Or, she concluded, maybe Christmas gifts of cast iron stoves? (Folks not yet accustomed to the draft mechanisms?) How her glances had longed over both a double layer Shaker heater and an ornate Bangor cook stove in a store window right before church. But she knew better than to linger long. Poverty was doing without basic needs, she reminded herself. Being poor (as she and Jacob were) meant just waiting, for what they considered wants, until God, in His infinite kindness, decided to bless them.

(Or, until Jacob's mother paid her son what he was worth, she second opinioned.) Better yet, if Joseph would face facts, demand a fair wage, or else change jobs. Heir or not, she had to bite her tongue when their "unapproved" marriage became the reason his mother cut his wages back to no more than a clerk at her fabric and notions counter. Unfortunately, the same marriage ostracized her from many church members.

Maybe bad drafts were not the cause, though, was that *haze* at the end of the street?! "Oh, Lord," she groaned, "let it just be snow laden lamplight!" Each chilly step nearer drove Bethany's thermometer heart higher. Suddenly prayers swept silently upward, *Heavenly Father, keep Jacob and little Josiah safe; please…keep our home safe!* Hardly their home in the possession sense, but the rent was all they could afford. A tenement building like she'd always known since leaving the farm, still it was a nice friendly neighborhood where she mostly felt safe.

Suddenly she hung her head with fresh remorse and contrition. *I really must keep reminding myself to be less self-centered.* (She hadn't once thought to pray for the neighbors!) As a postscript she added, *And the Cullens, and the Petersons, and the McDuffs, and the nice couple who just got married, Tilly and her mom's place, and…*

Turning the corner her eyes, thoughts and prayers mired into wretched worst fear paralysis. Beyond the hill, just barely visible against the blackness of the night, was a billowing gray that flung flashes of orange against the windows. Forgetting all that was perilous to bodily injury, she flung herself forward until gasping, startling the few who half peered and poked out windows (also aware of the thick smell of smoke.)

"Fire! Fire!" roared from an open window half a block beyond her. An enormous man, with red hair, suspenders and a white bowl pipe clenched in his large teeth, disappeared for just seconds before returning to pound a washtub with a stove poker, just as Bethany was passing beneath!

A further disjointed orchestra sounded within each house she passed. Doors banged, windows flew up, then down, thuds from feet jerking into boots, adults rousting children from sleep, and jolted articles hastily assembled. Hubbub emanated from within and without. Stair steps pounded as doorways spilled humanity; frantic voices shouted as orders were flung into the cauldron of panic. Soon she shared the street with a deluge of frightened inhabitants.

Floundering through, around, and between, Bethany still had blocks of uphill climb to go. Why couldn't she have stayed home? She hadn't planned to go out, why didn't she just finish the wash? With each step, dark eyelashes now fought smaller flakes, her mind chanting a recurring demonic song, *it collapsed again, crashed again, spilled out again…*

In an effort to minimize sideways resistance, hands and the small Bible with its metal clasp clenched in front of her throat. Nostrils and windpipe stung with an acrid stench, but all she wanted was to stuff her hands into her ears to block the preying demonic chant. (Although, with a shovel bonnet of gray wool surrounding a thick scarf, any further muffling appeared purely imaginary.)

"Mrs. Clark!" shrieked a short cloaked, gray-haired woman. Bethany refused to be detained so jerked ahead of a small woman and baby. She had to get to *her* child, didn't she? And Jacob would want to help, not be saddled with Josiah? All the women and children hurried down the street as most men swarmed up; she was like a salmon fighting surging currents. "I *must* know they're alright too." She mindlessly swallowed the ever-enlarging lump in her raw throat. Ignoring the painful stitch in her side, she elbowed further.

Finally she crested the hill. No longer could prayer avail for their two small rooms and loft. Utter futility evidenced before her. Smoke billowed from their address; fire shot upward as it shattered the windows of their apartment only. She knew the bottom two apartments' occupants were away visiting family, not only because of the abnormal quiet, but because their apartment was so much colder. (Heat from below usually benefited their feet. Today the cold lay at least a foot deep, the layer of chill hampering tasks until she'd felt like an icicle.)

In the distance resounded the clanging of a fire company. Everyone hurtled to the sidewalk, huddling. Her way impossibly barricaded, until the charging white steeds' heavy bodies and dangerous hooves passed, the crowd released its abated breath into the street once more. Dazed, she resumed the pushing squeezing quest.

"Grab her, George!" That shriek seemed somehow familiar yet hollow. *Male or female?* She couldn't tell, didn't know why she needed to or why it had caught her attention. Why *had* she allowed it to break her stride? Just as she edged between two black coated men, she was caught in an iron bear hug.

Muffled behind her flared hat she heard, "Ya can't git any closer, Missus Clark, 'nd ya shouldn't need ta. Gotta keep outta the way o' the horses, ya'll never know when 'e' kin bolt."

Wildly her eyes turned, then upward to her huge captor. "Mr. Cullens, sir, you...do you...have you seen them, Jacob, and my baby, Josiah?!"

William Cullens let her go slowly; his thick licked lips feigned to either eat the top or the bottom one. Finally, he just shook his head. "But," he brightened, "I's just cum 'ome meself, no way of knowin' now, eh? E's probably right t'round da corner!" Bethany recoiled from the alcoholic evidence of his former whereabouts. Then from the fact that he had presumed to embrace her, Jacob's wife! And, further, that she had not instantly reprimanded him! And, worst, how could he be so cheerful in the midst of such dreadful circumstances? (Must he be presumed entirely heartless?)

"Beth, Beth!" cried an out-of-breath woman behind them. Leaned in half to glimpse past Mr. Cullens' bulk, she saw Mary Lou Cullens shuttling her small bob of a form through the mob. "Ah, William," she collapsed upon them, grabbing an arm of each, "t'ank heavens yer 'ome! E's beginning ta worry."

"Oh, sha, sha, woman. Na don't ah always cum home?" William blurted indignantly.

"Aye!" Her skinny, mob-capped and moth ridden shawl wrapped frame drew up to meet his wide girth, her pinched mouth grim. "And usually wid a pint or two in yer fist, as well. Or, did ya imbibe all yer pay afore ya thought of 'at? Ah think," she glared, "from ta smell of ya, ya'd best get well back frum da fire line!"

"Now, Mum…" His scraggly mouse gray head shifted bloodshot eyes to wide booted feet, pleading with stolen glances and sad puppy repentance.

"I'm not yer mudder. Nor will I be wiping yer sniveling nose when ya lose yer job, nor your hat, nor your coat. And if the landlord loses 'is house, 'e's well shut of us, so it's a comfort iffn it comes to it! Com'on, Beth," she banded skinny arms around her, "ya be going to Sarah Townsend's. And, *you*, William Cullens," she irked, "ya kin hope to find yer own place ta save—as tho' I'd know anyone'd 'ave ya! And, see ya tell mister where I've taken 'er, ya hear?"

Swept up in Mary Lou Cullens' persuasive rocking side to side stride, Bethany both marveled and feared the tiny-framed lady. Who would think, as short as she, that Beth could be propelled with such gripping strength? Though, one needed to be strong to put up with the likes of Mr. Cullens she rued. Well was it known that she, not Mr. Cullens, who's own strong back put the bacon on the table, so to speak, not that they ever afforded such luxury as good slabs of bacon on her char woman's pitiful pay.

"Mrs. Cullens, please!" she wailed with all her protesting twisting energy. "I've got to know if Jacob and Josiah are alright!" She flailed and tugged, but Mrs. Cullens had been known to commandeer full-grown sons. Resisting her determined efforts could better be spent holding back the tide.

"I's already sent me Thad ta check," she confided along with a severe shake. "Ya've walked over 'alf of Boston to that church yer so fond of, and ya's na got to be chilled to the bone. I don't like these 'ere winters any better than me hears yer be doing yerself. When me Thad finds 'em, 'e'll bring 'em to the Townsends'."

It was useless to argue. Not only for the small dynamo's sheer force, but also for the evidence she'd seen. If they were out of the burning house, she wasn't helping them by filling her lungs up with soot and smoke. And, if they weren't…well, no one could help them…now. She could only wait. Hopefully, it wouldn't be…long…until she were held safe in her loving Jacob's arms, clutching her dark Josiah's hungry round body again. Demons accused her mental meanderings throughout the long walk to the Townsends…*you said it…shouldn't have married…wasn't enough…should never forgive your sin…serve you right…*

The Townsends' home was so many blocks away that after slogging one weary demon taunting foot ahead of the other for nearly a mile, it actually seemed normal that the Townsends should invite them in like old friends. Only after thawing out considerably did it strike the disconsolate Bethany as a terrible imposition. "Oh, Mrs. Cullens," she suddenly burst out sobbing beside the Townsends' cheery cast iron fireplace, "I've been such a poor, pitiful example…of a what a Christian woman should be…complaining about the cold when I've everything to be grateful for!"

"Now, dearie," Mary Lou Cullens soothed her work chapped fingers over Bethany's similar clasped hands, "we's all a need to complain about some'in' now 'n' agin. Yer no different frum meself. Ya's just worried, as 'r' the lot of us. Ya be praying now that the storm don' kick up a wind. Staying calm as it tis, a fire'd be out afur ya knows it." Her patting and prattling on made waiting no easier. Silently Bethany worried how Jacob would take it—having to walk so far to find her? Wouldn't he be vexed beyond speaking to her? What a Christmas that would be! And where would they all go after he did find her? What if they had to impose on his parents again? Oh, that'd frost him and them for sure!

Her wet dark blue eyes scanned the drab blue paint of the wood paneled parlor. That contrasted with white and deep blue willow chinaware in the small mahogany hutch. Pewter shone from constant use on the narrow ledge that ran the length of the wall. The comfortable padding of the chairs, the dark patterned rug and the elegant navy damask Regency couch bespoke the Townsends' increasing wealth. Mary Lou Cullens, their once a week cleaning lady (as well as other more affluent folk,) seemed obviously quite at ease presuming Mrs. Townsend would put up with them for the evening. But, it's Christmas Eve, the worst time possible for this to happen!

"I's lost me all meself, lass," Mrs. Cullens confided. "A drunken 'usband 's a danger as well's a shame; and 'es nigh burned us in 'r beds twice. But," she smiled a bright toothless grin, "we's all alive 'n' well and na worse fer the wear, as ya can well see!"

She wondered again at the cheerfulness of the comment, but she didn't think Mrs. Cullens heartless. Probably not her alcohol saturated husband's fuzzy brain either? Where were Mary Lou's own nearly grown children? Still, she decided not to pursue it. They were enough of an imposition on their hostess, a gracious lady with silver hair of great girth and kindness, who had immediately taken their wraps, stripped their foot gear, and laid warm bricks under their feet as she bundled them up into blankets. With her own plump hands she had placed their socks to dry and chaffed the circulation back into their chilled feet and toes. Her flurry of ministrations nursed the chilled young mother back to even more acute anguish. Now a cup of tea sat in Bethany's lap, cooling unnoticed after the appeasement of winter's cold pinch.

Plump cheeks evidenced throughout the entire Townsend family, two girls, four boys, assorted in-laws, their children, and dear kindly Mr. Townsend. His mutton chop sideburns and wax curled mustache shook and bobbed with, "Pity, pity, poor missus, and on Christmas Eve!" He must have said it half a dozen times before he and a brother-in-law excused themselves to investigate Jacob's and Josiah's welfare. Bethany felt relieved that someone more responsible (and sober) than William Cullens originated the task.

Thad never came that night. Henry Townsend and brother-in-law returned very late, but with a shaking head, tongue glued for long minutes between hidden teeth as his heavy scraggly brows furrowed into how best to tell her he knew nothing. His assurance, that the firemen still had the street in an uproar and "you couldn't get close," couldn't do much to appease terror nor grant hope. She knew him to have been gone long enough, and Hanah Townsend, his sprightly wife, assured her later of his thorough diligence in telling everyone he met that Bethany Clark was at their house.

Bethany knew, knew in only a very few hours that the heinous chant was prophetic. If Jacob were alive, he'd have sought her out by now. By the middle of the long night (that she'd insisted on spending fully clothed on the first chair she's landed on,) she knew Josiah should, in only a few hours, be howling for his feeding. One last hope was they were in some hospital. But even that slim chance produced anguish. To think of them lying burnt, in pain…she could pray no longer (nor had attempted it for more than an hour.)

Jacob had insinuated Bethany was becoming a nag about the unsteady leg on the fire-grate. She should have earned the money herself, hired out washing, ironing, and such, regardless of how ashamed he'd feel. Never should have depended on her husband, her high brow furrowed into a repentant stare that ignored the now glowing coals. It was too important! Something as critical as keeping fire in its place, in a city of so many people, a wonder this had happened on a calm night. The whole block could have caught fire, even the entire city wiped out. *Then how would I feel? If I felt guilt-ridden before, how would I ever survive that?*

As it was, the occupants, Mr. Townsend said, on the street and the houses behind, were evacuated while the fire companies stood watch—lest sparks ignite another home. Poor people, poor firemen! What a cold wretched way to spend Christmas Eve! Her heart broke over their negligence causing all these families' dismay and separation. Maybe her mother-in-law's last heartless comment rang true. *Was she a curse?* Or, worse, was it *divine punishment* for knowingly marrying an unbeliever?

BRIDE OF PROMISE

Morning never arrived so slowly. In agonizing drips the stately grandfather clock eked out a now bleak future. Her early breakfast sweet roll was obediently but laboriously swallowed. Her mind reeled over and over what she could have been done differently. What might have happened IF she hadn't gone to church, or IF she had tended to the fire herself instead of starting the wash to soak, or IF Mr. Cullens had come home earlier, or IF the church service had been shorter, or…? Mists from already-shed and yet-to-be-shed tears gathered in deep blue pools making her heavy lashes all the more noticeable. Long dark semicircles blinked against pink cheeks recently scrubbed to undo the previous night's torrent. A soggy hankie twisted around and around her work worn fingers.

As much as she hated to think of herself at such a time, chanting demons sang a new ditty that insisted: *back to the mills, goodbye sweet baby, back to the mills, goodbye loving Jacob, back to the mills*. She didn't know if she could have held in her accusers' screaming thoughts any longer if Mrs. Robert McDuff and Tilly's mom hadn't shown up around nine. Standing and rushing to face whatever, her wavering eyes pleaded. The host family, caught in the limbo of loss, had tried to go about a normal Christmas morning. But crisis held no option but bear the load of bad news as well.

Carefully shaking off a slight snow dusting from their capes, the ladies crossed the room with her to the heat, standing on either side of her. Tilly's mom stroked her glove against the narrow blue cotton sleeve of her ruffle-yoked blouse as Bethany's hand strayed into its high collar. Softly came the words: "Ya must sit, lass." Mrs. McDuff's cold leather gloved hand descended on her heart. Despite the warm compassionate look in her weathered face, the impact chilled to the bone.

"No!" she wailed, then collapsed back into the padded chair, dark curls and thick hair waves sobbing into the folds of her full, wrinkled, slept-in and out-of-style wool skirt. She had never had much in life, but to be reduced to homeless, destitute, alone and "the clothes on your back?" To lose her precious husband and baby *all in one night*, it…"*was sin*"…"*what you deserved*" whispered the demons from the pit. She braced herself against the mental onslaught and fervently silently quoted, *I will keep him in perfect peace whose mind is stayed on ME.*

"I'm afeared so, lass," choked Mrs. McDuff through her own tears. "They found them, the mister and the babe, both asleep in their beds. Mary's William and Thad looked along with most of the men in the neighborhood. 'Twas a labor of love, that's what it was. Your Jacob was well respected, bless you." No other words of comfort could be produced. She, Tilly and her mom had been praying for Jacob's conversion too.

"Where...are they?" she finally summoned some reasoning.

Not understanding that she meant her husband and child, the women continued to stroke her heaving shoulders. "Ey's gone to locate e's parents," soothed Granny Hendersen (Tilley's mom and the only name she'd ever heard her called.) Her red coloring was now more in her mottled skin than her hair. Jacob had teased her so often, calling her the neighborhood's "grand dame" and "resident all-round gossip." "We's figured since all ya has be gone, 'spects ya needed their help with the telling."

Through now clenched teeth came, "Ummm, of course. That's...very...so kind of your men, Mrs. Cullens." She wailed contritely into a shrill gasp. "His parents, of course...need to know." Silence reigned.

"Mrs. Cullens," she remembered her manners, "I'm so sorry! I've been such a nuisance, and on Christmas Day. You all need to be getting home to your families." The ladies instead took a seat for several more minutes, but eventually they all did leave, looking forward to complete holiday preparations.

Bethany's Bible lay on the fluted edged side table emanating only the blackness of its cover. Bethany licked her suddenly dry lips. She knew it was unlikely the Clarks would want to help *her*. They'd only stopped short of disowning their son when he'd married her. They met after the fact. But, even Jacob dismayed when they refused to accept them and their marriage. His father had persuaded his mother, albeit resentfully, to allow their staying in Jacob's room for three days (the time it took Jacob to find other quarters.) With great household division, yelling and even occasional screaming, she stung still from remembered slanderous comments. Always she'd received "curses upon your head" from Mrs. Clark at the three evening meals they'd shared. Jacob had tried to shield her as best he could. He just was no match for his large boned mother who shrilled "Silence, traitor!" each time he'd protested. How could their grief possibly soften such severe misgivings? Obviously Mrs. Clark's ambitions for her son considered her an interloper and denigration to their family. Why would they ever want her when no related heirs existed?

At eleven thirty-five came, "thump, thump, thump, thump" from someone's heavy-headed cane. Their door was in danger of splinters! Heedless of Mistress Townsend's intent to respond, Bethany flew instead, hoping irrationally that somehow her family members had only temporarily been separated from her.

Instead, there on the threshold stood a droopy thin mustached servant. His dark green livery, olive skin and scowling skimpy brows beneath a bowler hat seemed familiar. Then she recognized the only once introduced man as Mrs. Clark's secretary. "Yes?"

"A letter for you from Mrs. Elisha Clark," he dramatically sneered with exaggerated condescension.

Seeing him turn on his heel to walk away, she called, "Wait! Don't you want a reply?"

"Shouldn't think one necessary," his icy insistence matched the shimmering frost, dispensing entirely with even the courtesy of a returned glance.

Reseated and reheated, she allowed the chill of the opened door to slowly dissipate back into the corners of the faintly sunlit formal parlor. Slowly she turned the letter in her hand. "Best to read it, missus," uttered Mrs. Townsend's soft suggestion.

She brought herself to carefully remove the tucked envelope's flap. Another pointed barb, by Mrs. Clark no doubt? She withdrew a black edged letter, which seemed so unreal, like everything else in her life right now. Resolutely she snapped out of her partial trance. Moving away from Mrs. Townsend, she sat upon Mr. Townsend's graciously offered chair by the window. The parlor space absorbed the noon aroma of coffee, baking poultry and yeast bread; its homey comforts and children ecstatically enjoying seldom seen cousins contrasted with the dreadful reading. Sadly she noted being considered such an ignominy it didn't even address her by name.

December 25, 1842

Regarding Jacob,

Since you are without means to bury my son (or yours,) you have ultimately presented yourself as the conniving charity case and money-grubber we declared at first knowledge of your shameless deceit. Since we must provide for Jacob, deluded to his death by your vile lying face, we hold you responsible for his death! Never would it have happened otherwise. Hence we rightfully and emphatically insist on the following:

(1) Do not attend the funeral!
(2) Never visit the grave!
(3) Never contact us!
(4) Leave Boston immediately!

> We will NOT tolerate your person anywhere near us even one day longer! Comply completely and never vainly imagine we will bear any sentiment otherwise. We spit on you!
>
> Professionals are now searching, and if we can find the proof we need, to show you set the fire that killed him deliberately, the world shall soon know you by your true occupation: "murderess!" I assure you, by every means at our disposal, our intent focuses on your ruination.
>
> But for you, our Jacob would be alive today. Your charm (or your hand?) has poisoned those whom you entice. That hell may soon receive its most skilled cursed serpent remains my sole consolation.
> Sarah Clark

Bethany had never anticipated open arms. In fact, animosity *had* been expected. Why could the vindictive women not even endure writing her name? But, forbidding her attendance at the funeral? Or denying her to ever see their graves, or to even seek employment nearby? That constituted revenge beyond reason. And the injustice and slander overwhelmed. Not just that, his bereaved mother meant her ill far beyond abject poverty.

However, she could not deny Jacob or Josiah a decent burial. And what alternate recourse existed? She indeed *must comply* with this outrageous shunning. Stunned into looking into an even bleaker future, how could she find work outside Boston? Cautiously she steeled her emotions, not only where but how? Return to the Bershires farm? Without money, how could she ever get there, especially in winter? The farm being inherited by older brothers that never corresponded, they'd resent the intrusion too. And, she'd be a burden forever? Never could the farm support more than two growing families, if that. She'd never received much indication of affection from them, not even when she'd left home to help provide during hard times (and be one less mouth to feed.) No, that was a definite last resort. Perhaps get back to Lowell, apply for work at another mill? (Any factory would do except the one where Jacob had met her.)

Her mind shifted into recollections of their first meeting. He had been on a buying trip for his mother's fabric shop. Since Sarah Clark had originally treated his father like a hired hand, his father had gone into a small grocery business of his own. Consequently, since the age of fourteen, Jacob had been the family buyer for his mother. She could well have accepted what samples the traveling salesmen showed her, but she insisted they could swap a lighter weight fabric later, wanted Jacob to be sure he selected only quality goods to preserve the store's prestigious reputation.

Jacob said his father endured endless reminders of who had supplied the start up cash for the grocery store. Still, Jacob thought it gave the small sagging head and shoulders a slight lift to be out from under his domineering wife's immediate thumb (at least for a good portion of the day.) Jacob's small build and handsome dark looks reminded her of his father. And, he evidenced much the same personality, endured persecution well and without complaint.

He had waited for her at the exit of the mill that spring evening. The forsythia buds had barely started to wave their clutched hard fists. It was only by chance that they had been entering the factory entrance at the same early morning hour. (As usual, she'd paid the well-dressed young stranger no mind.) Since the boarding house was serving cabbage and pig hocks, when he approached her at day's end, she had considered his invitation to dinner strictly as a meal alternative. Since payday followed, the landlady might not think it strange if she dined downtown? (And, since it required being accompanied by a man, it'd be easier to request forgiveness than permission?)

Thinking he'd expect something romantic, she'd insisted (before acceptance) that she'd have to leave for "home" immediately after the meal. Not only agreeing but adding he had to catch the train, he had taken her to a modest low-ceiling establishment that faced onto Middlesex Street. At a white small table near the window, she had enjoyed fashions parading past, and he proved a most intelligent and charming gentleman with fine table manners. He had walked her all the way home: up Rogers Street, down Appleton to Canal Street and up the narrow lane to her boarding house door. His only hint at touching her was assistance via the elbow when they crossed intersections and then a slight squeeze of the hand when they parted.

But, the next day brought about a different attitude on the part of the factory workers! The lecherous supervisor that usually patted, shouldered, and bumped her when and where he carefully chose became overly solicitous. The paymaster, who smirked and usually hissed a foul lecherous remark under his breath, was glaringly but blessedly silent. The few girls who usually suggested she was a deliberate temptress turned companionable.

Only one actually acted catty, saying, "Who's the sharp dresser I saw you with last night?" Even the owner, who usually raked over her with hungry eyes, glanced at her face with curiosity (versus her generously endowed chest, narrow waist and generous hips where he usually stared.)

Slowly it dawned that Jacob was the reason for this new respect. When she quit work and he was again waiting for her, she was both surprised and delighted (obviously of great personal benefit?)

"I hope you won't think it forward of me," he had begun hesitantly, "but I thought you might consent to attend a small concert? It's being held at my grandfather's home tonight. It will end early," he'd quickly hastened to add. "Grandfather is not one to stay up past nine." He had smiled such a wistful smile that she might have complied even if not conniving to utilize him for defense. He'd suggested dinner at the same restaurant, a carriage drive out along the river and then back to her boarding house. Originally the idea of being alone with him in a covered carriage rankled, but then, since 1) she desired continued protection and 2) he had been such a gentleman, she had decided to risk it.

The dinner was nice, his intelligent attentions flattering. However, the carriage ride seemingly embarrassed him as much as her. Trying to appear interested in the scenery, she couldn't help thinking it strange that the river appeared to barely move. Inside the mill the river's power was a teeth-rattling, head-spinning maelstrom. The quiet soothed and the awakening lime fuzz of spring scenery entranced, but she couldn't figure out why he suddenly seemed at wit's end to cover the distance with conversation. Gradually she accepted the solitude as a comfortable way to unwind from a hard day's work. It would have been nicer to have had time to change clothes. Although she had brushed the lint away, combed through and rearranged her hair before leaving the factory, there was no way to consider the dark beige, with red and green flower motif, a party frock. Its demure unadorned white high collar and long sleeves had tapered into tight wrists without cuffs. Yes, she'd featured not a frill in sight, even the bell skirt skimped. Nor, she'd rued with a frown, did the draped bodice style require much imagination. Well, at least she hadn't been sweaty. Her thick waves of hair had stayed secure in its hastily rearranged side curls and pins had tucked the rest into a thick crown ("bird's nest on a branch" her older brothers called it when tormenting her.)

The tiny ensemble had performed rapturously. The soft lilting voice of the flutist turned lone soprano, who sang in Italian at the presentation's end, was as charming as she was startling in costume—heavy gold jewelry and satin red sash over a white lace dipped collar on a black gauzy mull gown. She complimented the gentlemen in their formal stiff white shirts and black bow tie and suits. But the flashing smile, white teeth against her olive complexion under two dark clusters of curls topped with red satin bows set her far apart. Bethany received the distinct impression Grandfather was playing cupid.

Were that the case, his accomplished soprano presented a most charming and beautiful young woman for competition. To win his grandson's affection should entail little challenge. Bethany had congratulated herself on her own maturity (in light of her willingness to "lose him to the other woman.")

On the way home, Jacob had oozed personality. He couldn't have been less shy, more talkative, formally respectful, or widely smiling. When they stopped at Canal Street, he had dismissed the carriage, after asking if she would "mind" walking with him up through the tenement neighborhood. She had gratefully accepted, knowing it instead for a kindness to shelter her from curiosity and idle gossip. Little did he know then that he would soon share a tenement flat very similar.

In front of the deep red shingle encased three-storied boarding house he had clasped both her hands. She'd supposed he was going to say goodnight as he had done before. Instead he had said, "I know we have not known each other long enough, but I do not want to allow someone else to take such an initiative first. Will you…consider…becoming my wife?"

She'd been open-mouthed, stunned speechless. Never in her most outlandish dreams had she ever imagined a proposal so sudden and unrequited. Jacob said her eyes just got wider and wider. "I know it's too soon," he'd groped for an explanation, "but I will not get back to Lowell for over two months. I give you that time to consider my affection and proposal. I will write you, if you allow me, and will see you on July 10…if you do not tell me otherwise."

He had left her standing on the bottom step without even a backward glance. He did write; she had written in return and they saw each other on July 10. But, she still couldn't give him the "yes" he desired. She had laboriously examined every facet of their lives and the only truly large drawback (for her) was his disregard for religion. But, that was a very big and tremendously important one. He had merely smiled his shy grin. She remembered him concluding one argument with, "But, I thought Christians believed in loving everyone. And, if not that, then how about considering belief in miracles?"

On a sunny amber and garnet Sunday in September he had a picnic prepared, meeting her after church. Beyond the bandstand in Slater Park he'd requested she wear his token ring—promising a gold band to follow…and, his patience to wait for a "yes" answer. Again, she had accepted, not for love (although she thought him the nicest man she'd ever met) but out of personal convenience. 1) She would not have to hurt his feelings, 2) it presented hope and time to convince him to become a follower of Christ, and 3) she'd enjoy the safety of engagement to one of the mill owner's important customers.

She had prayed, searched Scriptures, and pleaded in her letters to Jacob to read the New Testament, especially selected passages in the writings of Paul, so he understood her dilemma.

Then the mill changed hands. All the old managers and supervisors moved to Lawrence. Sinful new men, more vile than even those, were now pressing and groping against her at every hidden opportunity. The ring on her finger meant little to them; Jacob now did business with the mill in Lawrence. Her prayers were fruitless, Jacob's letters pressing, and sleepless nights exhausting. She forced herself to stay at her spindles and loom often when nature demanded otherwise. (Nothing could persuade her to be caught in the darkened recesses of the factory halls.) Finally, exhausting dawn to dusk work, six days a week, over thirteen hours in summer and over eleven hours in winter, wretched cold and lint induced illness wore her into abject humiliation. Reluctantly, yet knowingly, she'd agreed to marry Jacob, not in good faith, but in desperation. God forgive her, she *was* responsible for his death. *It was her fault!*

"I need to attend to some matters tomorrow," she finally looked up at the expectant fidgeting holiday assembly. "Can you bear my presence another night, Mrs. Townsend? I'll try to make other arrangements as soon as Christmas is over?"

"Of course we can, my dear," assured the kindly lady over tiny round reading spectacles resting at the end of her similarly round nose. Her full bosom flowed into a lap now filled with yarn and a half-knitted sock (a pair of socks to clothe some child of the extended household.) Somehow Bethany needed to find someone in need of her services that would allow her to have new socks (hers were now two days into the wearing.) She also must wash herself and things (if they were to be dry by morning.) But, on Christmas Day, she could hardly hang them in front of the Townsends' fireplace. How could they dry?

In desperation she sought the kitchen. The cook was glad for company and finally she became tucked out of sight of holiday celebrants. Why hadn't she gone here right away? What a wretched eyesore she'd been! Would she *never learn* to put other people first?

CHAPTER 2:
Secrecy and Seclusion

    Just past Christmas the wind rose off the ocean, snatching at Bethany's thin cape with intermittent swirls and vicious gusts. At times its fierce attack required a grip onto a post, rail or building's woodwork before resuming her quest. Fresh snow, just fallen off a building, now infiltrated between her shovel bonnet and collar. Her pale blue mitten wiped it away easily enough but it depressed her in the doing, having even the elements fight against her. She had no idea how to get out of Boston; however, she was indeed willing and would walk if she must. Also, she had no idea of what occupation to pursue to facilitate it. Only experienced at farm or mill work, she supposed she possessed the skills of a maid or cook, but wasn't so sure without a letter of recommendation?
    A burly smiling policeman with immaculate uniform and pleasant shaven face approached. She summoned courage to move right and partially block his path. "Excuse me, sir?" she shouted against the wind.
    "Yes, miss?" he shouted back, giving ready acknowledgement of a bright diversion from his normal cold watch.

"Would you know if there'd be a domestics' agency?" The calm between gusts promoted sudden consternation over her shouting at a constable and she lowered it to add, "anywhere near here?"

"Yes," he nodded, pointing a black mitten in the direction he'd just departed, then leaned towards her against a new gust. "Kin ya see that candle shop, ahead, beyond yon wagon of barrels?"

Tiptoe-raised to peek past his redden ears, she nodded. "Well, you turn left, then right at the bakery, the third right I think it is; go straight for five or six blocks more. I don't rightly remember the exact name." He frowned as he removed his hat to wave in the general direction. He quickly replaced it to protect a wavy auburn combing from whipping into snarls. Now placing a left mitten over the ear that faced the wind, he added, "I do remember 'tis beside a large church, granite stone—handsome place o' worship—with a square steeple rising straight up over three arched doorways."

"Thank you so much," she concluded by mentally reciting his directions and gracing him with a weary smile.

The policeman watched her progress to the first turn with admiration. He conversed seldom with any young female without family, let alone one so attractive. He wished he'd had the leisure to direct her in person. "Back to yer route, Brian McAneney," he commanded out loud, saluting the knowing grin of Mr. Briggs standing in his hardware store, thumbs tucked beneath his long coat into wide suspenders amidst his nail kegs and shovels. (Besides, he required finding his nice warm police station.) Nasty day for a young woman to be out alone, especially rough seeking employment!

Bethany's frigid form trembled as she stared at the front of a large church. It must be the one the policeman described, tall square steeple, three arched vertical plank doors and bold black wrought iron nail heads and strap hinges in a gray stone exterior. She looked right, then left, then across the narrow cobbled street. She didn't see any agency though. Disappointed, she continued ahead rapidly, searching desperately for a sign. By the time she finally located it, she'd been frustrated to almost tears. Between and beyond the middle of the long slanted block's set of offices, a door diagonally recessed three or four feet. Dark wood and shadows almost obscured the small block print: "Domestics, Nurses, Teachers" on the top line, then "Seek Work, We Shall Find" on the second.

The first line gave her a few more choices than she had considered previously. She knew how to read and write, and could do sums well beyond most folks. But, she didn't have a diploma, so maybe teacher wasn't feasible? However, she'd nursed her own mother until her final passing. That didn't require a diploma. She was obviously capable of running a home and cooking; there were surely many things she did well. Walking up three flights of stairs did little to improve her opinion of the establishment's small obscure sign. Obediently, reaching the top of the landing, she followed the instructions on the door and walked in.

Entering, she was practically in front of a lone man in a tiny room. The stale air reeked of coal soot, greasy coal oil and musty crackers. "May I help you?" The huge bald gentleman had a square face, abbreviated white whiskers on his chin, brown waistcoat, striped tan pants and shiny beige vest over an un-collared white shirt. He sat enthroned behind a huge wooden table where stacks of paper overflowed on either side of the improvised desk.

"I need work," she stated meekly.

Was that the best I could do, when I'd been so optimistic just moments before? If so, what could she expect but the lowest paying drudgery, if anything? He motioned to shut the door, then to the lone wooden straight-backed chair in front of the desk. She closed the door reluctantly and sat down. Mentally she reminded herself to sit straight, legs together, hands clasped loosely in lap, feet square on the floor. She also decided to let him tell her what he had to offer. First, though, she needed to be most specific regarding Mrs. Clark's demand, not only for compliance, but possibly to avoid being hung? Anything found in the building could be construed as evidence, every floor must have owned fire starting products, even a candle could be used?

"I would like to find employment outside the city, sir," she declared in a firm tone, "preferably, miles away from Boston, but I'm afraid my circumstances would suggest said employer must be willing to provide transportation. Do you have any such positions?"

He lowered bushy white brows into a glare. "Running away from home?"

"Oh, no, sir." She blinked. "In fact, it's more…the home," she gulped, "that has run away from me."

"Relative's death?" His pudgy face offered a heartfelt grimace.

"Yes, sir." She gulped more nervously. If that was all he asked, she'd be glad that was all that was necessary.

"Well," he turned all business, taking a pencil and paper off one side of the table, "name?"

"Bethany Clark."

"Miss or Mrs.?" He continued writing out her name without looking up.

Her heart sank a notch. "Is it a problem if I've been married, sir?"

"Well, it makes a difference to your husband, I'd expect." He raised his heavily folded neck and voice several notches. "What's a married woman," his baggy lidded hazel eyes turned suspicious, "wanting work 'well outside the city.' Unless…you running away from a bad marriage? That's it, isn't it? Or, maybe, he just got drunk and didn't come home fer Christmas until he'd slept it off? And you're going to show him a thing or two?"

She saw this was not going to work, this conveying only the minimum. "Sir, it's my husband and child that I've lost," she revealed with regret and a sniff. "They died in the South Boston fire of Christmas Eve; it's in the papers. The obituary only mentions them as the son and grandson of Mr. and Mrs. Ezra Clark. You see, his parents always opposed our marriage. Since they despised me from the first day they met me, my name is deliberately not included. They are the ones who insist I leave Boston," she added softly, blushing over what wasn't the most honest reason, "to help them cope with their loss." Renewing an attempt at honesty, with a slightly quivering chin she added, "I must make my own way and am anxious to start immediately. I impose on strangers as it is."

Stained teeth, behind the man's swollen top lip, now bit into the pencil which had twirled between his beefy hands. Then they were interrupted by a thin middle-aged woman with gray streaked brown hair entering and shutting the door. She slowly removed the pins from her unadorned brimmed hat, shed her coat and scarf with a snap and shot the gentleman an inquisitive sharp look. Taking her modest outer garments to stow in the room beyond an open door behind him, she could be heard adding coal to the fire. Obviously that was what heated the two rooms so inadequately.

"You say you lost a child?" His voice raised as though to assure the woman's hearing.

"Yes." Head down again, eyes on her folded hands, she could give no additional answer, lest she give way to convulsive sobs.

With a candle lit tree, carols and all, she'd been an ashamed teary eyed nuisance in the kitchen. All day long she had tried to help but mostly stared into space, not eating enough of the bountiful meal to "even fill a thimble," so said motherly cook Thelma.

The gentleman unexpectedly arose in the midst of her reverie, "Just a moment. I need to confer with the lady that just entered."

After several whispered comments, passed in the back room amidst sounds of rustling paper, the thin lady returned to perch on the edge of the chair seat and peer at her with a hawk-like brittleness. "Been in the family way unwed?"

A thin digit hand's emphasis leaned with an elbow braced against the table like she would pounce if she got the wrong answer.

Bethany returned a shocked, "No!"

"Ever been in trouble with the law?" she continued as though oblivious to the impertinence.

"No, certainly not!" Bethany was irate, to say the least, nor did she approve of the plain brown wool dressed woman's poor manners, especially seeing as how she had just revealed the immensity of her sorrowful loss and destitution, which (in light of the newspaper rustling) was surely confirmed.

Luckily it irked her enough to fight flight against such ruthless rude conduct. Much more in control of her emotions than a few minutes ago, she presumed this would probably not work out but resolved to hold steady. One couldn't control the reactions of others; one simply had to endure whatever was dished out. The recurring poverty problem: *no options at all* chanted a heinous mental barb.

"My name's Di, Dietra Durost," her inquisitor revealed, sensing the impending flight of her victim. "I don't deliberately offend; I just have to be able to tell an employer the answers to those questions. Have to get the unpleasantness out and done with." She gave Bethany a straight-line-across-the-face smile, falling far short of her hazel eyes and untidy salt and pepper brows. "How old was the child?"

"Six months next week," Bethany answered in a terse tone, fresh sorrow welling into her tightened throat.

"Nursing?" the woman queried without so much as a blink.

Bethany was aghast and ducked her head. Her voice finally strangled out a low, "Of course."

Di counted on her chewed-to-the-quick fingernails. "Since it's been over thirty-six hours, you *should* be a little uncomfortable?"

"Uh, yes…yes, I am." Bethany's admission was a little less tense. Did the outrageous female actually have some concern for her well-being when she asked?

"Were you aware we hire wet nurses?" she asked. "Was that the job you sought?"

It took a minute for the term to register. "No, I…that never occurred to me," Bethany admitted with a dazed shudder.

"What's your name?"

"Bethany Clark. I told the gentleman, he wrote it on that paper." Bethany pointed to the sheet now resting up against the right stack. Her opinion of the woman's lack of warmth and good rearing deteriorated with their shared suspicious stares. All she managed was silently praying, *Lord, glue me down!*

Di's eyes suddenly narrowed. "I think I've heard of you." She chewed the right side of her thin top lip in a moment of scrutiny. "Old Mama Clark runs a fancy notions and fabric place. And she near had a purple fit from what I hear! So her spoilt rotten son eloped to marry a farm girl mill worker, ha! If she'd had another egg in that pitiful basket of hers, my guess is her spoiled son wouldn't have continued in her employ. Although maybe that was punishment enough, am I right?" The accompanied chuckle appeared more a cackle of derision than mirth.

"He wasn't spoiled," Bethany protested, chin held high, "not a bit." Internally she seethed. Where was the dignity one normally afforded the dead?

"*Are* you willing to nurse someone else's child?" Di Durost continued as though the personal accusations she'd made required no apology or defense.

"Do you have such a job right away?" Bethany asked. "I mean, it would have to be soon." Already Bethany felt perhaps milk fever was progressing?

An irritated toss of Di's bony hand preceded, "I know! That's why I'm asking!"

Bethany hesitated before inquiring, "Do you have other openings?"

"Not much to offer a body right after Christmas," Di Durost revealed little concern for her penniless listener. "Anybody thinking of hiring a domestic would have done so before Christmas. Teachers are usually signed up in the spring or early summer. Nurses are more on an as needed schedule but still, usually folks try to avoid getting sick around Christmas, right? Pretty much it's a quiet business from now up until around Easter, unless a plague breaks out." And the smile of anticipation seemed morbid at best.

Bethany sighed before her second hesitant question, "This position you have. Is it outside Boston?"

"It's here for a while, but only for a short span of time. The infant requiring such a service is with its parents' friends on Beacon Hill. Eventually, you'd take the child home to Providence, Rhode Island. They're waiting for a warm thaw. We usually get one sometime in January, true? You'd go there by train. In Providence, servants of the baby's family will have cash on hand to pay for your hiring a private cab."

"I presume the mother and father would have to interview me?" Bethany cautioned herself as well, thinking instead, *What if they don't want me?* She knew many a woman who would not want a widow woman in their home who looked like her. If indeed the employer refused, what would she do? She could waitress, at a hotel or restaurant, but the risk of dealing with the public (plus housing concerns) had temporarily been set aside in light of Mrs. Clark's scarcely veiled threat.

"Actually, no, the child's family is dead," Di informed. Bethany's startled expression hurried an explanation. "They came here to visit for Christmas. Their friends had other guests, so they followed in a public carriage to attend a play. Their driver tried to beat a trolley. The carriage slid, a wheel wedged into the track and summarily dumped the carriage in front of the oncoming trolley. Even so, they might have escaped. The sliding motion threw one of the horses into a stone abutment and was terrorized enough to haul them off the track. However, half unhitched and badly wounded, the horse thrashed amidst their exit. Both died under their hooves. I can give you the article if you wish."

Di Durost was actually proving a baby was as recently bereft as she. The old adage about misery liking company was NOT true. Appalled, she felt her grief burden double. However, this *was* someone who needed her, needed her as much as she needed a job, maybe...she could believe that God provided them for mutual benefit? "But, if the child's parents are dead," Bethany wondered, "who would be hiring me, their friends?"

"No, actually it's a Providence attorney. But, he will accept anyone we send as long as the child is safely transported back home. After that, he'll be the judge of how well you fit his own requirements."

"I'll take the position, Miss Durost," she firmly accepted. She wasn't sure whether Di Durost was a Miss or a Mrs., but she despised presuming the old bit of horseradish was anything but a mean-spirited spinster. She also didn't inquire about salary. If necessary she could renegotiate in Providence, blessed far away Providence. Indeed, it appeared *"providence" from the Lord*, her weird jumbled thoughts concluded. Soon smitten with realizing it for a hideous thought, though, she instantly repented silently, *Forgive me, Lord, I didn't mean that! Only that we're both so needy and you've supplied, meeting those needs!* Dual tragedy was hardly a blessing from the Lord. And, that God cared (despite her miserable failure as a young Christian) was also remarkable mercy.

"Good! I'm having a cup of tea brewed," spouted Miss Durost. "If you'll allow me the time to share a cup, I'll pay for a cab to take us over to Beacon Hill."

Bethany allotted her the time but declined the tea. The compelling tightness of her chest wall, even bound up as she was by Thelma's thoughtfulness in providing rags for the task, could not afford the liquid.

CHAPTER 3:
Mansion Management

The fine home she joined teemed with activity. Business, plays, parties, and visiting filled the lives of the childless couple who had been friends of the baby's parents. Once introductions were concluded, she immediately was taken to see the infant. Information conveyed included merely his name, Jonathan Long, and his birth, September 3, 1842. He was therefore about half the age of Josiah. At exceedingly less than half the size she marveled that the young couple had traveled with him at all.

Left alone until the noon meal, she quietly despaired over his ineffectual nursing. A few frequent feedings transpired before the process became more normal. Each time she lifted the strange child she shuddered anew at the thought of what had happened, and especially what she had become. Stray thoughts weirdly scuttled about her brain, like soap shavings gone, or about losing her twelve-cent bandboxes. Then, lacking a few skimpy sewing items convulsed her sufficiently to weep again.

More interest in the child himself took over in time, but the blond skimpy hair contrasted so to her Josiah's thick dark curls. His faint mewing cry constantly compared feebly, versus Josiah's lusty howls. Almost a full month passed before she could think of him as "Jonathan" rather than just "the child." Tears flowed intermittently for a full two weeks before constrained only to nights. But, alone in the darkness of night, she could cry afresh over Jacob and little Josiah, now buried in a grave she knew not where. Eventually, she quit protesting the injustice. She must now listen for someone besides her own lost beloved child.

More or less she occupied the space between the baby's room and the oft smelly English water closet. She even took most of her meals in the nursery, courtesy of the full staff of servants. Blond elegant Lucile Brewer, well educated and cultured, admitted, "I was stirred to 'maternal instincts' at first, but am certainly delighted to finally find a nurse that can tend to his every need, including the milk situation." Her elegant curl framed head and cosmetics exuded such a cosmopolitan air that Bethany presumed the lady could have had similar instincts over a stray kitten (at least for a day or two?)

Bethany would actually be happy to leave Boston, the lovely brick home and even her church. She dreaded Lucile's frequently secreting away visiting ladies (from the gentlemen of the house,) telling them quietly, as they crept up to the third floor, to "come see the gorgeous little wet nurse we've found for baby Jonathan!" They'd titter, marvel over the four-month-old child, "tsk, tsk," over his orphan status, and then gaily placate her with "you are both so good for each other," "truly a God-send," and many other such painful expressions. Blessedly, it was apparent Di Durost had not told Lucile Brewer Bethany's surname or the fire details. In a house filled with servants, surnames were minor details no one cared about. It was also a blessing that her in-laws did not circulate in the Brewers' large group of friends. Just the same, she kept to herself and held her breath whenever strangers were admitted. Oh, if only the weather would break!

Old servants uniforms (starched aprons, ruffled hat and all) were immediately expected to be worn. That certainly worked much to her advantage. When asked if she needed anything else, Bethany assured them nothing more was needed. She washed out her own under things each evening, along with the baby's clothing, until she received her first week's pay. It promptly was spent on new undergarments, personal items and long cotton hose. Eventually, Lucille asked again if there was anything she needed before leaving for Providence. That allowed her mind to question, caused her to consider having to return the uniforms.

Hence, the lady's maid was given her second week's pay to buy dress lengths of black wool and dark gray cotton. Luckily a collection of sewing items presented in a nice small basket with a lidded top had been provided by her church friends. Free time between washings and child-care were spent stitching for the trip.

Then, one dark lonesome night she thought of one thing more. The fifteenth of January, when the slightly built lady of the house appeared upon the nursery scene again, Bethany asked, "Mrs. Brewer, when Jonathan and I go to Providence, on our way to the train station, would it be possible for us to pass through the cemetery?"

Mrs. Brewer insisted she accompany her in locating the robust, ruddy-faced Mr. Brewer in his dark paneled study. His spectacles made his brown eyes appear larger than they were and his wife's eyes mirrored the exact same shade of brown. Were they slightly related somehow?

"Certainly, Bethany," he'd flustered after she had been instructed to ask him. Sticking his wide chest out to hook a thumb and fingers that crushed his gray satin lapel, he added with concern, "Your family's gravesite you'd like to visit?"

"Yes, it would be a great kindness. If you will allow me to send young Roger, the butler's boy, on an errand, I'll try to have it all mapped out so we wouldn't waste any time?" She then deftly avoided any more direct response.

"Splendid idea," he beamed approval, "just as efficient as they come," he turned to his wife for affirmation, "that's our Miss Beth, right, Lucile?"

Lucile agreed with a nodded smile, noting that her husband's Southern roots were showing with the "Miss" phrase. But, in this case, who knew? Anyway, she was uncomfortable with her husband's praise of another woman. Her kohl rimmed eyes flashed Bethany the message that she'd be along in the carriage when they finally dumped their tragic responsibility at the train station. No more was intimated and Bethany interfered as little as possible in the household's daily routine.

She utilized young Roger to make her the map that would allow her to catch sight of Jacob's and Josiah's graves. But she would stay too far away to ever be considered "visiting." There was no way she wanted to stir up more Clark wrath, even if immediate dire possibilities were remote. And, she had not told Roger the true gravesite name, but mentioned instead a large headstone just to the front of it that bore the name Chester Patterson. Along with it, she gave him all the details she had received. *Blessed Tilly! What would I do without her?* Details she had copied over before she'd destroyed Tilly's letter in the fireplace.

The first Sunday after the fire she had managed time off for church attendance. (The same church she had trudged so far to reach from her old home was now quite near.) After the ladies had presented her with the sewing items, basket and a bag of hand-me-downs, unfortunately none of them suitable for a widow to wear, she had met Tilly and visited in a remote corner of the chilly foyer.

She'd promised to find out where Jacob and Josiah were buried and check out the cemetery for her so she could recognize it easily from a safe distance. Tilly was more than sympathetic; she'd seen firsthand the wrath of Mrs. Sarah Clark. It had been her sorry duty to show Jacob's parents how to accompany the undertaker, then how to get around behind the site of the fire and come in with the hearse. (Mr. Cullens and Thad had endured "that foul mouthed female" only until they'd flung themselves off the box in front of the Townsends in order to fetch Mrs. Cullens home.)

Tilly shuddered, recalling the clenched fists, oath-laden tirade and angry vows against Bethany uttered in the morning light. "And, on the precious Lord's own birthday," Tilly commiserated, "and just as we was all coming back to our own blessedly spared homes!" Sarah Clark had also demanded Tilly impart the message that Bethany should never live again in Boston, nor even Massachusetts, or the irrational woman would prevent it any way available. Finally Tilly had run away from her shaking claw gloved hands. Both agreed the inconsolable woman easily wished her dead.

Tilly advised, "Bethany, don't give away your address to anyone until after you've long left town, and…Bethany?"

"Yes?" she'd answered.

Tilly grimaced. "I don't think you ought to come to church for a while either; you could be followed or even stalked, I'm sorry to think."

The potential stalking threat filled soul and mind with fear. If a gentle, cheerful young woman like flame headed Tilley could be afraid for her, then wasn't the danger extremely real?

Then they agreed that only Tilly would know where she stayed. And, the information about the graves would be placed in a letter left with the Brewer's butler. That way it would never allow the suspicion that she knew anyone in the house personally, but was running an errand for the sake of someone's coin. Beth had slipped out the back basement door and furtively glanced behind at each corner. Now even her Sunday devotions were confined to the remote nursery.

Quite often lady friends of Lucile Brewer tried to pry gossip tidbits by asking, "What was your husband's name?" or "What happened to your own child?" She delayed an answer by becoming overwhelmed with grief, would close her eyes momentarily and ask to be excused to procure a glass of water. Then she'd dawdle until they left and descended from the nursery. The first time, it was a genuine reaction, but twice later it had become a defensive pretense.

Versus no longer grieving, it's just that the same questions would have been impossible to produce an identical reaction. But, since requesting to tour the cemetery, it appeared no longer necessary. Lucile informed the recurrent ladies' parade, long before they entered the nursery, that she was Bethany Patterson and "don't, for Heaven's sake ask her about how she lost her family. It convulses her into a weeping heap. It's no good for the baby, I'm sure."

"God, forgive me," she prayed daily, "I know it's wrong not to go to church or to admit my name, but I'm afraid for my life. Just until I get out of Boston, please don't be angry? My fear of death may be irrational, but an attempt to ruin my employment chance here is not. I *must* keep this job. Please, Lord, please protect me!"

When January 24 arrived both warm and bright, it was declared a perfect day to attempt the train transfer to Providence. Unfortunately, Lucille had a charity benefit meeting already scheduled. She managed, though, to insist that the Reverend Maynard Fields accompany her husband, Bethany and Jonathan through the cemetery and onto the train. After all, it was *his* charity she was helping with and "the least you could do for a *poor widow and orphan*." Hence, husband, clergyman, Bethany and baby Jonathan rode out into the brilliant sunshine overlooking the sparkling Charles River. The sight of some open water caused her to mist over, once again she reminisced a Merrimack River view with Jacob. Was it only a couple of years before?

Truthfully, she could no longer be totally regretful. Their few months of marriage had been the only truly happy days of her life beyond the idyllic days of childhood. They might be the only happy days she would ever have as an adult? And she'd always honor his memory for the love they'd shared. Well aware that it was a self-absorbed thought, she refused to deny it. Nor did she solely blame herself for the fire. Jacob was a grown man, well aware of the danger as well as she. Just the cost of a couple bricks to steady the wobbly leg might have prevented it! But, it could also have been caused by just a wild stray spark, a tragedy with no one to blame.

Besides, the weight of it was more than she could carry alone. Strength and courage she possessed enough to survive. And she preferred to recall instead a loving man who honored her by asking her to marry him. She had done God wrong, yes. But at least Jacob and she had always done right by each other.

If she hadn't known just where to look for the headstone, it might have taken hours to locate. *Thank you, Lord, for Tilly*, she silently gave credit where due. It was a comfort to finally see their massive plain headstone shining in the light of day. "Clark" lettering looked just as impressive as "Chester Patterson," even if it did lack a tall ornate angel. Quickly she lifted her wounded eyes to Mr. Brewer. "Thank you, sir, you can have Jules go on to the station now."

"You're sure you don't want to stop and step out for just a little while?" He frowned beneath his silk hat, hands clasped over his silver knobbed cane. "There's plenty of time."

"No, sir, the baby ought not to get any more chilled than necessary. Best we worry about the living."

"A most sacrificial sentiment, Mrs. Patterson," the reverend commended. "And one I most heartily approve. Most young widows are much too grief ridden for living in the present. Time is the ticket to healing. And, you, blessed more than many, have little Jonathan to give you new motivation. Many say it's a great shame when a father is taken and leaves a young woman with small children, but I say she will heal faster and have less time for self-pity. I've seen it far too many times. Believe me, a child is good medicine for grief."

Since this was the first time he had offered much more than comments about the weather, Bethany chose not to argue with what appeared to be his doctrinal statement on human suffering. The fact that the child in her arms was not one she had been "left with" appeared a minor detail conveniently ignored?

Having seen that she and the baby were comfortable and safely seated, Mr. Brewer put out his hand in a parting gesture. She stood in front of her seat with the baby clutched to her body for support. Once in public view he had requested Reverend Fields and the driver to wait on the side street to avoid heavier traffic.

"Please tell your wife that I deeply appreciate her hospitality. I was in very dire circumstances when I accepted this job. But, to be honest, sir, I must also confess that my name is not 'Patterson.' I can't go into details as to why I let you assume so. However, I'm not in trouble with the law," she pacified, sensing his great alarm. "Furthermore, I apologize to be best served by remaining anonymous. If anyone should ever ask, you'd do me a great personal kindness by never giving out my forwarding address. Please, it'd be an extreme favor if you'd avoid details of any kind, not so much as to admit I'd ever been in your home. I know, many of your wife's lady friends could testify otherwise; but, unless mandatory, please do not confirm it?"

The confused gentleman appeared bereft of comment for several moments. At the conductor's last call, he managed a final grand effort to close the awkwardness, "Well, good bye, then," he patted the hand that clasped around Jonathan, "take care of yourself." He fluffed the hair of the sleeping baby in her arms. "I already know you to take great care of Jonathan. Yes, indeed," Mr. Brewer broke away, retreating with, "you should be very comfortable in Providence. Although I dare say, it's as beastly cold there as here, if that's possible. Good luck," he shouted a little louder than necessary, "and I trust your future improves with this opportunity." His confused frozen smile remained beyond the window until they were long past view.

The Providence home did indeed possess, as promised, every possible convenience including a steam engine laundry. She was delighted with the friendly staff (which might well have been a little more formal had there been a master and mistress to supervise?) However, almost immediately, they came to view her as the authoritative mistress. All complaints or worries about this and that wound up in her lap. With prayer, wisdom gained from experience, or the searching of Scripture, she managed to keep everything going, although she often worried over how well.

They kept assuring her the solicitor would come in time. Since wages were always paid promptly. As if by magic, James the butler (and now grounds supervisor) appeared with weekly pay packets for them all. She relaxed in the spacious mansion marveling at this most unusual circumstance. Mattie, the cook, had insisted she "see it all," and Bethany had enjoyed going with either James or the maid, Heidi, or Charles, the stable hand, into the closets, attics, basement, barn and sheds to explore all that had been left intact. It seemed like Jonathan's parents were merely out visiting. All four (Mattie the gossip, Heidi the diligent, somber James who lived off the estate and Charles, the stable hand and lately also helping with grounds keeping) seemed to take great pride in having worked for Mr. and Mrs. Long.

Only Charles, big, loud by times, also secretive, uneducated and occasionally leering, had caused her any concern. One encounter and she was glad he stayed outside or in the heated tack room watching over the remaining two saddle horses that were now utilized to pull a light carriage or cart. The women, who stayed in the house with Bethany, expressed their thanks to James who took Charles' meals to the tack room.

All nonetheless missed the other three servants who had been let go.

"Each of 'em had family, tho," Heidi confided. "I t'ink da 'torney took our lack of family into consid'ration. Ah feel bad fer t'em, but dey had better chances than ve vhoud. All 'ave found jobs, 'cept Timmy Martin; he only delivers nevspapers so needs somet'in' bet-ter."

So, it was an expected letter that arrived in late March announcing the lawyer's visit. Mr. Samual Roberts, Esquire, would appear on the morrow at eight o'clock Tuesday morning, Bethany read for the third time today.

"What should I wear?" she absently asked Heidi, as blond and light of eyebrow as she was light of heart, but then, she was only seventeen. By comparison, Bethany, now past twenty-two, felt a great age older.

"Vy, I don' know," Heidi pondered, "most yo' vhear black. Yo' are mournin', so yo' vhoud. But, maybe yo should have little color som'vhere," she replied while in front of the long mirror patting loose blond strands back into her upward encircled braids.

"Like what? And where?" Bethany questioned from the padded Windsor rocker.

"Vell, maybe vhear one of Mistress's scarves, tuck 'round yor neck maybe?" Heidi gestured in a fluttering gesture around her own V-necked white collared uniform. Bethany, who hadn't been asked to return the uniforms, had decided the light gray color of the former household's uniforms were too pale for proper mourning. Since there was no one to say her nay, she'd followed her own inclinations.

"Oh, no," protested Bethany, "I couldn't!"

"Vell, vhat you ask me fer?!" Heidi threw her hands up and grimaced impishly.

Collapsing in mutual hysterics, they both shook their heads in unison. "Yes, a silly question," Bethany admitted. "Maybe I'm just nervous. I've hardly seen half a dozen men in three months except for James and Charles. And for him, once was more than enough!" Both hooted gales of unladylike laughter. James was a dear man and old enough to be their grandfather. Charles, although young, appeared working on becoming as wide as he was tall. Both Bethany and Heidi admitted to sharing apprehensions.

"Mrs. Bethany Clark, I presume," the solicitor greeted Bethany upon her descent from the sweeping marble stairs with wrought iron geometric railings and long brass top rail. "Samuel Roberts, at your service, madam." He bowed sweeping his hat slightly to the left of waist. After the briefest kiss of her hand, he added, "And please, do call me Sam." He handed away the cap to James as a man accustomed to servants. James closed the front door and added the headgear to the hall tree.

Sam figured he'd find it hard not to gawk. But he was having all he could manage to not look or feel like a country clod. He'd already heard she was extremely beautiful, but he had not quite expected overly generous hourglass proportions or gorgeous facial perfection that might rival porcelain.

Bethany, on the other hand, was not sure if almost three months of few men was too wise. She had the distinct impression her head spun in a cloud of overwhelming masculinity. If her memory served her right, the solicitor was the embodiment of a Greek god. She blushed not only from his now near proximity but also from that thought triggering the remembered scandalous book that Jacob had secretly shown her in an old friend's home. He had teased her about her red flaming cheeks all the way home. "Bad enough," she had blustered back at him, "that we needed to visit to conserve on fuel without you exposing me to sinful nakedness!" The Scripture that haunted her every time she recalled it was Psalm 101:3, "*I will set no wicked thing before mine eyes.*" She wondered if she were even blushing at the recall.

"Sam" obviously had called during, before or after his morning ride. He had thick auburn hair swept straight back into his upright collar, straight brows, square jaw, broad forehead, full mouth and dark eyes with small crinkle lines that presumed he must smile often. His chest was massive, waist slender, and feet shod in knee high black leather riding boots. Light wide hipped tight leggings, clean hands, and neat fingernails portrayed a fastidious dresser. The most up-to-date styled short black lapels outlined the front on the long tailed red coat. When opened, a lined vest in white brocade matched his shirt.

"I trust you have been well this long winter, Mrs. Clark? We haven't seen you out and about much. May I call you Bethany?"

"I suppose so," she heard her constricted voice reply. It was normal for underlings to be called by "first names." It always amused her how quickly a newly appointed supervisor suddenly demanded "Mr." and his surname. And, owners, well, they even had to be introduced by Title, First, *Middle initial* and Surname, and maybe even followed by "esquire" or some such addition.

"You may wonder why I've never requested a meeting before," he smiled benignly, "but you see it hasn't really been at all necessary."

"Why ever not?" She riveted to attention.

"Because, my dear lady, I live right next door. Your Mattie gossips with my Rita and Joe in my kitchen. I usually hear all I need to without asking. You see, my study adjoins and there is a big space under the door. Also, Joe usually sees to it that I'm fully informed of any tidbits I may have missed." Noting her discomfort, he continued, "It seems the entire household here is most taken with you. Also appears you are doing an excellent job with baby Jonathan, but I finally had to come over out of pure curiosity, nothing more." His smile oozed of the intimate as though he presumed a secret friendship for his knowledge of her over the few but long winter months.

"Curiosity satisfied about exactly what?" Her hackles raised in dread.

He grinned deliciously. "How gorgeous could one raven-haired beauty be?" Grinning wider at her sudden discomfort, he added, "Joe says he'd glimpsed you a couple of times downtown, absolutely raving over 'glorious thick raven hair, serene of face, and fabulous figure.' He suggested a resemblance to Russian royalty. It instigated his Rita coming right over to see, purposely close up, to assure it wasn't just distance that flattered you. I have to report it just as she told Joe and me that afternoon. 'Not a prettier girl in the entire county and then some.' Yes, she did," he nodded at her disconcerted embarrassment, "that's exactly what she said. And I considered that high praise for a woman with four marriageable daughters!"

Bethany resented attentions so superfluously fixated on her physical features. "There's little one can do about how one looks, sir," she replied off handedly, "and I'm sure time will erase all reason for praise soon enough. Better a pure heart and productive hands, you can tell them for me, Mr. Roberts."

"Sam, please," he urged. "I suppose so, but you are still quite the picture *now*!" His raised brows and forward wink were not to be taken as offensive, she was sure, but such was nevertheless how she viewed them. "And, since Mattie says you have a reduced staff on a better schedule than they ever were, I'd say you have fulfilled those desired admirable qualities as well!"

"Please…Sam, if you don't mind." Her head and shoulders slid forward. Her shoulders slumped so her right palm clasped the back of her left hand between knees hidden in the deep folds of her full black skirt. It was an old defensive posture. Raising haunted eyes to his now contrite gaze, she pleaded, "I'd just as soon we discussed Jonathan's future, and mine. And, how long I shall be needed?"

Mr. Samuel A. Roberts, Esquire was impressed. The capable lady came directly to the issue at hand. If she were not so stunningly beautiful, it would have been rare enough, but…ouch, a woman of perfection, almost too wise? Such a woman would well be wasted if…well, he might as well spill the spoiled beans? She obviously wanted the truth of the situation. And, he admitted in admiring recognition, she likely could handle it as well. And, if she couldn't, well, although he didn't normally wish a woman to faint in his presence, he might make an exception in *her* case?

"Jonathan and I...Sam?" Her expressive arched brows and penetrating dark blue eyes prompted him to consider where his train of thought was leading.

"Ah, yes, Jonathan Long. He is a problem, to be sure." His straight nose inhaled but then he lost his thoughts again. She was absolutely gorgeous from delicate hands to immaculate grooming, admired up and down he couldn't find the slightest fault. Lovely females always made concentration hard, but this lady went way past distraction.

"Why a problem?" she interjected into the uncomfortable span of time it appeared to take him to continue. "Is it just the obvious long growing up process?"

"No. There's much more to it than that." Sam exhaled as he slid into a languid slouch and lifted lanky arms to knit long fingers behind his pensive head. Dark eyes peered long and hard at the cherubs peeking out from the corners of the ornate gesso ceiling trim. Obviously he was at home here in the Longs' pale green and gold gilt paneled formal parlor. Before her, massive white marble fluted columns flanked green botany tiles surrounding the fireplace. Its smooth edged mantle was supported by heavy sculptured marble quoins and featured a slightly tilted mirror over its precious objects d'art.

Generous male shoulders hunched further down in the massive Italianate chair that matched the rest of the lovely green and gold jacquard patterned upholstery. Bethany had chosen the footstool of the chair opposite his. Near the open double sliding doors, she viewed the spacious chandelier centered foyer. Beyond stretched a similar double door. That was for the privileged few (herself now included,) a book lined private library. Shelves and shelves balanced another marble fireplace, equally impressive but much more masculine, the room decorated in tones of brown with plain Mission style stuffed leather furniture.

In dealing with the few visitors who inquired of baby Jonathan, she had found it an advantage to choose the padded stool. Just inside the double doors, it left no space for a man to sit next to her, and she could conclude the conversation by leading guests toward the foyer before her progress became impeded.

A man as handsome as the solicitor posed a dangerous distraction to herself. But a distraction she had no reason to presume would be anything but an insincere dalliance. His flattery and admiring looks she'd heard, seen and resisted before.

BRIDE OF PROMISE

"Jonathan's sole living relative," Sam finally broke into her admiration of the surroundings, "that I ever heard tell of is a British cousin of Mrs. Long, a Mrs. Lois Mott. Her husband Ernest runs a trading post inland from the Oregon coast. Soon after I received news of the accident, I luckily happened to have an investment appointment with a man who supplies their post with trade goods. It was his plan to sail down to Panama, cross his goods overland to the Pacific and find another ship north. We're old friends from college days so he promised to leave immediately with my letter advising them to direct me as to what they want to become of little Jonathan.

"Unfortunately, Joseph Wright, that's my business partner's name," he turned toward her, "was pretty sure they'd want Jonathan to be taken west to Oregon. Yes," his nod agreed. "I was as appalled as I can see you are." He turned his unusual dark short-fringed eyes away again. "However," he hesitated before continuing, "I am resigned that final possibility may well be their intended plan. If so," he sighed, "he also tells me they will never send the child by sea. It appears they nearly perished when they went around the horn. Then, only a few days from their final destination, a shipwreck actually did occur during a storm off Oregon. They managed to be rescued only after they spent two and a half days in a life boat on the open sea. Badly injured, Mrs. Mott lost their first child, never to conceive again. Two years in their first port of call concluded—I'm not sure I remember him telling me exactly where, on the Oregon coast I suppose—before they journeyed up the Columbia River."

Both quietly allowed the grim words to sink in. The ornate porcelain clock ticked against the hard marble mantle. The intermittent strokes emphasized their deadly dread. Despite the well-fueled fire, the dampness of a cold spring wormed into their midst.

Finally the Greek god resumed, "So, you see, Bethany, if they want him to live in Oregon, which my friend says is likely not only because they have no children, but because he doubts they'd ever attempt a return trip themselves. Mrs. Mott's health is frail at best, and they are considerably older than Jonathan Long's parents. He's presuming the baby will have to be transported to them." Clock ticks filled another interval.

"Do you know what I'm suggesting?" he apprehensively inquired.

Bethany was staring at the side bay windows. Five ninety-inch triple hung windows were festooned with dark green velvet drapes and gold scallop shell catches. Previously she had thought them magnificent. Somehow the conversation had dulled the setting. She also held less admiration for the minor deity before her. He was expecting her to sacrifice herself on an altar of torment. That contradicted the belief that human sacrifice was not practiced in Christian societies.

Suddenly all she had enthusiastically read in the newspapers (that the Longs had subscribed to) about Westward migration and Manifest Destiny became stubble. She drew her emotions together. "I suppose," she replied carefully, "you are inquiring if I would be willing to accompany Jonathan on a trip overland to Oregon?"

"I'm afraid so." He admired her composure that revealed almost no trace of anxiety. "I have urged Joseph to use all of his persuasive powers, and I assure you he is most persuasive when he puts his mind to it. He's to point out the advantages of returning to this fine home and the Longs' extensive trust funds that would be totally at their disposal. Also, I stressed how impossible it is to think any woman and child could safely reach them, among that would be Indian uprisings, disease and land travel that condemns even strong grown men to their graves!" Sam now half bent over his elbow-laden knees. Gesturing with expressive hands, their agitation clearly indicated his opposition. "I'm so very sorry," he confessed with a defensive shrug before he unwound back into his former slouch. "I'm sorry to have to convey this and apologize for getting so opinionated. I had every intention of utilizing my most professional detached manner."

The long silence was broken only when Bethany suddenly giggled. Her nerves were so frayed; she couldn't help it.

"Well!" he exclaimed with mock horror. "You're taking it well enough it seems. If you can find humor in absolute madness, maybe you see something I don't?"

"No." She hesitated before answering, "I just couldn't help it; you were just so far removed from…'detached.'"

Shyly she glanced sideways through thick charmingly lowered lashes. He was trying hard not to smile. The harder he tried, the more he grinned. Bethany's mind wandered wondering if, as a boy, he must not have been quite the darling rascal?

He succumbed to merely marveling at her enchanted peaceful composure. It was a comfortable silence. Too bad, he mused, that there hadn't been someone to play the gold leaf and mother-of-pearl inlaid grand piano. It seemed appropriate that there be music to celebrate their shared "togetherness" over caring for little Jonathan in the only humane way thinkable. He should be raised right here, under his own roof, and Bethany could stay on as long as that took. He had heard how she kissed and cooed; so

Jonathan was obviously more than just a child to serve. They had become one in suffering, one in support. It would be sad to see her ever leave him, now or ever.

"You are most beautiful when you are pensive," Sam finally interjected.

"Really, sir," she protested the familiarity, "you shall force me to call you Mr. Roberts."

"Then I repent profusely. Please, Bethany, do consider me your friend and Jonathan's. And know that I shall do everything in my power to prevent this from happening. However," he changed to his most serious facial expression, "please realize that I am essentially powerless to do what I know the Longs would have wished. I kept pleading with them to make a will, to appoint a legal guardian. They had no close family and few friends they considered appropriate to accept the task. They refused to hear of it until I finally agreed to become Jonathan's guardian myself. They, unfortunately, put off making it a formal agreement until after they'd returned from Boston. But for the lack of two or three weeks' time, none of this would be an issue."

His sorrow was obvious, and the gesture helpless, but Bethany's senses were suddenly on alert. Complimenting her so outrageously appeared suddenly most inappropriate. *No parent considered a bachelor a proper guardian for a child!* She wondered if Mrs. Roberts were as lucky as she might presume. In fact, had he been one of those men who had never even thought to include his wife in such a major life altering decision?

Bethany rose and smoothed her newest black wool skirt and tugged at the points of the short over jacket's gray piping. The white blouse, similarly trimmed high neck and long sleeves with bound gray buttonholes contrasted with the gray dome buttons she'd rescued from the Long family's "button graveyard." With reservation and stiff demeanor she indicated the conversation concluded. "You've given me much to consider; I trust you will update me as soon as, or whenever, you hear from your associate."

"Oh, sure," Mr. Roberts agreed, uncurling to rise. "As soon as I hear, I'll be right over."

"I'm sure you shall," she inferred in even tones but turned rapidly for the foyer.

Bethany's hand soon became encased in his. "Bye now." He patted her hand boldly before taking his leave. James presented his cap and soon both were standing by a now open door. The tall hall mirror revealed Samuel Roberts smiling at his deliberate delaying cap adjustments. She shivered as chill musty earth smells slid in from unwashed winter covers. Reminded of the world she'd left behind, and that her husband and child lay under that, a sigh formed but fought escape.

As the door closed, she explored becoming a man-hater. If so, it was good she had married Jacob while young (and foolish?) Otherwise, she'd be called a man-hating spinster. (*I suppose Di Durost hated both genders equally?*) Immediately her black mood was penetrated by a Holy Sprint pricked conscience. She knew better than to hate. And, she didn't *really* hate, she was just *infuriated*, maybe at men, maybe more being considered a helpless female. Or, more that she *was* one! She knew it; that man knew it. Since Rhode Island was the last state where even men couldn't vote unless they owned property, what could a lone woman without property expect?

If he became a nuisance, she would have few allies in the household, regardless of how well liked. Servants had a way of not intruding (but gossiping about) the folks who gave them orders. And, as much as she was unaccustomed to having authority, she was mistress for the moment. And obviously, she'd already provided fuel for gossip. Because of its position next to the nursery, she even occupied Mrs. Long's magnificent cream and blue bedroom.

James looked at her rather strange. "You all right, missus?" he inquired.

"Fine," she'd assured him, pulling upward as she hip leaned to help propel herself up along the brass laden banister. After silently peeking at Jonathan, she retired to Mrs. Long's bed to assess her few known options.

Lord, she sunk to kneel on carpet cushioned knees, *isn't infuriated like righteous indignation?* Better search the Scriptures, came her obstinate conscience again. But, she procrastinated. She had too much to ponder right now to be concerned about Greek gods that conducted themselves like demons. *Keep me safe, Lord, and little Jonathan and me healthy, that's all I ask. I am blessed to be here and I'm thankful for Your provision and safety. Most of all let any of my future decisions please You. Amen.*

CHAPTER 4:
The Church Soloist

On Samuel Roberts' second visit, Bethany arranged for Heidi to retrieve her knitting, James to tend the fire, and Mattie to occasionally inquire about tomorrow's menu or the shopping list. But "Sam" still settled in as though approaching the most natural domestic setting. He commented about the weather, the soggy country roads, and eventually related how an alcoholic client had returned home one evening with a rooster, with absolutely no recollection of whether it belonged to him or not. "I've had to hire a detective to track a rooster!" he concluded uproariously. Against her better judgment Bethany found herself laughing too. Well, it was a funny story.

Then Sam turned melancholy. For no apparent reason, he poured out the tragic loss of his parents to a fever in the Carolinas just before he finished his apprenticeship. "I was glad, though, to have had them while growing up," he continued, "and to have been as well prepared to handle their affairs. My own complicated inheritance and holdings gave me much of my experience to help other people with their estates. He admitted with a bit of embarrassment, "I'm afraid I liquidated most of the real estate. I kept the local stuff that I could easily attend to, but I had no desire to end up burning with fever over a few thousand acres of swampland. Guess that's why I so admire my friend, Joe Wright. He goes to the ends of the earth and back, heat, cold, insects, disease, knaves, Indians, and thieves; thinks nothing of it!"

Up to that point Bethany had knitted away at Jonathan's tiny sweater and listened with a detached ear. But Mr. Roberts was not going to use his comely "buddy" to elicit sympathies. What she wanted was a clear confession of his being in the wrong place for the wrong reasons. And, she would tolerate his visits no longer unless he had a sound business reason. She had enough put by now that, if he did fire her...well, she'd survive, for a while at least. But she didn't think it a likely prospect as long as Jonathan needed her.

"And did Mrs. Roberts share your lack of enthusiasm for extensive travel?" she insinuated.

"My mother perished at the same time. I just told you, my parents died within two days of each other."

"I meant," Bethany persisted, "did Mrs. Roberts, your *wife*, not care to travel?"

Sam Roberts, not often stunned or speechless, was suddenly bereft of response. When the mental gears finally meshed, he couldn't imagine what kind of man she thought he was. No one in all his days had ever so impinged his honor! It was obviously a mistake but why, or how, had she presumed this? *How dare she suggest such a thing?* His face suddenly darkened into a hardened mask, "I am a lone bachelor, Bethany Clark," he protested through clenched teeth. "I have no idea how you received a different opinion, but I assume you presumed me a cad of the crassest sort. I shall not burden you with my pitiful life's history any longer. Good night!"

Bethany watched him angrily stride away, slam himself out the front door with a decided bang, and listened to his boots stomp along the long brick walk. The mantle clock's rhythmic pendulum measured the room oozing into fresh composure. "Humph, likely story," and that charade was pretty outrageous, pretending to be a bachelor when you lived right next door. Although, no one mentioned a Mrs. Roberts next door; but then, how much time did he spend there? Probably they lived in another part of the city? Or, how likely he left her in the country to tend his acreage? She had heard of men wealthy enough to maintain several residences. Certainly an inherited home would cause little suspicion; instead, it offered excuses galore. Would that explain why Rita and Joe only stayed a few days every so often? Well, what did it matter? And, who cared what he said or thought? Single, married, handsome or not, he was not making folly's fool of Jacob's widow! Let the man fume. She'd still not be duped.

Determinedly sauntering off to the kitchen for a cup of tea, she informed Mattie no second cup, nor sweet cakes, should come to the parlor.

"Whad'ya mean, he's gone?" Mattie demanded.

"He went home already." Bethany blinked back calmly.

"Why?" Mattie's tilted mobcap wanted to know.

"Why not?" Bethany bristled. "You can hardly expect an important lawyer to fritter away his time with a servant."

"Now don't give me that," Mattie's pursed up mouth decreed, plump fists on both hips. "You are the best looking female anywhere, hereabouts at least, and to not want to spend time with you when all he's got to do is jump over a two foot hedge, well, I say just don't give me that, that's all!"

"Mattie!" Bethany's shocked expression emphasized renewed mortification.

"What?" plump matronly Mattie demanded, a gray hair strand now being poked back under the freshly starched mobcap with careful floured finger.

"How could you? Why? I'm...oh!" Bethany flustered. "I can't believe you'd..." Bethany was calm one minute and burst into tears the next, ran out of the butler's pantry with its glassed top cupboard doors extending up to the ten foot high ceiling, streamed across the kitchen, and stumbled up the narrow back stairway. She'd escape to the second floor.

She would soon have to wake Jonathan anyways (or he'd never sleep through the night) but she couldn't think of that now. She shouldn't feel sorry just because of evil thoughts, especially when they were someone else's, but she did. That's because, she would never have thought it of Mattie!

Oh, Lord, she wailed out her despair, *I just want to be respected! Is that so much to ask? Must a woman alone do without respect until married again?*

"Bethany?" called Mattie from behind the second floor's heavily carved mahogany door. There an inner balcony semi-circled the center foyer.

"Yes?"

Mattie tentatively requested, "Kin I come in?"

"If you must," she replied begrudgingly, quickly rising off her knees and pushing herself into the nearby rocker.

"What's wrong?" demanded Mattie's sweet dimpled cherub features. "I'd never do anything to hurt you, yet it seems I've committed some capital crime. Please, you simply *must* tell me your heart. I want to know what I did; or didn't, or if Mr. Roberts did or said something wrong?!"

Ever so slowly and painfully Mattie dragged it out of her, but not easily. It must have taken three quarters of an hour for her to admit that she thought Mattie expected her to keep company with a married man. "I'd never!" Mattie exploded. "I'd do no such thing. And, I should think you'd have known us all well enough by now that, well, we just wouldn't. And that's that! But, I think there's something else you should know about the handsome Mr. Samuel Roberts." Mattie drew herself up to boost her flagging ego. "Mr. 'Sam' Roberts is about the most handsome and eligible bachelor in all of the state of Rhode Island, that's all! That *fact* is in the society pages of the public newspapers."

Bethany's crying jag was well over and early on she'd retrieved Jonathan. He now happily played with bright tin cups on a doubled up blanket between their feet. In a dull drained voice Bethany replied, "I don't mean to argue, Mattie, but he must have a wife somewhere. He offered the Longs to be Jonathan's guardian, at their insistence. What single man would offer to take on the responsibility of a child? Even if he did, no sensible parent would expect a bachelor to do so, especially if not related."

"You thought that just because of that?" Mattie placed a plump hand over the "O" her mouth had formed.

"Well, cause enough!" Bethany tossed back renewed irritation.

"Bethany, honey." Mattie placed a warm motherly hand on the again bent over shoulders before toe-tipping the cup to return Bethany's way. "I'm sure a country girl like yourself doesn't have much experience with legal things, but you need to learn that lawyers can act as guardians without ever lifting a finger."

"You mean," Bethany gasped upright, a retrieved tin cup in hand, "you mean, just like he's providing for Jonathan now…by hiring me?"

"The very same, they just arrange things. They don't actually ever *do* anything!"

"Oh, no." Bethany's hand covered the bottom half of her face now forming a duplicate "O." "Whatever must he think of me?!"

Suddenly Mattie laughed hilariously, her hands pounding upon her knees. Bethany stared at her with trepidation. Whatever had set her off? It was hardly funny, more the worst breach of etiquette imaginable. And, she'd jeopardized her job for no good reason. No, worse than that, she'd insulted a total stranger who was also her employer! "Oh, Mattie, how can you possibly think this is funny? He will likely fire me, and then what about poor Jonathan? He's only seven months old!"

"I'm thinking, my dear," Mattie held on to her heaving sides, "that handsome Mr. Samuel A. Roberts, Esquire has never had a female rebuff him, never! And, if I'm thinking right, it will not only make him mad, it will drive him crazy! My dear girl, you've the makings of a heartbreaker and don't even know it. It's just too juicy, too rich...and I can't wait to tell Joe and Rita!"

"Well," Bethany stated, "maybe it's my turn to tell secrets, dear Mattie Slade. Mr. Roberts hears everything you say in that kitchen; his study is right next to it and he hears all the gossip you share. He says there's a large gap under the door."

"Oh, *we* know that." Mattie's downward hand gesture emphasized dismissal. "We just never say anything in the kitchen that we don't want him to hear. How would the misters and missues ever know anything that was going on if the help didn't let them hear a few things?"

"Mattie!"

"It's true. A body needs sources and I'm proud to say that there are no secrets afoot in any house I've served in. Keep things above board and ship shape, that's my motto."

Jonathan was rolling over more lately; Bethany decided she'd better retrieve him to keep his little fingers from getting crushed beneath the rocking chair's sharp edges. Drawing his soft body to herself, feeling his soft blond curls by her chin, she kissed his cheeks as she absently stared into space. What would it be like not to have this baby to care for? She didn't even want to think about it. He was her lifeline to sanity, as well as the Lord's provision. But, as much as she hated to admit it, right now Jonathan seemed a bit more tangible.

"Are you going to let this misinformation fiasco somehow 'slip' to Mr. Roberts?" she hinted.

"I almost don't think so," Mattie twinkled. "Nope, think I'm going to let him stew in his juices for a while."

Bethany protested, "But, he doesn't need to. I mean, he hasn't done anything wrong. And I have!"

"No, you haven't." Mattie waved a plump index finger into her frightened face. "It was an honest and understandable misunderstanding. There's nothing to be ashamed about that."

"But, what will I say whenever I have to face him again?"

"I don't know," Mattie declared with delight. "But, I sure wish I was a fly on the wall when you do!"

"Oh, Mattie, you're no help at all." Bethany despondently watched the now departing cook's back shaking with mirth.

Days passed, then weeks. It at least looked like Bethany was going to keep her job. However, by late May of 1843, she realized Jonathan (at almost nine months) was not going to need her forever. He was holding on to things and walking in place. Before long he'd walk on his own. Even if he did have to travel west, couldn't anyone do it? What if they wanted to save money by sending him with someone planning to go there anyway? She determined that she would start weaning him. Both because she knew it was time and because she didn't particularly anticipate going west. She didn't want to lose him, but she would eventually anyways. A few more months could hardly be worth risking her life over someone else's foolhardy decision.

She began walking with him in the perambulator to get him used to the fresh air, bundling him up well, but staying out longer each day. They both enjoyed the bright tulip and hyacinth surrounded front yards; the neighbors enjoyed admiring the boy as well. By mid June she was out with him twice a day. On many occasions she showed off the now thriving youngster to admiring ladies and gentlemen in the park. She thrived also; and it was good to be "out and about." The little church she'd found, just a Bible study really, in a nearby school "down the hill," suited her needs and she spent her evenings in contemplative prayer and Bible reading.

Heidi and Timmy were encouraged to join her at church also and she adored their company. However, they did have one prerequisite: Heidi would have to welcome or discouraged one or all of the three eligible men in the congregation.

That wasn't counting the young bachelor minister, of course. But he presented no such concern, cause nor lofty aspirations. He came to the house from time to time, but usually for no more than five minutes. It became a second Thursday or third Friday ritual to request her substitution for the small children's Bible class. The lady who usually led the children suffered from frequent colds, even in summer. She pitied the poor lady, but happily enjoyed the sweet youngsters.

One evening in late June, though, the minister asked her if she would sing a solo during the main service two weeks hence. "Why, Pastor," she replied, "I'm very flattered, but I think I have few talents in the singing department."

"I think you have more than you know, Mrs. Clark," he had countered. "I've listened to your voice singing to the children. It's really quite lovely. You just need to find a song that suits your range. If you would be willing to let me suggest a few selections, but in a lower key, you could practice with Maria Strum until you and she felt comfortable. Can I count on you to use your God given talent instead of 'hiding it under a bushel'?"

His smile both unarmed her totally and tossed in a liberal dose of guilt. "Now, Pastor Terrell, how am I supposed to refuse after *that* pointed sermon-in-a-nutshell?"

"I'm sorry," he laughed, "but we need a soloist and I am not above coercion it appears."

Her wry grimace warned, "You may be better off without *my* singing."

"I doubt you could do anything without being a tremendous success," he assured her. With his and Maria's help she did indeed sing a church solo:

> *O worship the King, all glorious above,*
> *And gratefully sing His power and His love;*
> *Our Shield and Defender, the Ancient of Days,*
> *Pavilioned in splendor, and girded with praise.*

She'd managed only one verse before signaling her limit. With polite praise ringing in her ears from male (single) parishioners and a few older ladies, she decreed her singing career to be short-lived. Whether a pleasant voice or not, she couldn't tell. But no amount of public inspection flattery was worth the nerve-racking, palm sweating and heart palpitating effort.

July's request was staunchly refused. "But, your voice is lovely, Mrs. Clark," Pastor Terrell cajoled her, "I was blessed enormously last month. Please, won't you reconsider?"

"You flatter me, but I must insist. I'm sorry, Pastor Terrell, I know you mean well. You likely are even doing the Lord's own work by encouraging one of your flock's hidden talents, but I am definitely not cut out for public singing. You may think I should pray for boldness, but—quite frankly—I not only lack it, but abhor any thought of acquiring it. Please, do not ask me again. I do not care to be your 'problem parishioner,' but I've no church soloist ambitions either."

Later, in telling Mattie and Heidi about it, as she gathered up her cup of evening tea, she remarked, "Honestly, I don't know why he looked so disappointed. I never thought I had any great voice, and he admits I can't reach any high notes. Wouldn't you think he'd be satisfied with Agnes, Timmy, and Maria? I mean, Agnes can reach high A, for heaven's sake. We're just a small congregation, it's not as though we expect such great variety. It's as though," she continued, "you'd think I'd insulted his sermon or something. Why, he swung his hat back and forth and acted like a forlorn orphan who hadn't been offered supper. I shouldn't say it, but if I didn't know him better

I'd think his authority has gone to his head. I know, a Christian should be kinder than that. So perhaps it's best we surmise he's just young at his job and too enthusiastic? But, really, he'd best soon learn that folks do know what they can and can't, or want and don't want to do!"

All she got out of Mattie or Heidi was, "Ummm" and "Yup."

As they watched her grasp half her skirt to climb the servants' "wooden hill," ever watchful of her full cup of tea, Mattie turned around to roll her eyes heavenward and again toward her retreating back.

Heidi was nearly in stitches before they heard the door close upstairs. James hurried to shut the back stairs' hall door, commanding, "Shush," to the ladies giggling behind him.

"Vell," Heidi gasped when it was finally safe to do so, "fer reading all dose books, yo'd think she'd be too smart ta be sa dumb, don' yo' think?"

Shaking her gray head, Mattie added, "She's *too quick* to pick up on ill intent but slower than January molasses to pick out pure hearted attraction. The poor thing's been through so much she's pure prickles and barbs. Why, she couldn't recognize a gift in a glass box! That preacher fella was looking to hitch her into a yoke he'd already built, never once measuring whether it fit. No shame fighting a tight set of stocks on your shoulders!"

"Mattie!" exclaimed Heidi. "Don' yo' think our pastor's nice?"

"Sure," agreed Mattie, "if you like them skinny, freckled, and slicked down half 'n half. But tell me, given a choice, would *you* want him? Versus the one next door?" She winked at the oft smitten Heidi who began blushing about three shades of red.

"Ooo, yo' meddle!" Heidi pointed a threatening digit. "And just vhat makes yo' think e's coming over vhere she is ag'in? He's no been since March."

"It's looking quite promising, that's all I'll say," Mattie replied knowingly.

"Humph!" James crossed wiry arms across a sunken chest. "You act smug enough, but I'll make you biscuits before he courts that one. Beauty is as beauty does, that's what my mama taught me!"

"And I'll see your biscuits before the month's out, James Stafford," Mattie decreed. "And she's done nothing but protect her reputation, and don't you forget it!"

James rose to don his black hat and matching long coat. "And I will say 'good night, ladies,' before we all get thrashed by my missus for me getting home late. It's staying light so long, I forget the time. But, I'll deny I ever said that!"

"Good night, Mr. James," sighed Heidi with a dreamy stretch of her hands down over her extended gray covered legs, "seems vhould be so nice ta go home to yer fam'ly."

"Indeed it is, lass." James patted her shoulder affectionately. "Indeed it is."

As soon as the door closed behind him, Heidi pounced on Mattie's fallen morsel. "So tell, vhat do yo' know? Yo' goin' ta tell, aren't yo'? Ve needs ta know, yes?"

"I will tell all," Mattie swung around, "soon as I freshen up my cup here." But all Heidi heard was wood being added to the cook stove; obviously the kettle must be either not quite warm enough or else drained too low?

"Oooo, yo' kin be mean, sometimes, Mattie," Heidi complained. It seemed to take forever for the kettle to boil. "I dance pins an' needles. Vhat's going on dere 'at ve don' know 'bout?"

"Well," Mattie seated herself back down, "his lordship pretends to take no notice," Mattie stirred in a dollop of rich cream from a flowered china pitcher, "but Rita tells me, whenever she's there, she watches to take in a cup of tea just as James hauls out the perambulator to the front walk. She goes in easy like and says he's standing up but back from the window, as though not to be seen. But he's so engrossed craning his neck, half the time he's oblivious Rita's come into the room. When he does notice, he instantly pretends he's looking for a book. Then she goes out fast, but closes the door *real slow*. Well, he's back craning out the window before she gets the door latched!"

"Oh, Mattie." Heidi sat with her tiny chin resting on downward intertwined fingers. "So romantic, like ve hear of star crossed lovers!"

"Star crossed fiddlesticks. He'll be here tomorrow."

"Vy?" Heidi's blue saucer eyes blinked bewilderment at the infinite wisdom of her elder.

"Because he has to, that's why. Mr. Wright's letter arrived. Joe delivered it with his supper; says Sam near turned inside out. Says he bellowed, banged doors and finally devoured Rita's sugar cookies by the fist full. He'll be here all right. If not tomorrow in person, then at least there'll be a notice from him, and then himself to follow."

"But, if 'e vas upset, maybe dey ship da little boy off ta vilderness. Mattie, vhat vill become of him, 'n' us too?" Heidi sniffled into a swiftly procured hanky.

"We'll make out just fine." Mattie patted the poor dejected girl's slender hands. "Who knows, maybe they'll need more help next door?"

"Ooo, yo' are cupid, Mattie. But, jes hope if anyone comes with 'pure hearted attentions' fer me, yo'll just up and tell me 'vake up an' smell blossoms already bloomin', stead of vaiting for ones in bud. I don' have much hope fer yer Mr. Roberts," she pouted. "I think 'e gets past his prime." With a maturity born of caring too much, she primly sipped her now tepid tea.

"Past his prime, what are you thinking? He's not yet thirty, you young child, Heidi. Someday you'll know just how young that is!" She shook her head at the audacious impatience of youth but then wisely determined not to pursue a protracted argument with a child. "I'm about ready for bed now, how about you?"

"Yes, ve might as vell sleep," Heidi agreed. "Can't vait til see tomorra," she added, making a wry face.

Mattie called after the girl's departing back. "Ya just wait, Miss Heidi, and then you tend to catching a fella yerself!"

CHAPTER 5:
Sacrifice of Life and Limb

James waited by the steps, having dawdled most of the morning diligently watering the summer flowers that Charles had, as usual, sadly neglected. Placing the watering can beside the hydrangea (thankful the suspense was finally over,) he accepted "the note" with a formal bow. "Thank you, Joe; I'll see that Mrs. Clark gets this right away."

"Thanks," Joe winked, "guess it must be pretty important else the mister wouldn't have sealed it so good."

"Umm, sure does look official, doesn't it? Well, I'll just go take care of it. But you watch that brick in the middle on the left," James pointed, "Charles should have taken it up and reseated it; must have frost heaved this winter."

Joe glanced casually back down the walk. "I will watch out for that old brick, James, thanks again." With a wave and grin they returned to their normal tasks.

He'd no sooner shut the door than Mattie grabbed the letter and held it up to the window. But it revealed no naked eye secrets. Heidi came out of the parlor, feather duster in hand, to watch Mattie sashay toward the stairs, waving the letter like a hankie at a maypole dance. Heidi and James merely observed until Heidi turned and thumped her duster into the Queen Anne chair. As though on cue they simultaneously lit out like sprinters to reach Bethany's door in a clump. "Mind your manners," Mattie quipped, straightening her shoulders majestically. "Let's be real solicitous, right? Ya never know about letters from lawyers."

Mattie's quick knock produced a grunted, "Come in." The door opened onto a wrestling Bethany and the prone-to-squirm while being diapered Jonathan. "Oh, wonderful!" exclaimed Bethany. "He's getting so strong; I need an extra set of hands!" Mattie hid the letter, James retreated, and happily the two ladies rescued Bethany from her usual "overheated and losing patience" ordeal. "I don't know if it's worth making him 'fresh air' healthy," she moaned as she collapsed across the bed backward, task finally completed. The energetic boy now happily pulled Heidi's obligingly dangled braids.

Mattie thus felt confident of an uninterrupted audience. "The reason we come, Beth," she began importantly, "is this letter come over from the lawyer's. It might concern us all, so we'd kind of like to wait until you…if that's okay with you?"

"Oh, no, I don't mind." Beth hesitated as though it might bite her. She also took awhile straightening herself off the bed before sitting down on the straight-backed chair by the window. Beth's mind reverted to that "other" letter and how its disaster misconstrued into months of guilt. She visibly gulped as she read the contents.

"He just says, 'I have received direction from Mr. and Mrs. Mott, concerning Jonathan, and would like to come over at one o'clock if that's convenient. Respectfully, Sam Roberts.'"

"Not much ta tell, es it?" whispered Heidi.

Bethany shook her head. "I'll write a note that I'll expect him. Think James would mind taking it over? If he doesn't have time, I'll take it myself, when I take Jonathan out."

"Oh, no," blustered Mattie, "I don't think it would look right for *you* to take it over; I'm sure we can get James to do it. Or, we could call Charles to take it. Course, he might not want to be no messenger boy for the 'stuck up lawyer' as he calls him. If all else fails, well, I could call through their kitchen window and have Joe come out for it."

Bethany's confused glance shifted from Mattie to Heidi. "What would be wrong with me delivering it?"

"And wouldn't that look great to folks!" demanded Mattie. "A pretty woman, with a baby no less, bold as all get out waltzing up to a bachelor's door? Before you'd know it, busybodies could start rumors flying, enjoying a gossipy scandal all over town, and for no cause at all."

The intended nicely turned tables led to hastily procured writing materials that decorated the former mistress' lacquered drop down desk. The two ladies and baby accompanied her to observe careful penmanship. Hushed silences interspersed the pen being inked, excess shaken off, wiped against the side of the inkwell, and then careful stroking. With finality she cast sand on it. "You think that will do?" Bethany asked Mattie as she shook the excess off into the inkstand's glass receptacle.

"Oh, yuh, it says, '*Mr. Roberts*' and '*We'll be expecting you at one o'clock. Sincerely, Bethany Clark,*' That ought to tell him everything he needs to know," Mattie declared with a decided toss of her cap. While Mattie candled a good gob of wax, Heidi guided Jonathan's chubby hand to mash down his family's household seal. "I'll see to having James deliver it," Mattie commandeered the missive. With a regal swish and a rustle she was gone, the door closed behind her.

"Do you suppose Mattie is upset with me?" Bethany whispered to Heidi as she crossed to the rocker.

"Oh, ah 'spects ve jes all vhondering how long jobs vill last. 'But, Mr. Roberts tell Joe if house sells, m'be ve cud stay on vhith new owner. Know Mattie vhould hate ta leave friends next door." Quick as a scat, she deposited the baby.

Jonathan quickly wrapped death grips around Bethany's neck. Prying him lose, she began to bounce him in place and tickled his now pudgy middle to enjoy his glorious chortle. "You, sir, are getting just too rambunctious! "Come on, now, let's get you dressed and see who you can flirt with today. By the way, I was quite jealous yesterday, you smiling so big for Grandma Jensen. You keep that up, and every heart on the whole long street will be smitten. You *know* you're a rascal." She teased her fingers through his quite long curls. "And, I think it's time we got you sheared? Huh? Suppose we can meet a Delilah today?"

From his joyous response he was indeed ready and willing.

"Mattie," she later peeked in through the kitchen door once she had the baby's hat and mosquito netting in hand, "could you ask James if he'd arrange for us to take a little ride to the barber next week? I think it's about time our baby Jonathan became a little gentleman."

"Ooo, now, must he?" Mattie hustled out of the kitchen all soft and gentle.

"Well, his curls are starting to hide his eyes, so I really think we should. We don't want him cross eyed!"

"Guess so," Mattie beamed weakly. "But he's so cute with his little golden curls. Maybe we could just trim them back from his eyes?"

Her nod joined Mattie's. "Yes, he is, but I think we're perhaps a bit blindsided, don't you?"

"Go on with you, ya scalawag," Mattie scolded. "Think we might be partial to the boy after all these months of trouble from him, the idea indeed."

Laughing and tickling him, they managed to easily trick him into ducking into the perambulator. Bethany promptly predicted, "He'll probably be asleep before I reach the fifth mailbox. Everyone thinks he's such a perfect little gentleman, but that's because they rarely see him awake!"

"You've got to be real careful now, that sidewalk's a mess in places, what with elections coming!" Mattie instructed. It was not her only concern, but she knew Bethany was not one to willingly invite trouble of the other sort. Now, she must apply herself to the chore of figuring out what to serve the one o'clock couple. Might tell Rita not to serve the mister dessert, tell him to save room for apple dumpling? Yup, that'd do fine; he'd come for that any time. And she'd just tell Bethany it was late into the oven due to the impending visit.

"Good afternoon, Mr. Roberts," James greeted their expected visitor and thus alerted the expectantly hushed household. I trust you're finding a little relief from this sticky heat. Unusually early this year, isn't it?"

"Yes, but it won't last; never does in New England, especially with us so close to water."

James nodded acquiescence. "I hear you're part of a rowing team, 'spect that could cool you off a bit now and then."

Sam laughed. "Oh, well, it's not an official college team, just a gentlemen's club. Thought we'd show the youngsters up, I suppose. Not much fun challenging the old-timers."

"Right you are, sir," James smiled. "Yes, I'm sure there's nothing like it. You have a seat in the parlor, sir; I'll fetch Mrs. Clark."

"That won't be necessary, James," Bethany stealthily descended the stairs. "I heard the knock and came down lest your summons awaken Jonathan. Don't worry. Heidi is nearby; she'll listen for him."

"Yes'um," James replied with a slight bow, "if you folks will excuse me, I'm sure Mattie can use my help in the kitchen."

Bethany nodded. "Of course, James, thank you."

Bethany faced Samuel's dark brown eyes and both felt the need to glance elsewhere. Finally, he waved gallantly toward the parlor, and she swept past him in a cloud of full petticoats and new dark gray linen. She had been sewing on the simple cartridge gores, white lace collar, below elbow flaring ruffles on the narrow sleeved gown for weeks, but had stayed up late last night to finish the hem. She hoped it did not seem too soon to be wearing a lighter color, but black was awful hot during this heat wave. At her customary footstool, she gallantly extended her hand toward the chair beyond.

"You're looking lovely today, Bethany," he offered polite admiration.

"Thank you, Sam. I'm afraid you're much more gracious than I deserve. Please, do be seated."

Sam smiled with trepidation then added sincerely from his quickly assumed slouch, "I'm amazed at you taking the child out every day regardless of the temperature. I'm told he thrives on the effort though; must say it's improved your winter complexion as well."

She was too frugal to buy a hat and too intimidated to wear one of Mrs. Long's. "Well," she shifted hands into a clutched knee grip, "it's rather hard to manage a perambulator and a parasol at the same time. Although, perhaps the pale look mandated by the ladies magazines is healthier." She determined not to force him to reveal his purpose. *Give him time*, she reined in her impatience.

"I think that will change," he prophesied. "After all, if the sun is such an enemy, why do we all so long for spring, right?"

Sam's eyes lit with a soft glow that warmed Bethany's repentant heart. He was a fine man. How *could* she have been so *insipidly stupid*?

"Well," Sam proceeded, "I asked to meet with you to reveal the contents of Mr. and Mrs. Mott's letter."

Just then Mattie came in bearing a full tray of dessert and James the teapot and cozy. "Just never mind us," Mattie bustled about viewing the side tables and utensils. "We'll be outta here in seconds. Now, Bethany," she directed, "you and Mr. Roberts come over here on the couch if you will. I think that'll work better for the tea service. Mr. Roberts, sir, would you mind being mother-of-the-pot? It's quite heavy." James pulled the rolling teacart in front of the couch, presuming both would comply with Mattie's request.

"No, I don't mind, Mattie," Samuel reassured her. "And may I say, this dessert looks as good as I remember. When Rita said to save room, you can be sure I didn't overdo. Any more out there if I might get a late-night craving?" He began carefully pulling one dangling apron string.

"You mean," she yanked the string away, "you want to take some home. But instead, I'll send a little over to Rita and Joe and tell them not to eat it all, how's that?"

"Just right, Mattie," he beamed, "you're the best!"

"Ah, high praise when you eat Rita's cooking most the time," she acknowledged the compliment. "And, Joe doesn't do so badly either. You excuse us now and we'll pack your 'second helping' over next door."

James added a dour, "But it's to be a toss up if it's me or she who goes, right, Mr. Roberts?"

"I doubt you'll lose any hair worrying about it, James," Sam grinned.

"Oh now, that's pure relief." The stray stranded fellow glanced upward and sighed.

Bethany would have reprimanded Mr. Roberts for teasing poor James about his thinning hair, if she were on better footing, but decided James' sensitivity was not her concern today.

"Sugar?" asked Sam when they heard the kitchen door squeak shut.

"No," she answered, "just straight tea, thank you, but please pour now; I like it quite weak."

"Like your minister friend?" Sam raised a curious eyebrow.

Surprised at the question, she asked, "Are you referring to Pastor Terrell?"

"Forgot the name, but know the type," Sam smirked.

"Well," she flustered, "I'd hardly call a pastor 'friend' just because he calls on one of his flock. Although, in a small church, I suppose we all do get to be sort of friends."

"Nothing more than friends?" he persisted.

She twisted nervously. Why could he irk her with no effort at all, and why had she agreed to leave her safe footstool? "Mr. Roberts, really, can we find another topic?"

"Nice dessert, isn't it?" he commented pleasantly.

"Yes, it is. Mattie's a lovely cook, the Longs were blessed. She's told me she felt the same towards them." The pleasant warm apple and cinnamon odors reminded her of Mother and the farm during happier days. Nostalgia rose like a suffocating pillow.

"Mutual benefit to both parties, nice arrangement, everyone happy," Sam stated with some kind of hidden meaning behind his root beer eyes.

Thinking he was intent on his dessert, she was startled to have him suddenly demand, "What are you thinking?"

Bethany's color rose in her neck, then into her cheeks. How embarrassing to be embarrassed and show it! Why couldn't she outgrow such childishness?

"Well?" he prompted. "You've either thought of something you need to confess, or else, could all that color result from just hot tea?"

"Thank you; it's kind of you to think of such a possibility. I'm afraid my own mind was searching for just such a logical excuse," she confessed.

"Well, I won't press you, but…I *am* intrigued. If you ever have need of confession, I assure you I shall be more than willing to absolve. Of course, after I hear whatever delicious secret sin you've committed," he promised with a lick of his full lower lip. She wasn't sure if it was over her presumed sin or Mattie's rich dessert.

"Really, it's nothing sinful at all," she protested. "I think I shall confess just to reassure you your imaginings are far astray of the facts. I merely was struck by the color of your eyes, rather the shade of root beer."

"I have eyes the color of a root." Sam nodded thoughtfully, gazing into his now finished dessert plate, a handsome ornate wine and gold band surrounding a giant rose. "Great, I always wanted a beautiful woman to say that."

Bethany giggled; it couldn't be helped.

Sam responded with an irritated, "Do you always have to do that!"

"Do what?" Bethany's instant contrition questioned.

"You giggle, I look to see why, and I forget why I'm pouting."

"Grown men," she replied as skillfully as any coquette, "shouldn't pout, should they?" She even turned on the long batted eyelashes.

Sam scowled. "Maybe not, but I'm told they generally do at one time or another."

"But why now?" she inquired with genuine interest.

"Because, Mrs. Clark, I'm madly in love with you," replied Samuel A. Roberts, Esquire, "and angry at the same time."

Bethany stared at her dessert self-consciously before placing her half-empty dish on the tray. A small sip of tea looked away to the French peasant boy and girl figurines on the Provincial side table. Finally she decided to ignore the first part of his declaration and addressed the other. From the depths of her heart she needed to repent. "You have every right to be angry with me, Sam. I have wallowed in guilt for three months and wanted to seek your forgiveness almost every day since. I would have, but the knowledge of my own self-absorption shamed me so much, I felt I deserved your wrath. And, long term, 'I'm sorry' is never adequate when the insult is so unjust. I hope, over time, I can prove how very sorry I am."

"If I'd known how you felt, I'd have come over much sooner," he admitted with a half smile.

"Please know I have only my own self-centered presumption to blame for my rude behavior. At no time did any person place any evil thoughts in my mind. As the Bible says, *'the heart is deceptive and desperately wicked.'* I may try to be a good Christian woman, but just when I think I'm succeeding, I trip over my own conceit."

"No, Beth," he protested, "you've had a real rough time. I know. I guess I should confess too; I had a detective check up on you."

"You what?" she gasped, eyes widening in horror.

"I hired a Boston detective to find out all about Bethany Anne (Brooker) Clark. Born December 29, 1820, you were the smartest girl in your class, but you dropped out of school one month before finishing the eighth grade to care for your ailing mother. In addition, you milked cows for your father who'd broken a leg in an argument with a horse. For nearly six months you managed the farm until your older brothers returned home from lumbering. Mom died when you were a month shy of sixteen. By sixteen and one month, you worked in a Lowell, Massachusetts, textile mill, sending money home to help Dad hire help until the next winter.

"You were harassed and outraged by numerous mill men for four years until you eloped with Jacob Clark and moved to Boston. Instead of security with the well-to-do, his parents ostracized you both.

"Five days before your twenty-second birthday, he and your almost six-month-old son died in a fire. If not for attending church Christmas Eve, you likely would have died too. Your in-laws blamed you for his death, took over funeral arrangements, and—capitalizing on your poverty—forbid you to attend or visit their graves.

"Two days later you secretly defied their 'don't seek work in Boston' orders, to be employed by myself for that one month until you came to Providence.

"You now attend church where you occasionally teach children and have once sung for the congregation. The minister says you have a very sweet voice but don't care to be a church soloist, a fact which distresses him greatly. Mattie says you conduct yourself like a saint, or at least a nun. Did we miss anything important?"

It was a new thought, that she might have perished in the fire too, but she merely whispered, "Why?"

"I told you; I was mad. When I get mad, I hire a detective!" Sam was staring at the same pink and blue figurines. "Hardly the healing balm most people recommend, but it did help me to see that you were not an empty headed female with nothing to do but suppose every man wants her. Unfortunately, in your case (as is often the case with rare beauty,) many men *have* wanted you. I think you're exceptionally beautiful too. So I understand that, but you must have endured many who were less than gentlemen in their pursuit."

"Enough to want to change the subject, may we?" she asked in a small voice, her shoulders slumped, her hands sliding into her knees, and her body starting to rock forward.

"Suppose we get on with the Motts' letter. I'm afraid it's exactly like Joe Wright predicted. They don't want to set foot outside their own Oregon community, but they insist they *do* want little Jonathan to live with them. There's nothing I can do to change their minds, so I have to start selling off the estate to finance the baby's trip west. They also mandated I at least request that you go along with Jonathan."

He turned to take her cold hands in his. "I also take my liberty to say you don't need to go. I can find someone else, someone who's going west anyway. They couldn't expect you to go until I've arranged it, so it will be several months yet. There's plenty of time to get him ready. I understand he's already weaned so it shouldn't be that hard to find someone willing to be paid for a trip they planned anyway."

A long silence preceded a decision that surprised her. "Don't postpone it on my account, Sam. Do everything you can to comply. Hopefully the rest of the servants can stay on with the new owners? But, I'll do my best to take Jonathan to the Motts."

In one leap Sam had pushed the cart away and was kneeling before her, clasping her two hands in his strong and surprisingly callused ones. "Haven't you heard anything I've said, Beth? I admire and love you. I don't want you throwing your life away on some forsaken plain or mountain range. I want you here, not just with me, but that you stay where you'll be safe!"

Heidi, observing from the upper balcony via the hall mirror below her view, suddenly threw an apron into full eyes and backed away silently into the master bedroom. Alone to have a good cry behind closed doors, she also knew she had no right.

Bethany looked at this stranger who had just declared his love for her. In so many ways this reminded her of Jacob all over again. But this time she would not be so easily swayed by danger. He was like Jacob in another way too, an unbeliever. For once in her life she determined to hold firm. "Sam," she said quietly, "I've known Jonathan for six months. I've known you for three or four hours all told. You may think yourself in love, but I'm only a beautiful face, self-sacrificing, church-going, self-sufficient woman who nurses orphans or runs an efficient household. Love's much more than ideals, Sam. And, there's a whole lot more to marriage than physical attraction.

"I married my Jacob for both good and bad reasons. We had a wonderful marriage on the surface, but the roots were always hard to intertwine. Do you know what I'm saying, Sam? Our backgrounds and life experiences will never draw us toward each other; we'd always be growing further away, maybe even like separate pots."

He sighed in defeat. "So, you're quite sure?"

She was not going to let the church issue drop. "You envy my church friends, but don't go to church yourself. Yet you respect my doing it. How can you know it's a good thing and not attend also? I don't condemn you; but I do heartily recommend you find peace through believing in Christ as Savior. Until you've know God, invited Him into your heart, you'll never know what love's supposed to be all about. It's not about pretty or handsome, it's similar hearts and goals merging. It's really quite…spiritual," she whispered so low he bent closer to hear, "when you know what it should be, then the merger is obvious.

I had the most loving husband possible, but there were these huge big gaps. Please, I know the difference. I saw it in the lives of my own parents. As you can imagine, there were plenty of hardships, but always there was a patient trust in God and each other that both reinforced and superseded fidelity. I want the best for you *and me*. I'm sure, no matter how much I wished it, that I couldn't stay up on that pedestal long enough. Maybe you need to find a way to deal with your anger too, Sam? Find a way to let God heal your pain, from losing both your parents so close together? Am I not right on that score at least?"

Sam just knelt there on one knee, their heads nearly touching. Finally he raised soft root beer filled eyes to nod slowly. "I know you're right, Bethany, I just never knew where to look. Maybe your Pastor Terrell could help me too?"

"You've no idea how he'd love to try." She smiled back pure delight.

"You still don't have to go to Oregon, you know," he continued. "It's pure madness. You're under no obligation, to me or any one else. Please, if I thought for one minute that you were going because you thought I would pester in any way, I'd move out of the neighborhood tomorrow!"

"No, Sam, I know that isn't so. Plus I know I don't have to, but I will.

Please, be my friend and counselor? In fact, let's sit in church together. For as long as I have here let me try to show I trust you? We'll grow together in faith and become great friends over the next few months? Who knows? Maybe there'd even be hope for reconsideration? But for right now we're going to plan on me going.

    I love Jonathan with all my heart; I really can't bear to part with him. For that or whatever other reason, Jonathan's 'Manifest Destiny' may also be part of God's plan for my own healing? Perhaps only physical hardship can overcome my emotional void? If I can return to some semblance of living again, that would be worth any trial imaginable."

CHAPTER 6:
To Shoot or Not to Shoot

In the worst heat all summer Sam rode alongside the perambulator to inform her to prepare for travel. "Joe tells me you've got to reach Saint Louis, Missouri, by March of forty-four. But you've got to travel overland from here too. He's on his way to Missouri now, planning to load up wagons with trade goods. He says if he has to go overland, he's going to make it pay along the way. You're to wait on the east bank and he'll accompany you over the Mississippi River. But, the Motts insist you not cross any water during the route unless it's absolutely necessary, and always with Joe's help. That means you travel by land unless it's absolutely impossible. Obviously their fear of water is as much a phobia as Joe intimated.

Normally you'd sail up the Hudson River, take the Erie Canal, cross the Great Lakes and down the Mississippi River by steamer. That wouldn't take more than several weeks. But you, Jonathan, Charles, Timmy and that wagon will take several trains. After Albany, trains follow the Mohawk Trail and turn south. Past the Alleghenies, it's all mapped out with names of people to meet, dates to make it by and where to stay for the winter. But, when you get opposite St. Louis, you're to stay at a wharf hotel until Joe contacts you. He says you're absolutely to wait for him; the Motts insisted on his being with the baby when you cross the Big Muddy. Just remember that you're in charge of Jonathan, not Joe Wright."

"Do we go on to Independence from there?" Sam's procured guidebooks made her only slightly knowledgeable of the route.

"I don't know," Sam shrugged, "Joe just said meet him opposite St. Louis." Poor Sam looked like he could bite his tongue out. "You don't have to go, Bethany," he whispered beneath the shade of the overhanging chestnut tree, amidst the smell of cut grass and fresh boxwood trimmings. His mouth drooped like the wilting petunias that lay exhausted beside the walks.

"I know, Sam." She looked up and patted his leather gloved hand. "I'll probably hate every minute of the trip, become an old crone by the end, and pine over 'what might have been' for a lifetime."

Clasping her chin in his free hand, he gently shook it before lecturing, "Don't tease me, Bethany Clark. This trip is serious danger!"

"Just pray for me, Sam." She removed his hand gently. "And, I'll pray for you."

He nodded. "I'm already praying, but I'm telling you right now, we're going to sell, salvage, and convert everything in that mansion that isn't nailed down. You are going to have whatever is necessary to be as independent from Joe Wright as is physically possible.

He is NOT the easiest guy to get along with, even around men, but especially around women. Might be he's the last guy in the world I'd want to send a woman west with, or any place else for that matter. I don't know what the Motts see in him. I deal with him too, and I invest money with him because he's as honest as the day is long. But don't expect him to coddle you. He absolutely won't!"

"Are you trying to frighten me into staying, Sam? If you are, it wouldn't work. And if not, please realize I'm almost terrified of my own determination. I need support, not chastising. Don't you agree that Jonathan will be best taken care of by me?"

Bethany turned to lift the toddler out of the perambulator in response to Jonathan's pleas of, "'orse, 'orse."

"Of course I do! That's not the issue, it's Joe. I don't know what's wrong with him, Bethany, but stay clear and don't get him mad. I saw him once send a Southern belle from Georgia near *flying* up the steps of her grandmother's house in New York. He'd so reduced her to tears that she never came down until the next afternoon. And, she was supposed to be the guest of *honor*! Worse, she was so mortified no one could ever find out what he said to her. Every one of us eight guys tried to physically shake it out of him, but he wouldn't budge an inch. I don't think he'd hurt you, physically," Sam added thoughtfully. "In fact, it's more the opposite. I'm serious; he despises women. In a tough situation, I'd worry that he might *abandon* you. He's grumpy around females, just walks off. If not that, then before you know it, he's yelling, 'get lost,' or 'get out of my way' for absolutely no reason."

"Well, I'm glad to know he's honest!" Bethany smiled with relief. "And, I *think* I can handle all the women haters you can throw at me!"

"Hate to say it," he grinned as he replaced his jaunty riding cap, "but I might feel a tad better knowing you're with ol' Joe, myself." And they both shared a good laugh. "Anyway, I'll be over tonight. We'll go through the Longs' jewelry, china, silver, and such. Anything of a personal nature, I'll have you take to Mrs. Mott. Joe says she's a plump lady of generous proportions, so there's no need to take her cousin's clothes except in your own trunk (as *your* personal property.) I've got to meet a client, but I'll be over as soon as I'm done. You think about what you want. I may not be able to do much about your destination, but you'll get a tangible reward out of this outrageous imposition if it's the last thing I do!"

As August cooled down, activity in the Long estate heated up. Sam didn't trust Joe not to thrust Bethany in among his muleskinners and trade goods, so he had a special wagon constructed. Interlocking and stacking barrister bookcases constructed of cedar with thin cedar front panels had leather strap handles added to each end. Three back stacks were used to store valuables before straps with buckles attached all to metal floor and side rings. Front ones were for personal storage. The addition of wood slats allowed a cedar fence section to stand across the entire wagon, its purpose to contain Jonathan during washing, cooking, etc. Next, a commode with a lid and chamber pot was fitted for privacy with curtains hung from the ceiling beyond barrels of flour. On top of those stood two smaller barrels of corn meal on the left and buckwheat flour on the right. From the ceiling they hung two narrow boxes with canvas tie downs for diapers.

Over the double stacked barrister cases were canvas covered horse hair mattresses that would ride on top of extra sheets, pillowcases, winter blankets and fancy comforters. Pillows with cases, sheets and a lightweight blanket covered the whole.

Another canvas-covered mattress on the floor, beside her bed, provided a play and sleep area for Jonathan. There was little room between so it produced careful packing. Packets of cash, gold, jewelry and sentimental items were kept from rattling by Mrs. Long's scarves, linens, gloves and silk stockings.

Sam reiterated his afternoon promise. "The clothing items will be *your* property when this trip is over, to keep, sell, or use any way you see fit. You are more than going to earn them so you are not to turn them over to Mrs. Mott, do I make myself clear?" he scowled in his most authoritative tone.

"Yes, Sam," she placated, "and thank you. I mean it; I really appreciate what you're trying to do for me."

He waved away the thanks. "Well, let's call it a little '*canker worm*' restoration, okay?"

"You are becoming quite the Bible scholar, Sam!" she rejoiced.

"Don't know about that," he grinned, "but I need to thank you for the best blessing that's come out of all this. And, I do, with my whole heart. If I hadn't hoped to be near you, or thought I could win your heart, I don't know if I'd ever have gone to church or not. If I've become any kind of Christian at all, you're the reason."

They smiled in contented sharing of his newfound faith while the carpenter added tall stacking and latching field bureaus. These were strapped on the end, leaving little space to stand or squeeze between (this storage filled with baking utensils and supplies.) Slabs of bacon, ham and salt pork filled one drawer and dried beef above. Dried apples, dates, raisins, pears and nuts filled cloth bags, and white and brown sugar filled wooden bandboxes in between. Pots, pans, skillets, a spider and a small tin reflector oven sat in a carpenter's version of a two foot piano hinged shelf. It hooked up behind her cupboards or else flopped down supported by chains on the sides of the wagon.

Outside, the most obvious tool was a medium size shovel firmly tied between two of the water barrels. Two watertight sets adorned both exterior sides between the wheels. Front and end barrels carried grain for the horses. Grease and tar buckets swung from beneath the front drivers' box.

The canvas on the sides could roll up and be tied out of the way against the square spars, but the roof was low and solid ship-lapped cedar extended out over the heads of the drivers by decorative metal braces. The ceiling and its sun onion lantern barely missed Bethany's height; close quarters for months to come. Of course, the chicken coop that hung off the front made her know others would be more confined. Food would be replaced as farmers provided but they had to be well provisioned in between.

"Best to think of rain as well as sun protection," Sam fretted. "You get sick and Jonathan could perish for sure." Castor oil, peppermint, quinine, camphor, hart's horn, citric acid, physic pills, and even laudanum were packed, bearing witness to the serious nature of "no civilization." A book of diseases and known cures had already proven helpful when Jonathan's tooth cutting accompanied an earache. She wasn't sure whether the heated salt placed in a sock was effective or merely soothing; but, either way, he'd recovered nicely.

More bandboxes contained sewing notions, crochet hooks, thread, pins, needles, hatpins as well as hairpins, a couple of gift broaches that were considered merely "costume jewelry." Baby paraphernalia hung within a net bag that tied to the same brace as curtain hooks. As they made and remade decisions on what to take and what not, the dangers became clearer. Mrs. Long's beautiful silk dresses and petticoats became padding for glass bottles of food, medicines, and spices.

A tool kit, including hammer, saw, drill bits and press, plane, square, ax, chisel, clamps, glasscutter, block and tackle, ropes, etc. filled the entire space under the wagon seat. The most frequently used (determined by Charles) were packed in a drawstring canvas sack that featured a leather strap for easy loading and unloading. All the other tools were packed in a similar fashion, including her "secret" possessions.

Rolls of canvas filled the back corners between the inside barrels and cupboards. Jonathan's diapers and two years of clothing barely fit into the exposed cases along with extra flannel. Her minimal clothing and personals fit below. Wooden textile spindles along the roofline held her four dark dresses. A new multi layered winter cape of dark wool was added plus Mrs. Long's theater mink, now repaired for cold weather versus impressing the elite. Beneath it were four of Mrs. Long's casual dresses (Bethany shouldn't act like a widow forever, Sam urged) and elaborate petticoats. Summer and winter shovel hats hung by ribbons from one corner. However, in the other was her one extravagance: Mrs. Long's fancy wedding cap and mauve lace wedding dress. It was too beautiful to leave, else she couldn't resist hoping to use it, someday? Both resided in a generous sized hat box. The blue flower garlanded paper covering added a bit of bright color and hopefully it would urge cheerful thoughts when the days' labors proved too rigorous?

Mrs. Long's slightly too large riding boots, shoes and winter boots were sold to Timmy's teenage sister. Beth would thus have the advantage of new footwear. These got bagged as well, along with four sizes of shoes for Jonathan. In them were stuffed cotton and wool socks, double knitted mittens, and leather gloves.

A larger hooded bunting was made for Jonathan out of two layers of a new blue wool blanket. Two fur lap robes were laid out under Jonathan's oil cloth covered middle floor mattress. Pounds and pounds of soap and candles were stored between coils of thick rope in a top drawer. A shaving mirror, several combs, a silver brush set, toothbrushes, and two large wash pans hung from canvas pockets that draped off the back of her "cupboards." A large oval copper canning tub with clamped on laundry rollers sat on top of the commode due to the lack of any other space.

For several days they worked at either liquidating or adding forgotten items. Luckily Bethany was well adapted to getting by without. Six silver porringers with handles, pewter tankards, pewter beefsteak plates with hot water recesses, a basting spoon, stuffing spoon, soup ladle and a fish slice that would do double duty as a dessert server were added to several knives (some for trading.) Silverware for only six was due to Sam guarding her against playing the too generous hostess. Salt, pepper, baking spices, a mustard pot, and a small silver wine strainer pretty much completed her outfit.

Samuel insisted on her personal preparation as well. Clouds bumped and fumbled over the rifle range vying to view his latest accomplishment.

"Sam, I don't know why I need to learn to shoot a gun," Bethany hesitated. "I mean, Mr. Wright must be hiring many men who can shoot. I'd image most of them better than I could ever hope!"

"Well, you still have to learn," Sam insisted. "If you could hear Joseph tell about the snakes, hostile Indians, cougars, bears, buffalo stampedes and roust-a-bouts, you'd know I'm right. Now load, cock, aim and squeeze, just like I taught you."

The sports club they frequented took special interest in a gorgeous widow woman's "great western adventure." Unfortunately she wanted none of the hubbub. Luckily Sam did most of the talking while she muzzle loaded the single action five cylinders of the new Patterson percussion revolver. The small octagon barrel felt weird in her hand and the holster felt heavy against her black bell skirt, but the worst was how the noise impacted already taunt nerves.

Samuel also insisted she know how to load and shoot a similar self-cocking long octagon barreled rifle, but was content with her knowing only the basics due to the heavy caliber. The few times she'd fired it, her shoulder had ached for a week and the bruises were still fading.

"You're doing great, Beth!" Sam praised her efforts. He knew it took great effort to be out in front of this group of men. Nevertheless, she'd encounter many more where she was going. If he had his way, she would over achieve at every skill he could possibly bestow.

"Sam," she sank wearily into the carriage beside him, "do you realize you are expecting me to walk, ride, bounce a baby, shoot snakes, cook with weeds or buffalo chips, keep us clean without water...and I'm exhausted before I even take the first step?"

"You could always stay here," he suggested with a pleased expression.

"And get in Heidi's way?" she posed melodramatically. "I think not! If I *must* pine my life away regretting 'what might have been,' at least it's better than watching her take you right out from under my nose."

Sam laughed and pursed his lips together. "Okay, so she *is* cute, I admit it. I just don't know how to introduce the subject of courting her. She's awfully young!"

"Well, it would appear no one *else* notices. But, since she's from a fine family in Norway, your house would have to shine from top to bottom. No more once a week maid if you marry Heidi, you hear what I'm saying? More expense, more people in and out of your life—she's *very* sociable!—more demands to straighten up your library, maybe even new furniture and curtains?" Then she warned, "You aren't getting any younger but then she isn't either. In fact, if you didn't have such a stubborn streak, you'd have been married years ago...not to Heidi, of course, but another poor pitiful creature."

"Pitiful!" he protested. "Thank you very much, Bethany Clark! See if I take you shooting any more."

"Promise?" Her pathetic blue eyes pleaded hopefully.

"I promise." His eyes evidenced sudden dread. "You need to leave soon. We can't wait for autumn; you've got to leave right away. You have to get as far inland as you can before winter. When you get over the Alleghenies you still need to wait until you're almost to the Mississippi before you find a place to winter over. You can't plan on traveling much in the spring. I know Joe; by the tone of his letter he's pretty ticked off already. He'd leave by sea and tell the Motts he'd pick you up next year."

She reaffirmed her resolve, "Tomorrow?"

"Okay, tomorrow," he confirmed the finality.

"I'll miss you, friend Sam." She swallowed a lump in her throat, breathed deeply and changed the subject. "But don't be too long letting Heidi know your feelings. She's not going to find it hard to get herself a husband. Did you know Pastor Terrell's already asking her to sing church solos?"

They smiled over Mattie's shared wisdom and Sam's confirmed detective work. "She's too good a chance. And I happen to know she thinks you just about put the shine on the apple, even if she does think you're getting 'past your prime,' *old* friend."

"Oh, thanks a lot," grumped Sam as he slouched deeper into the corner of the cobblestone jostled carriage. "You really know how to hurt a guy. And, should I also point out that my hair is starting to thin?"

"She's already noticed," Bethany winked. "Ask her yourself if you don't believe me. That is, if Jonathan isn't too loudly protesting her love of shopping by now!"

"Ugh! With a friend like you, I should hate to have enemies," Sam retorted. After a comfortable smiley silence, he seriously took possession of her right hand, knowing they would soon reach the downtown appointed meeting spot to pick up Heidi. "You are my best friend, Bethany. Before I met you, I didn't think it was even possible for men and women to become best friends. So I don't want to lose you. Not only did you show me my need of Christ, you've also helped by always listening to me pouring out my anger, confusion, or loneliness. I can never repay you for that."

"You're welcome, Sam, but we all need Him." She gently disengaged her hand. "Because so few people ever really take the time to find Him, you deserve some personal credit too! I just praise God that I was His instrument to help you in your search. Right now I have to believe that God is carefully *working all things for good*, for both of us."

CHAPTER 7:
A Captain's Wishes

"Mr. Joe!" yelled Captain Bradley Neal above the din of the busy freight yard. Everyone teased him about his name. Many declared him running from the law, insisting he just switched first and middle name around because he was so absent-minded. He'd otherwise never respond to an alias?

Joe Wright squinted his already tanned face into an early April morning's sun before shouting, "Bradley! Over here." Joe lifted his flat black felt brimmed hat before he used it to push back the mass of escaping black curls that needed a haircut before he headed west. His back was near twice as wide as Bradley's and he stood a full head taller when Bradley finally gained the granary platform and panted a small fog into the early frigid air. The man, Joe knew, made up for size with ability, daring, and style.

"They be come, Joe, a big man, young boy, babe just walking, and a woman! Oh, Joe, listen to me! You will tear my heart away if you take her with you. You must find someone who needs exercise, a nice spinster who wants another chance to catch a husband. You can find all kinds of these everywhere, but this one should stay here, in St. Louis, this you must do for me, okay, Joe?"

"Sorry, Bradley, but she's the one Sam says I've got to take. Believe me when I say this, 'I'd be more than *happy* to leave her.' In fact, nothing would please me more!" Joe wiped a large callused hand through his hair again, replacing the hat low to shade neat black brows and wide set blue-gray eyes against the morning rays.

"Who's Sam and why he doesn't want me to keep her?" Bradley looked ready to duel.

"Well," grinned Joe, "for one thing he's a fancy Providence, Rhode Island, lawyer who's financing the whole thing. Second, he claims she's *his* girl."

"Pshaw!" Bradley disgustedly shook his thin mustached face. "She is *not* his girl. He makes her go away. Now, me," he bounced a raised bejeweled digit on his chest, "I like her to stay here always and will make her *want* to stay!"

Joe laughed rarely, but it was stated as such a fact! It really tickled to see the sly smile and dreamy eyes on the fancy dressed riverboat owner. From his polished shoes to his brass buttons and braid, Bradley Neil exuded marine magnificence. The fact that his new steamship was barely more than a glorified barge made him all the more comical.

On second thought, Joe didn't know why it tickled him. If Widow Bethany could turn both Samuel Roberts and Bradley Neil into instant mush, what would she do to fifty ratty muleskinners? It was bad enough he didn't want to travel overland. With a woman along, this was going to be the trip from you-know-where!

"Well, let's go get them, Romeo, can't win fair maiden from afar, can we?" Joe managed before hammering out last instructions to his crew of three to continue stockpiling cream of tartar, baking soda, oats, oatmeal, flour, beans, mash and grease buckets.

"I tell you, Joe, I'm serious." Bradley brushed at a speck of lint on his sleeve. "I never fell in love at first sight before this! Maybe I'm in love in twenty minutes before, but this is different. But, she is such a lady! So, I need proper introduction, from you, okay, Joe?"

"Sure," Joe appeased, but he really wasn't listening because otherwise he would have informed that he didn't know her either. Instead he was eyeing a new Kentucky greenhorn exiting from a side alley. His unsteady gait at this time of the morning was sure trouble if he managed to join their outfit. Mentally he noted the man's wide nose, v-notched black hat, and slight scar above the left eye that divided one of his brows. He'd recognize him if he came around. Soon Joe would be on his way with whatever the Lord and his own good or poor judgment provided. (He exerted great care dividing credit, versus blaming God for his own decisions.) He also liked to wait a few days before he let anyone know he was hiring. Cases similar to this one had spared him more troubles than any innate ability to size up men.

Bradley sang of love and brushed his uniform all the way across the Mississippi, his tiny black and white flatbed burbling happily behind the small pilothouse. His was not the largest or fanciest paddleboat, but it was the cleanest and safest in Joe's opinion. Since only Joe, Tom (the elderly colored fireman,) his son Tom Jr., and Bradley were aboard, he could hardly tell the owner to knock off the caterwauling. But Joe's mornings were not usually accustomed to tolerating top of the lung music. He wasn't terribly jovial by nature. Still, it irked him to be irritated. All the same, enduring singing before seven in the morning was expecting a lot!

Ex-slave Tom, who usually stayed aboard with Tom Jr., was right beside them on the gangplank, bow legs tipping his wide belted girth from side to side. Obviously, Bradley's great infatuation was a justifiable case of hired man's curiosity?

"There, Joe," Bradley whispered loudly, breaking into a wide smile. "In front of Goodwin's, the lady with the baby, they are a sight, hey? Madonna and child, this is not so?"

Joe could only groan. She exceeded his worse nightmare!

"She sure 'nuf is purty, Capt'n Neil," Tom agreed, folds of chin working like an accordion.

Joe stomped a small rock beneath the muddy road. "Let's go!" He led out without waiting to see if they followed.

Bradley hissed, "Joe!" within a few feet of the outdoor arrangement of tables,

He stiffened and turned impatiently. "What now?"

"Your hat." Bradley's hiss reminded him of his lapse of civilized manners.

Joe self-consciously swiped the offensive headgear into his left hand but continued swiftly proceeding toward the lady's table before he lost his determination to see this impossible imposition through.

He'd never seen lashes that thick and long, not even on the big Frenchman he had helped bail out of a fight at his father's mining camp in thirty-three. At only seventeen, the lesson of sizing up the competition had come at quite a price. He'd be twenty-eight April 12 and he still had Maurice to thank for what he'd taught him. "The Frenchman" had learned to fight real good because of those "girly lashes." Constant tormenting had motivated him to develop every muscle into a finely tuned fighting machine. How could he have conveyed so much about self-defense and God's grace in just three months? How he wished he could be that effective a witness. Silently he wondered where Maurice might be today; and he chuckled, wondering whether he'd conquered the Jews' harp?

"Widow Bethany Clark?" Joe addressed her curtly.

"Yes?" The raised startled face with dark blue eyes reminded him of his sister's dolls. Dolls his mother had bought in London or Paris but considered much too delicate for Claudia to play with, unless Mother supervised, which she rarely had the time or inclination to bother doing.

"I'm Joseph, Samuel's college friend," he introduced himself with a rush of fresh resolve. A tug on his shirt prompted him to add, "and, this," he beckoned backhandedly to Bradley, "is Captain Neil Bradley of *The Colonel's Lady*, our ship and destination to get you across the Mississippi, and also, this is the best fireman on that majestic river, Thomas…" He turned around to discover that Tom was nowhere in sight, probably never even came across the road? Just as well, he glared at Bradley's preening. He'd never heard the man and his son addressed as anything but "ol Tom" and "young Tom."

"Captain," the doll nodded while clutching the chubby child whose long blond curls ducked shyly into her shoulder, "I'm glad to meet you. I'm sure Mr. Wright has put us in safe hands with you and your crew."

One couldn't argue with the fancy dressed captain. There certainly were uglier women in the countryside and plenty with more flesh to lose. And, there was no denying she fit the term "physically spectacular." But, *he* didn't have to like her looks, and *he* didn't have to like her charms because *he* smelled trouble—*his*!

"Would you mind if we joined you, ma'am?" Captain Bradley inquired all the while pulling himself into the chair next to hers. "I should care for a slight repast myself."

"Not at all, you're both most welcome," Bethany smiled politely, removed the baby blanket from the back of the chair Captain Neil had tried to carefully occupy and pulled away some dishes.

After waiting for her to reseat herself, Joe continued doggedly. "Umm, I was hoping the rest of your party would be here too." Joe looked about the small open awning area expecting to locate the men Bradley had previously recognized.

"Charles and Timmy just left for the stable, to feed the horses," Bethany informed. "They expected to tour the rest of the town before you came to retrieve us, but I'm sure the town on the opposite bank will be just as exciting." Her dazzling confident smile left Joe depressed.

With resignation, he sat down and ordered eggs, sausage and biscuits. And then he marveled over the captain only wanting coffee and apple pie. (The man had eaten at least four raw ones on the way over. Was he so in love that Adam and Eve was all he could think about?)

Just as Joe was gulping down his last bite, a wide man and a narrow boy joined their table. "This is Charles Brodsky and Timothy Martin," the widow offered introductions.

"Charles?" He stood to shake the meaty hand that Charles offered after a slight hesitation. At his silent nod Joseph turned to the young man beside Charles. He would have preferred more meat on this one. If skinny now, what would he look like after six months? "And you must be Timothy?" He smiled an uneasy recognition.

"Yes, sir." Timothy Martin's firm handshake accompanied a beaming grin. He had begged Samuel Roberts to let him go west with the Long baby and his nurse. Lucky for him he had lots of younger brothers and a couple of toddler sisters. He had vowed to help Mrs. Clark and Charles get Jonathan to Oregon because he had "lots of experience with babies." Finally, when no one with better references showed up, Mr. Roberts had reluctantly agreed. Seemed he stressed every day how responsible, diligent, sober, and helpful he must be. And, it had surprised him to drive the baby's wagon, not Charles. That this was a huge responsibility was constantly stressed. Then, just a couple weeks before leaving (when he knew for sure that he would not be replaced) he'd had to tell his mom. He knew it was going to be tough for all of them to be so far away, but his older brother Henry brought in a decent week's wage. His own pay barely kept himself clothed; they sure didn't need an extra mouth to feed (especially one that ate like he did.) He'd already filled out the waist of his new twill trousers just since they left Providence. If he could, he'd try to send some money home after next September. By then, his half held back monthly wages given to his mom would run out.

"I understand you have two wagons, but only one is supposed to cross the Mississippi, is that right?" asked Joe of Charles.

"Yes," Bethany spoke up from his right. "The extra wagon has already been sold; the horses will be our spare team. Supposedly Charles will drive a wagon for you, which Timmy will share for shelter, but will also regularly see to the maintenance of our wagon and harness as well. Is that your understanding also?"

"Right." Joseph Bentley Wright III jerked around surprised. "If you've finished," he glanced at the empty dishes, "then we should see to transferring your wagon and baggage to the flat white stern wheeler at the dock."

"I'll be right with you," she replied, rising to bounce the already fidgeting boy and gathered up reticule, gloves, and blanket.

Captain Neil made a big deal of removing her chair, assisting her between his and the next table's chair, then resting his hand on her elbow as they headed toward the proprietor's desk. Behind her back he motioned Joe to stay put (playing the big spender?) Joe's hard eyes followed them, watched female as well as male patrons take note of her passing, and rued the day he'd allowed himself to be blackmailed. Astonished to see her pay for the three meals, he also noted how she commandeered the men. As Bentley paid for his food and Joe's, he noted how deftly she had seated him before sweetly asking if he'd hold the hefty baby. (Ha! The captain with a child looked as unnatural as a fish with a cigar!)

In the retrieving of their belongings, it amused Joe she innately recognized the captain should not proceed to a lady's boudoir. Although, he shortly learned she and the child had remained in her wagon; only the men had stayed at the hotel. Did that indicate unexpected thrift or unusual wisdom? Mostly he wanted to know about her being in charge of finances. Sam had said she had willingly and easily taken over running the Longs' household, but it had never occurred that included handling money. And, she seemed to make a point that *she* had sold the wagon; should have been a bit of an affront to most men, but sturdy Charles hadn't even flinched. Was she an independence-seeking female going west to claim her own section under the 1842 "Preemption Bill"? If so, that could explain her willingness to leave the States? He'd never before met a woman who came of her own decision, but he presumed there had to be at least one exception somewhere. And women weren't as likely to gamble or drink alcohol. He'd known a good many who became the family bankers because their men did. However, if either Charles or Timothy imbibed, he'd find out if one or both should come along.

Samuel may have started this group, but I'm in charge of seeing it finished. Whatever he thought was best he'd point out to Sam later. He knew Sam and he had a different perspective on matters, both personal and religious. He also needed to talk to Sam about the Lord. God forgive him, but how could he talk about the love of God to Sam when his own life was such a mess? For himself, even love of his fellow man was a joke! As much as he tried to live right, he appeared basically mean. As much as he tried to find a way to forgive, his temper or memories got the better of him. When he tried to repent, it seemed God waited for him to do more, much more. He did know that God was real, he claimed Christ for his Savior and a Friend he could depend on, and his repentance of past sins was genuine. But, he also figured he was God's biggest problem child. Learning to curb his tongue and soften his heart was the challenge, *but with God all things are possible* (Matt. 19:26.)

He needed God so much it hurt, especially for *this* trip! A strange and mystical thought occurred. Maybe this trip with a Boston widow was a form of penance, punishment, to purify the dross from his soul? Or would she become his albatross, like that guy in the "Rime of the Ancient Mariner"?

Joe paid little attention to the courtship of Bradley and Bethany. However, it soon became apparent (even to him) that the captain was beating a dead horse. The lady was charming and polite, but not impressed. The captain strutted, postured, bribed, tempted, and pleaded, but she maintained her duties to the child were not to be shunted onto another. In desperation, the captain attended church with Joe, Timmy, widow, and child. Even then, she could not be persuaded except to allow a pleasant lunch. The widow, Joe chuckled to observe, deftly made a point of presuming it included all of them (to the captain's dismay.) Timmy and Joe both knew what the dark looks were all about, but managed exceptionally well to "innocently" ignore him.

Joe might fear her face and form, but he was beginning to admire her persuasive intellect and manipulation skills. However, what if the same skills were used in the opposite way? Should she find husband material to her liking, what then? He thought of praying she *would* marry Captain Bradley; that would at least change the problems he'd face. Soon enough he dismissed the idea. (Figured God knew much more about matrimonial stuff than he even knew how to pray about.)

Bradley made an absolute fruit fly nuisance of himself, hanging around right up until departure day. It marked the first time Joe had ever felt really sorry for an adult female. It shouldn't have been such a big deal, after all, he'd felt a little sorry for his sister a few times. Just the same, it irked as he did not intend to play nursemaid, to her or anyone else! Bad enough, he rued, to be blackmailed into responsibility for the kid.

The Motts were usually real nice people, but when they heard they could have a child to themselves (after ten years of marriage without one,) they were ready to resort to even criminal intent. Add bribery to their list of ploys; the fur payment in advance had provided a lot of wagons and animals (as well they should, he justified the outrageous sum.)

When he had refused to take charge of bringing the child west, they'd just stiffened their jaws and said, "Then we guess we'll find someone else to trade with, Joe Wright."

He couldn't believe they'd stoop that low. Their one-stop trading normally saved him from lugging his goods up the whole Willamette Valley. If they stopped trading with him, whether he physically passed over them into the interior or not, others would soon refuse to trade with him too. Not because they would fabricate a lie; that would be too easy to dispute. But others would presume their refusal had "some very good reason." Out of fear, of either being cheated or tarnishing their own reputations, they'd just hang him out to get buried in an avalanche of suspicions. In time, stated imaginations would further erode previous doubts and suppositions.

Well, here they were: forty wagons of food, tools, trade goods, drivers, and herders, twenty seven wagons of settlers, plus a single widow's wagon with a child and a boy (plus big boy Charles who didn't quite match any pigeonhole niches Joe tried.) He'd noted alcohol on Charles' breath a couple of times, but it appeared he, like many of the male settlers, had been talked into a shared celebration of the westward trek. Viewing his physical prowess and carriage knowledge as a strong asset, assisting the widow's success, he decided to take a chance. That night heaven's full jewel box stared down at him. The calm was pleasant and soothing. Could he pull off an early start? On such a night as this, anything appeared extremely possible? Monday next, he calculated closely, three days.

Wagon wheels mired, making a bog of the early morning dew dampened clay, the cattle refused to move without herders' insistence and the horses and oxen stomped frustration over ended leisure. Everyone seemed excited except Joe. (He should have been enjoying a stiff sea breeze and a cup of coffee leaning over a ship rail, watching a fast wake instead of watching for trouble from either man, woman, or beast.)

If he managed to survive this, he'd a mind to retire east and hire other traders to travel. This Mott deal soured the whole process. Jed was as astute and capable as he; Chicky Greene was tougher. Mike (called "Moose",) an older mountain man and mariner, had more skill and knowledge. Joe also preferred not getting any older any quicker than he should, IF he survived this trip! He'd packed through with mountain men a few times in the late thirties, so he knew how grueling getting over the "top of the world" would be.

They probably should also wait another week, but he was going to start this second Monday of April and risk a late storm in light of clear skies and a potential long-term astronomical blessing. If he could pull this off (to get out ahead by only as much as one week,) they should certainly all thank him, cold or not. Likely as not, though, they would hardly be in a thankful mood, nor would they likely realize what they'd been spared. Didn't matter though; he'd learned to please himself.

They'd head northwest, spend a Sunday on the Lake of the Ozarks and head out for the California Road along the Platte (across broad yellow Nebraska to Ft. Kearney, then Chimney Rock and Scotts Bluff.) Follow the Platte until they hit Ft. Laramie, which he figured would be maybe one quarter the distance? (But that's hardly in travel time; that would be the easy part.)

The days after would be hot and the nights cool to cold when they climbed the broad plain of South Pass. In Sioux territory James Bridger had started a post on the route south of the Wind River Mountain range. Check for Indian problems there. He hadn't heard of much lately, but it had to happen someday. When it did, the Sioux represented a natural first choice.

The Bear River Valley led to Ft. Hall, Idaho (halfway?) Then, by following the steep ledges of the Snake River, they'd turn north to Ft. Boise, Idaho. (The ladies could put the hot spring to good use; the train would rest whether it was Sunday or not.)

He just hoped the Shoshones weren't too much on the prod. Settlers had started traipsing through to Oregon for a decade, but in earnest over the last couple of years due to this new Preemptive Act. It guaranteed a homesteader the right to improve the land, pay for it as though it were still raw land, and not be outbid by developers. (He presumed, as always, the real winners would be the fat politicians.) Supposedly some nine hundred settlers immigrated last year. He doubted the tribe was too keen on tourists shooting their buffalo, but maybe the extra trade goods and river ferrying fees were too valuable to object?

After Ft. Boise they would edge the desert before "climbing the wall" as he called the Blue Mountains. He had hoped never to see them again in his lifetime and sure wasn't looking forward to pulling his many wagons both ways. Hopefully he'd have emptied a few and sold a few before then. Last, but not least, the Dallas to cross.

How he wished the Motts could have traveled both ways. They'd realize the danger was just as imminent overland as by sea. He'd sooner go by stout ship round the horn in winter as to ferry across the Deschutes River on an open raft. They'd come to the final leg along the Columbia River before facing the Cascade Mountains. If they managed all that, then it was a flower-strewn walk in the park up the Willamette River Valley to Salem.

Only a few up and down mountains, deep canyons, dry deserts and several treacherous rivers, what's to worry? That is, besides revolting angry men, shivering or dying women, lost and stolen children, no grass, no water, hailstones from the size of peas to walnuts, animals with cut or separated hooves, Indians on the warpath or stealing provisions and animals, deserting hired help, getting snowbound in the mountains, animals eating poisonous vegetation or possibly humans facing starvation. Anything else this devil-infested country could throw at them?

CHAPTER 8:
Alone Together

    Bethany tired easily in the heat but so did huge horses. Joe ordered her to rest at least once during the day, though most women did not. She began sharing cold biscuits while walking in the early morning with Jonathan, whom she held captive in her apron. Extra straps pulled from the back crossed over Jonathan's back and she had sewn the apron half up into a pouch effect attached to the top of her shoulders by buttons. She fed him a prepared meal from the night before, about ten or so, and put him down to rest while she walked alongside the wagon until the noon meal. When he fussed from being over tired or too long constrained she often crooned "Nearer My God to Thee," praying every word.
    While she prepared their meal, Timmy Martin (medium height, skinny, auburn hair that hung straight just shy of his eyes, that is, it did now, thanks to her new barbering skills that had also shorn baby Jonathan of his re-grown girlish curls,) was off talking with the other settlers and Joe's hired men. At first he had carried Jonathan in his arms on his social jaunts. But when illness started breaking out, Joe insisted the baby be left in the wagon no matter how much he cried.

Charles usually chose this time to inspect harness and wheels, watching her every move, then fetched Timmy to eat. It wasn't exactly what she'd expected but it was a routine they accepted.

Charles had come to respect her authority and gave her no problem other than wariness. As they became ever more weary and accepting, to keep the conversations impersonal, she began to ask about their future plans. However, they offered an extreme contrast in expectations. Charles didn't know how to answer because he had no plans at all; Timmy had a different notion every two days. Gradually they accepted that "nooning" meant listening to what Timmy learned in his meanders.

When measles broke out Bethany scrubbed and cleaned with lye soap everything Jonathan touched. She kept Timmy and Charles away from him as much as possible and nearly became a recluse herself. The other women noticed her sorrowful separation but understood her responsibility to the child.

Regardless, Jonathan came down with it. She stayed inside the wagon whenever he awoke for almost two weeks. Toward the end she near despaired for his life. Forlornly she stayed a small distance away to attend the few funerals of those who didn't make it.

When all were on the mend, though, it seemed she didn't quite fit back into the women's social circle. She trudged, picked weeds and chips, searched for berries and greens along with the rest, but something never improved. Was it Joe always having them attempt the crossings first? Or did they resent her easier loading and unloading? Was it having the support of three men but only the cooking for two? Or, were her dishes and tableware too fancy? Were they jealous she had a clean dress more frequently or had a more watertight shiplapped wagon?

During late morning Jonathan played until he slept. Then she drove the wagon (to "rest my shoulders" meant zealous and affable Timmy could canter off on a horse to follow Joe or some other male hero.) By late afternoon, she and Jonathan attempted a rest together and Timmy now handled the reins from the ground to lessen the load.

Even *she* felt comfortable tying up the canvas sides a bit in over one-hundred-degree heat! At night propping the sides outward dragged in a change of air. Mosquito netting hung over her and Jonathan from the same hook that held the infrequently lit lantern (Jonathan slept the minute supper chores finished.) When awake, he walked, fell, pulled himself up onto the fence, and played with several presents of rattles. That made getting inside at night a little more difficult as she had to enter by the front to avoid them.

Charles was becoming quite acceptable as a partner to a rough mountain man named Chadwick. One noon he announced, "Chadwick says we can trap beaver and fox, maybe bear in the early fall, and live soft the whole summer long."

"Where would you live?" Bethany asked in astonishment.

"Chadwick knows of an abandoned cabin. No reason why we can't take it over."

"That what you want to do?" she inquired further. She amazed herself to be afraid for Charles, that maternal instincts could stretch to an adult she secretly feared. Mostly she worried whether Chadwick's plan included taking advantage of Charles' brawn?

"Might as well," he munched on last night's beans she'd laced with honey that Joe had found and shared among the cooks. Ordinarily a nice crusty biscuit and beans would have been a welcome meal, but they had been eating the same thing for two weeks now. How she wished to see a vegetable she didn't have to parboil for hours. "Won't be able to do it in a few years, Chadwick says the beaver are already getting scarce in the lower rivers. What about you, Timmy?" Charles' suddenly gruff voice demanded.

"Don't know yet." Timmy's frustration became apparent. "But, don't think I'd want to go off trapping the whole winter. Miss my family fierce, guess I'd want to stay near people if I could."

"Well," Charles rose laboriously, "guess we gotta git back to it. Beginning to wonder if I won't be worn down to half size by the time we see Oregon."

Bethany agreed. The saying was, "them that eat the most breakfast eat the most sand." Remembered more were graves they'd passed, in the lonely desert with a coyote howling. Three men had now drowned (fording rivers holding on to thrashing animals,) then a mother and newborn had passed away during childbirth. They'd led wagons over the grave to pack down the earth and hopefully obliterate any sign it existed. She wasn't sure which was more disrespectful: riding over it or Digger Indians digging them up for clothes and leaving them unburied (to be further desecrated by animals for more gruesome reasons.) In her mind, it felt right, but her spirit rankled against the fear this could happen to her, Jonathan, or any other member of their train.

Just as shocking were some of the quick marriages of the new widows and pitifully young teenagers. One of the young men she considered nearly abusive. *But, I have the support of three men; to what extreme would I have been driven if suddenly left alone?*

Naturally distressing, beyond the obvious physical effects of travel, was the silted dirt that made her skin resemble an old pincushion. Worse had been the thick layer upon layer of alkali dust. The desert she hated almost as much for having lain in her dirt, fearing sparing even enough water to dampen her face. Necessary cleansing of Jonathan and her hands was accomplished with animal fat. When they reached water, the fat had to then be boiled out of every precious scrap of cloth. Daily picking up bits of grass, weeds, and buffalo chips made cooking revolting and dangerous.

Thank the Lord she'd purchased that drum! At least she didn't squat like most. But, that also caused more resentment?

Most women held themselves in check against hardships. How she wished the men would resist arguing, fist fighting or vicious name calling. Thankfully Joe was tough enough to handle them. And thank God she was single, not bearing a child as well as carrying one, as were many of the women. Nor was she enduring morning sickness in a wobbling wagon or heavy with child in stifling heat. Most blessed of all, she need not endure a husband's flaring short temper.

That jolted her. More than anything else in life she'd thought she wanted a child again. She didn't relish giving Jonathan up after over a year and a half caring for him. But carefully she'd taught him to call her "Beff." At least she would not have "Mama" ringing in her ears when they parted. Right now, all she wanted was an end to this wretched journey (even if it meant giving up Jonathan to the Motts. Yes, likely by Oregon she'd be quite prepared to "get on with life," presuming she was alive to do so.)

Another jolt occurred when she realized her need of a child exceeded that of a husband. Not that she was about to produce one without a husband; but it was a revelation of how the journey had changed her perspective. Arguments you could not help but overhear in the close spaces and thin shelters reminded of how good her marriage to Jacob had been. (Of course, Yankee husbands were known for their gentle ways.) Daily she prayed for women who ignored how much the husbands suffered too, including the embarrassment of depending on Joe's hunting skills or their own wives trading with Indians for food. When alone with any of them, she'd often tried to encourage them to cherish more and complain less. Always she got the same sullen blank stare. Then finally she'd hit a last nerve of one who'd remonstrated, "Easy enough for *you* to say!" Probably shunning was the result of her being judgmental?

One was so put out she was ready to trade her husband for anyone who lived at Fort Laramie. Had she found anyone willing to face up to her husband's infamous Bowie knife, she'd be there still? As it was, she spoke neither to husband, her small children, or anyone else until they reached the cool of the mountains. Since then she only complained about the constant climb or descent. Regularly she sat and refused to budge. Finally she'd be put on a loaned horse and her oldest girl would lead it, the woman sprawled in a near stupor. Many questioned if her head were addled. At one point the husband had left her sitting. Joe had Timmy go back to fetch her up with the group. Soon after, they'd decided to wait for wagons coming along in the distance. One of Joe's men disappeared in the night. No doubt to join the other train? Joe very matter of fact passed a few provisions to the girl saying, "It's a gift, from Thurston."

And, Bethany noticed Joe trying to make sure little ones were well out from under the wheels whenever they started moving. Woman hater, maybe, but he apparently liked small children well enough. A fierce man when required, he also seemed extremely fair and God fearing. He seemed similarly cursed. Neither appreciated God's gift of beauty, he being as beautiful in a masculine way as she did feminine. Young single women would flutter around him; older married women would knowingly eye each other understanding why.

Joe felt Bethany's eyes on him and turned to stare back into weary eyes, slumped shoulders and dust covered clothing. The formerly immaculate widow shifted her attention to resume passing a damp cloth over Jonathan's head, hands, and feet. Soon she would toss the Indian drum she sat upon into the back of her wagon. He regretted she would be reduced to walking all day. Originally thinking the drum a stupid purchase, he acknowledged it hooked easily on the picket fence, was lighter than a chair, and alerted her to whenever the little boy woke up. Glad Jonathan was too young to be jumping in and out of wagons and dashing among the animals. Always he shuddered over how most young ones did so.

The widow's wagon he had not insisted on lightening before they started. And, her cedar roof and solid wagon had been freshly tarred above and below even before he'd mentioned it. Her handles and stacking gear could be disassembled and reassembled faster than any others so it was a given that she would ford or be ferried across first. His primary responsibility out of the way, his mind could then relax.

One thing he never would have given her credit for, being smart enough to buy high moccasins and Kiowa leggings. Tucking her skirt up as they'd traveled through sagebrush and prickly pear, many of the ladies had deemed it scandalous. However, she'd not needed the services of Mrs. Sims' tweezers, had she? No, she'd been less trouble than any (men included) he was amazed to admit (so far.) What would she do in Oregon? She apparently wasn't sweet on any of these sorry men. Did she expect to be hired by the Motts? Maybe he should prepare her for more realistic expectations? No, just talking to her might start rumors or worse. Nah, forget it; she'd survived thus far. Oregon would be a lot easier. Skimpy grass was his main problem. If they didn't get down off this mountain, their beasts would feed the vultures.

Bethany and Timmy lost two horses that came up lame. Instead of shooting them, they'd been let go into the wilderness. "Maybe the lameness would heal given enough time," she'd pled. Nodding, they'd saved ammunition instead. Besides, there was stench enough from dead animals along the trail already. Obviously they were not the first train to attempt an early start. Now, with only seven horses, they'd all start to worry. Needing a six-horse team minimum, only one horse at a time could be rested.

They were carrying Jonathan all day long too. Either he was too hot, too cold, too curious or too old to sleep two naps a day. So that meant they endured considerable more fussing. Just the same, Bethany thanked God for his strength to fuss. The small silent bundles in other arms lent more concern. Timmy, bless his heart, spelled her and she drove the team from the ground level, as he did, every other hour. He was losing flesh he couldn't afford yet they couldn't eat more than Joe allotted lest they also eventually worry about running out.

This somber terrifying thought was new. She had never noticed the need for food while she grew up on a farm. It had always surrounded them. It had been more of a chore to pick, wash, dry, jar, process, store, retrieve and prepare.

The milk cow they'd started with had dried up and been traded for more flour and salt.

Joe said they were lucky to have a full moon when they came to the desert. By traveling at night and baking like lizards feigning sleep by day, the old timers with the party said they'd never had such an easy crossing. If true, she prayed for those who didn't have bright moonlight. If she thought about it, her mouth still puckered with the awful alkali thirst. How unbelievable to go for miles and miles for days on end without seeing water.

Only in wretched contrast did she acknowledge the rare beauty of cool green and water wrapped New England geography.

"I'll swap, Widow Beth," Timmy came up behind her. (The name originally used by Joe had stuck to her.)

"Jonathan's just fallen asleep," Bethany whispered. They didn't dare put him into the wagon for fear the brakes would let go or the wagon could tilt or topple over a chasm. In the mountains there was always some task that would near pull the men's (and women's) arms near out of their sockets. Ladies more or less schooled in their resentment over being reduced to men's hard manual labor. Joe warned everyone to beware falling asleep near the canyons and plateaus that overlooked deep chasms. Now so worn out, it took immense effort to keep alert. (Bethany shuddered over the story told of a German farmer who had fallen asleep from fatigue. His horses had just walked off the trail, killing the entire family.)

Forgotten was asking Timmy how near or how far. Sometimes he volunteered, but it was never near enough. If the snow didn't come, if they walked far enough, if the horses stood up, if wild game held out, always it was one big "IF" after another. What she knew was that it was longer than the guidebooks estimated; she'd handed hers over to Timmy in disgust. When they had enough water and grass, there were too many mosquitoes. When rain stopped chilling them to the bone and drenching their contents, they broiled in the sun and basted in dust. When the air became pleasant, the vegetation and water turned poisonous or else it stunk from putrid carrion.

She also dreaded the unknown, of always being first at the constant water crossings. She did appreciate water for the chance to get clean again, but the currents and numbing cold terrorized. Yes, she knew how to swim (thank God!)

No, she need not climb monuments, look at vistas, or admire blooming cactus. Jonathan was slow walking and heavier carrying. She wanted an end before she turned twenty-three (December 29.) Today, September 29, was three months away but she felt at least fifty. Every day the same plodding, one foot in front of the other, thanking God for Joe, Charles and Timmy, eating the same boiled wheat, oatmeal, dried beans and peas. Wild meat became scarce and her depleted store of salt reduced everything tasteless. Everyone else endured the same predicament but that shared knowledge only depressed further. Mr. Wright held his part in God's plan to get them through, but remained detached except when crossing water or hoisting wagons up or down.

If she had a husband, would she be so patient? She knew she *would* like to have a good cry on a broad shoulder (a man's strength could be so marvelously reassuring!) And look at the sacrificing missionary men trying to convert the Indians. In so many places they had passed she sensed a magnificent zeal for the Lord's work. She almost looked forward to Oregon's inhabitants despite the trail's discomforts. That is, provided the British didn't declare war or their intermittent aggression against infiltrating American settlers didn't get her killed?

Rumors proliferated the closer Oregon approached. Would these helpful Indians really passively allow the white men to push them into the sea? Oregon was as far west as either race could inhabit, peacefully or violently. If so, Oregon posed a likely spot for an Indian war? The thought she'd traveled all this way, just to be killed, and over political disputes or clashes with primitives, ludicrous! Gritting already dust-coated teeth, she hauled aching limbs up a never-ending mountain.

Gasping on the crest, she viewed green trees with glimpses of a shining river. Oh, to just slide down, wash for hours…not clothes or dishes…just leisurely soak and play with little Jonathan (sadly, the cherished toddler never intended to be hers.)

Slowly everyone braced, roped, and otherwise prevented wagons from crashing. When they arrived at the river, it took awhile before she realized Joe would float her wagon away without her.

Timmy was going and Charles had been instructed to keep an eye on Timmy. However, when Joe had everyone drifting away, she was left to sit astride a horse with little Jonathan excitedly tied frontward into her apron. Flannel tied across her back gave extra support to keep him well connected. His small excited sentences forced sad realization that his baby days were ending. Along with them, Joe and several of his men herded horses to an eventual portage. They took several days and passed several Indian villages, sullen and impassive until Joe would bring out unexpected trade goods. Unfortunately, the horses were soon filled to capacity with furs. Now it became clear why he had not sold all his wagons as they emptied. He would need them to get his furs to the sea.

At last they came to the Columbia River. Every night she found she liked walking or wagon travel more than horseback. She was sore in places she couldn't even complain about. Charlie horses wracked her thighs; raw sores required salving whenever they stopped. And, of course, nature *would* have to remind her of being female.

From the last portage the settlers surveyed the land's attributes and decided to band into two groups based on their interests in coming. Joe sold wares to whites and reds alike and seemed in no hurry to get them on to the Salem settlement to find the Motts.

He'd finally explained a little about the Motts during a break in an extended haggling session with a British trapper. He concluded with, "Mrs. Mott is English, but married an American, Ernest Mott, so it's a difficult situation knowing which side of the fence they'll jump. More likely, they'll stay neutral until they see which way the wind blows. One thing's for sure, Oregon Territory claimed by two countries isn't going to last too much longer."

Bethany confessed her worse fears. "I hate to think I've brought Jonathan to where there will be war."

"You didn't have any choice just as I didn't." Joe clamped his jaw until his neck muscles bulged. "But we've seen the plan through as best we can. I'm sure we'd have both sided with Sam and left the kid in Rhode Island."

She gave him a wan smile, marveling he could be forced to do anything he didn't want, remembering Sam's warning about getting him mad. Had the Motts dared risk his ire?

"I wonder if Sam and Heidi are married yet?" she changed the topic. "When you see him, you *will* ask him to get word back, won't you?"

"Why didn't he marry you?" he asked the question he'd wondered since St. Louis.

"Not too much in common, for starters. Then, I had to take Jonathan to his mother's cousin. Not much future in courting a woman who's going to Oregon, right?"

"Sam said you fit into Providence high society enough to impress him into proposing. I doubt he'd stretch the truth or give me a totally unrealistic assessment," he insisted.

Bethany was amused that Sam's letters had discussed her to such lengths. If less exhausted, maybe she'd be flattered, or else take offense? Instead, she offered the truth. "When he asked me to marry him, I told him he needed to repent of his bitterness against God instead. In time, he came to a small church I attended and spoke with our pastor. Almost the same age, in time they became good friends. After he converted, he acknowledged his attraction to me was pretty shallow. So, I became his sister in Christ instead."

"He accepted my decision, took it upon himself to teach me to shoot and prepare me as best he could for my trip west. That, of course, was due to what you'd told him. Heidi offered to go along and take care of Jonathan in exchange for shopping downtown. By the time I learned to shoot well enough to please him, Heidi had Sam pretty well mesmerized."

Bethany's ability with a revolver was the one thing the women of the train sought her out for frequently; usually to kill a snake or put some poor animal out of its misery (hardly any female's desired task.) "Good thing he taught you to shoot," Joe shuddered. "I hate to think what might have happened if that buffalo that turned towards the wagons hadn't been stopped. You were pretty impressive, up on that wagon seat, sighting in on him. Too bad Sam couldn't have seen it; good reason to be proud of such rare insight."

"Huh!" she laughed, shifting Jonathan onto her other knee. "I knew if I didn't do it right the first time, a second chance was a whole lot less likely. I anticipated being knocked onto the ground from the recoil."

"But you stood solid! Even gave it an extra shot just to be sure. Heard later that you didn't even flinch much when Mrs. Sims insisted on administering her home made liniment."

Bethany grimaced and he half tried to hide a knowing grin. He'd had his own dose of that stinging foul brew (but only once.) He moved away to check her supplies again. She'd had a lonely trip; his fault, but he didn't regret telling the women to keep their kids away as well as themselves. As long as the Motts' baby cousin was alive and healthy, they'd both done their jobs well. From the looks of it, he'd better give her most of the few beans he had left. When he hit Astoria, he wouldn't have to worry about such things (although too tired to relish starting back east again,) floating down river and then off by sea vessel looked downright leisurely.

The Deschutes crossing had been so frightening she had stuck Jonathan in a small barrel, ready to clamp the lid on at any moment. The weather turned rainy and damp, the nights cold and clammy. Although the stunning and enormous lush flora flourished, the human species shriveled like old leather and resembled shuffling and sniveling convicts.

Crossing the Cascades offered more horrendous despair. Sometimes the ditch they'd called a road was so deep you could barely see the team even when you were right on the bank above. Bethany crawled, slid, straddled, hoisted, and generally exhausted every ounce of strength.

Thank God for these industrious Indians! If not for them selling salmon, or for farmers selling vegetables at outrageous prices, what would they have done? Eggs at $1.00 per dozen, almost too dear to bear, perked up Jonathan's appetite. Recklessly she paid whatever his family's money could buy. She, at least, could do so, which was more than most could. Did the money set her apart even more?

One frosty October morning, camped on the banks of the Willamette, she deliberately sought Joe out. "Will we see the Motts today?"

"Yes," he assured her. "It will be late afternoon, but we should see the post before dark."

"Then," she extended her hand, "I'd like to say farewell to you now. Let's focus instead on the Motts meeting up with Jonathan."

"Yes," he returned her firm handshake. "I guarantee they'll be quite overwhelmed with their blond prince." He kind of hated to see the little charmer go himself. Now that he was beginning to talk well, he intrigued everyone, quite the pleasing package.

She regretted to say, "I wish I could have presented him trained; but he doesn't seem to have much interest. Or, maybe I haven't the strength left for interest myself?"

"I imagine Lois would be heartbroken not to claim that honor herself," he pacified.

"Suppose so; anyway, I wish you a fast journey back east." She smiled a heartfelt sentiment. "I don't envy you the trip; but I do envy your return."

"Sure you're not sorry to be going back to Sam?" he couldn't resist asking.

She shook her head.

"But?" he prompted.

"But I envy him the life he—and hopefully Heidi—will share." She was very still for quite a few minutes before adding, "I spoiled quickly. And, I could easily want to become spoiled again, but not enough to marry either the wrong man or without a good reason."

"Guess any woman would, or should, want it easy. Maybe you'll see it someday out here too?"

"No, Joe," she denied any such "guidebook" reassurance, "we won't see that kind of luxury for many long years from now. Expected it to be rough out here, but I never dreamed how raw it would be. I'll get by the best I can, but if lent the chance, I'd return east some day myself."

"You've barely arrived! It seems you'd at least give Oregon a chance." He was less impressed with her, finally! Thought the trip would have toughened her enough to be glad for any kind of life.

Outlined in the tawny yellow light that filtered through the treetops, she stated, "Maybe I should run ahead, maybe I should run back. For right now, I'm just hanging on to Jonathan for one more day." On her return to her campsite, she leaned to pick up the pot of beans cooked last night and another kettle to add water for more beans to soak.

Something in the sad mournful way she moved struck a deep cord. He knew where she was coming from; he'd been there more than once. You come to the end of yourself, you don't know where you're going to get direction, or help from, and you just hold your breath until you do know. Or, you wait for someone to give you a push one way or another. He wished he could help her get a place going, but if he didn't get out of this country within the month, he could be staying the winter.

Risking the Isthmus was about equal risk next to that, at least at this time of year. Resolutely, he called Timmy to hitch up the team and instructed him to stick close to him after the noon meal. What a ridiculous idea, he fumed afterwards. He'd never wanted to build any woman a home before this one. Was she manipulating *him*? He didn't know how but placed himself on high alert. He'd remain vigilantly on guard until he was well shut of her.

"Joe!" Lois Mott cried out waving frantically. They had come out on the plow horse she and Ernest traded a few springs ago to help Lois plant her garden. Personally, he thought the animal required more care than he was worth, but Ernest occasionally used him to pack trade goods too so maybe he did earn his feed? Ernest nudged the old animal to approximate a faster trot. From the looks of it, there were settlers from miles around with them; there had to be nearly thirty? When they got nearer, Joe waved the freight wagons to veer off and follow the river on in. Only Bethany's lead wagon met the Motts in the high grassy meadow. Butterflies and lingering wild flowers performed their ancient performance in nature's amphitheater as a small fawn's second act cavorted through a far corner.

Ernest and Lois decided to dismount and hesitate while the wagon approached the last few rods. And Joe observed a lot more strands of gray hair. Would have been better a few years younger, but rotund and usually jovial, they should make good parents anyway? And, if you had to live in Oregon, living with the Motts was as good as it got as they usually had the lion's share of trade goods, what little there was besides tools and blankets. He regretted hauling only the cheapest calico, but marked up to fifty cents per yard, few could afford that.

"Is the child alright, Joe?" Lois asked with bated breath.

"Yes, ma'am," he assured her with a scowl and an irritated nod towards Ernest. He dismounted himself as Timmy hauled the team to a stop. Timmy leaped off toward the back and Joe led the approach of Jonathan's relatives around to their planned unveiling.

"Hand me your drum," Timmy instructed and Beth tossed it beyond the side of her cupboard. Joe could only see a bit of pointed toe, but noted the fence was already aside. "Come out; step down on the drum. Tim and I'll hold the thing steady. You tell me when; we'll fling the flap up. Might as well make the grand entrance, you worked hard enough for it!"

What Joe didn't know was that Bethany had decided she didn't want Jonathan to be a reminder of death. She'd hauled out one of Mrs. Long's casual dresses, rinsed it, and hung it to dry in the back of the wagon over night, ironing it early that morning. When they'd seen the company in the distance, she'd instructed Timmy, "Keep your eyes front and center, young man," and had slipped the dress over freshly washed skin and undergarments. When she said "Ready," Joe was not prepared for the gasp that arose from the assembled group.

Looking to see what had happened, he viewed a new Bethany. Or, perhaps he saw Samuel's radiant Bethany in a new dress, gaunt but absolutely stunning nonetheless. Wine color flowed from a high neck's white lace collar of ruffles that garnished an elaborate series of v-pleats that focused on her tiny waist and mother-of-pearl buttons. The similar white lace cuffs enclosed her elbow to wrist. The lowered waist similarly flowed from its point into a wide gathered skirt. He recovered quickly, but let Timmy assist her down. Her next graceful step led straight to Lois.

"Lois Mott?" she whispered in a soft confidential tone.

Lois returned a hushed, almost reverent, "Yes."

"May I present your cousin and ward, Jonathan Long. He turned two years old as of September 3." At that exact instant, Jonathan reached out for Lois' long dangling curls and it looked, for their whole world to see, like he wanted to be held by his newly adopted guardian.

"Oh," she gushed to Ernest. "He's the exact same coloring as my cousin Dora." Ecstatic to finally hold the child she had waited for over a year, Lois waltzed off through the crowd leaving Beth and Tim to just put the drum away. Eventually, the good lady remembered her manners and invited them all to the trading post's evening meal.

"Why don't you ride on the wagon, Mrs. Mott?" Bethany suggested. "I'm glad to get out and stretch."

Reassured by Bethany not trying to usurp the toddler's attentions again, Mr. and Mrs. Mott sat with Timmy on the wagon seat and Joe tied the old horse onto the back of the wagon. By the time they all arrived, Joe's now twenty-two wagons (many having been sold along the way, with or without trade goods included, and greatly reduced loads) were already circled up. The horses had received water and now contentedly munched in the fenced pasture.

By that time, Jonathan had the Motts wound right around his little fingers, literally as well as figuratively. Joe joined them for their anticipated celebration but he didn't see anything more of Bethany until they were about ready to eat. When he did, she was again more lovely than haggard. She looked like she'd make the long trek, of course, but there was an aura about her. She looked different. Was it because the other few women's faces mostly wore blank expressions?

"Joe." Ernest Mott beckoned for silence. "Joe, please say grace? You've done more for us than anyone else more than once, and we want to hear you talk to the Lord. Bringing a wagon train of almost a hundred people all the way from St. Louis, we know He listens to you!" Bethany felt a quick jab of neglect. A total lack of recognition for her efforts made her realize Sam's wisdom. Neither pay nor flattery would be received on this end. And it did little to make her feel welcome.

Joe waited for the silence to get respectful before he began.

"Father God, we are blessed of you to be here. There were times when we wondered if we were worthy, but you brought us to water out of dry deserts, hauled us out of horrible pits and helped us crawl off many a mountain. If our faith wavered, please forgive us. If it strengthened, let us grow yet more diligent. By your Holy Spirit help us daily to perfect Your peace.

We pray health and strength for the Motts, little Jonathan Long, those who came to stay, and some that travel further yet. Please heal the bones of the little Branson girl, be with those still sick, and help fulfill the hopes and dreams of all that desire to make this land flourish.

Help them spread Your love just as these kind folks have spread this feast. Keep us safe from harm; and bless this food we pray. May we be more like Your Son, Jesus Christ, who gave himself to save the world, amen."

It was noticeably quiet. All knew Joe's voice was as shaken as he was grateful to have managed a successful journey. Those who knew him better than others were pleased. Maybe he'd found real peace at last? Commenting on his new patience, many expressed hope that it wasn't mere exhaustion.

Bethany approached Ernest and Lois in the morning. Along with handing over a great deal of cash, jewelry and a few precious keepsakes and photos, she conveyed how she had been discussing sites available for a homestead claim. She had asked who would be the most knowledgeable and managed to seat herself beside older resident settlers. It seemed there was only one nearby site with a flowing stream that offered a steep rise. When she asked Ernest about it though, he dissuaded her. "The land was cleared of trees to build a fort down river in the early thirties. Tree growth's still five to ten years from producing timber large enough for a cabin. And it's pretty far out for a lone woman to live, plus it's a pretty steep mountain for building."

"I'd still like to see it," she insisted. "Could you find someone who could show it to me?"

"Well, the only one I can think of right off would be Joe." He scratched his neck and then yelled, "Joe, can ya come out here a minute?"

"But he must go on to the coast," Bethany protested, "I can't ask him to delay his trip for mine."

"Oh, he won't be going anywhere for at least three days," Ernest denied Joe's quick departure. "We need to move stuff and then we have to check inventory for next year's trip. He won't go until we get squared away."

And so Joe took Bethany riding into the mountains on her own huge horses. Six had managed to pull through. How, she was mystified to explain except for the skill of Charles and Joe's easy pace at the end. The morning was glorious with sun as the earth miserly hoarded its golden color lest the shortening days not get enough of it to get through winter.

The trail behind seemed a dream of endurance past. Here they ate more food for lunch than they had eaten in whole days. Renewed by sleep and lessened responsibilities, it was a fine day to be alive in God's great world. The trees looked greener, the stream sang cheerier, and not even the birds' and squirrels' scolding for trespassing could dispel their peaceful contentment.

"It's a nice stream, isn't it?" Bethany commented on the mossy bank that overlooked the property and river below. Their picnic things were now stashed back in the pack but she hated the thought of leaving the idyllic setting (or making the trip back?) Was she that ready to start nest building in Oregon?

"Flows strongly in winter and spring, less in the summer, maybe even trickle during dry spells," Joe informed. "It comes from a spring plus mountain runoff like many Oregon streams."

Bethany's farm girl reasoning knew the sparse grassy slope was not the best for farming, but she figured she could route the stream right past her home's door so it would be good for a building site. Also would be good enough for grazing animals. The trees growing on a slope that held fine rich soil *were* small, but there was a whole mountain full of big ones within sight. And, thanks to not marrying, she all by herself would soon own a lot of it! She might not be able to use most of these near at hand for cabin timbers, but there were enough. If her secret purpose could be accommodated...for her small needs...enough to by get by on alone.

In a couple of years, she might even have a crop of wheat to harvest. She doubted to see the $2.00 a bushel price, like they'd seen in the forts and settlements they'd passed through, but as long as settlement continued it was unlikely the price would ever go to the ten cents a bushel she remembered her father suffering through in eighteen and thirty-seven. (Luckily her father had raised sheep mostly, although the price of wool dropped plenty too.) Considerable profit was faster at the high price, of course, but she could be very content with much lower than what she'd been forced to pay.

And, the stream could be used to start her secret lumber mill, even if it was more or less seasonal. Jeremy (one of Joe's hired men) said he knew how to set one up (learned through Timmy's mealtime recollections.) In the bottom of the tools were saw blades and connections; the metal canopy supports for her wagon were actually shafts. Part of the necessary wheel hub, bolts and what not to saw lumber were now covered over in the depleted barrel that had once held flour.

Sam had said the Longs' family fortune was in Maine lumber. He had suggested it could be part of hers in Oregon if she could find the right help. Lord willing, maybe she had?

"Are you thinking of settling here?" Joe was actually more curious to know why but wouldn't ask outright just yet.

She dreamily answered, "Yes," with an elbow against a mossy stump and her chin in her cupped hand.

He warned, "Kind of far out."

Bethany nodded. "I know, but I'm told it's the nearest steep stream around."

"What's so important about that?" his curiosity couldn't resist asking.

"That's for me to know and others to find out." She still hugged her delicious secret to herself. She'd been hugging it ever since Providence; afraid speaking of it might make it less attainable. It was her secret and Sam's. (Dear Sam, she so hoped he was doing well, both spiritually and romantically.)

Thwarted to know her mind, he demanded, "You ready to go back now?" He impatiently led the horses toward her in anticipation of a positive response. The less he saw of her the better. Bad enough the Motts ordered him about. If not out of consideration for the widow, her having absolutely no one to depend on, he'd have flat out refused.

"Yes," she agreed. "By the way, what are your plans for Jeremy?"

Joe shrugged. "He's his own man now; I hired him only to get us to here."

"Good," she smiled secret delight, rising to stand upon the stump where he'd positioned Clyde (her one remaining Clydesdale.)

Joe presumed the manipulative widow must have set her cap for Jeremy? "Aware Jeremy's a married man?" The casual question was meant to provide her with information.

"Yes," she returned. "Jonathan reminds him of his own children, he says. He has three: a girl and two boys, Sarah, William and little James."

She obviously had some other reason? Well, he just wanted out of here. Hopefully the Motts could take their eyes off Jonathan long enough to get organized. He'd depart with enough furs to make him a rich man back east. But they'd better not haggle; that little kid was worth a lot more than furs!

CHAPTER 9:
Men, Machinery and Manure

Timmy and Jeremy got the stream damned up, framed a sturdy log building, and dug a ditch. A trough hung in place to catch the paddle wheel's spill, bringing a small stream of water toward Bethany's future home and barn site. Just when the mill's roof went on and equipment was readied for use, a cold snap froze the water to a trickle. Unfortunately the men lost interest (once paid for setting it up) and both went fur exploring.

So, Bethany sawed small trees and limbs, burnt brush over stumps and made Clyde, Dave, Bo, Barb, Martha, Sweets and Swede take turns pulling what she could fall and limb into the area around her small mill, its saw and shafts rusting more each day despite frequent oiling. Observing how the huge beasts devoured grass, viewed in light of her pitiful efforts at gathering it, reinforced her opinion to immediately sell all but two. No way to keep a spare regardless of "just in case." However, for such valuable animals, she wanted cash (for worker incentive.)

Lonely days filled her hours with hay and trees. Evenings merged into barn building, tool sharpening, and cold that poked into bones like a devilish tormentor. Each clear day at ten she took a break from sawing to scythe a load of hay from the nearby meadow. After a late lunch, she used a pitchfork shaped tree limb to gather hay into the wagon that was now reduced to an open vehicle. (Its sides the paddle wheel, its top on upright logs under evergreen trees, roped and ready for high winds, with its contents banked round with poles and boughs.) "Home" wasn't even a hovel or hut yet!

Foundations emerged by hooking the horses up to an ax sharpened tree root. Resulting ditches filled with shale similarly dug near the riverbank. She consigned all but Barb and Clyde for Ernest Mott to sell. Twice now Tim had stopped by from the post saying she had a credit to use, indicating two less horses to worry about. With two to go, she dreaded retrieving them. Renewed determination gathered more hay and worked late by lamplight on the barn.

When rains resumed, Jeremy and Timmy returned to erect a lean-to affair stretched from the base of two trees up to the side of the mill. Regretfully she saw her small pile of logs reduced and her offered shanty's tree boughs half confiscated. Finally though, the men turned trees into square joists and boards, enough for a barn roof.

Each bit of lumber belittled her previous efforts (stacked firewood cemented together with a lime, sand and sawdust mortar.) In desperation, to speed up her process, she'd discovered that even she could mill firewood (despite the slow stream.) To get her animals a temporary shelter, she'd drilled holes so pins inserted into heavy log bases (placed on the shale footings) accepted upright logs. Leaving a couple of openings for doorways, she'd laboriously drilled holes almost at their tops to receive both cross members and pegs.

Finally a log weighted strip of canvas made a temporary door instead of covering precious hay. Since the animals could still find a bit of feed now and again, it commenced looking more and more adequate.

Bethany bribed Tim's sweet tooth to pick up empty bottles from around the trading post. Paying him a penny for ten, she soon had enough to add empty bottles end to end (instead of a piece of firewood) every so often, which allowed a little south side sunlight. It provided barely enough to let her see the rough hay bins, but it was cheaper than a lantern and safer than now depleted candles. Although she had tallow (now reduced to shooting her own wild game as well,) there was too much else to do. A hollow log was hauled in, filled with dirt and planted with vegetable seeds. Next question was: would anything grow in the very pale light?

Unfortunately, jerking deer meat over wet green tree limbs consumed over half a week of intermittent efforts that should have been totally dedicated to sawing more small trees.

She couldn't spend the really cold months under her roof and poles, regardless of its protecting canvas. Hence she moved her double-sided barrister bed to the barn when the roof went on (animal warmth instead of a stove. Her past tenement's shaky leg grate and smoky fireplace started looking like luxury!) Both the sides and the back of her barn evidenced low hay mows laid over raised up logs for air circulation. The center featured a group of log stalls and tree limb woven mangers backing up to more hay mows. The two horses were led in between each night. There remained enough space to add two more stalls if needed. The sloped bank's fifteen-foot high mow (reinforced with poles between the firewood sections like the rest but much more difficult to mortar due to the height) had been dug away and reinforced with more firewood and poles laid to receive a full barn width of hay. But, any hope of filling it appeared remote. The weather drizzled and froze back and forth like a cat toying with a mouse.

Where she'd put the horses (if they didn't sell,) she supposed would be in the center behind the others but she worried about heavy animals there. Two hollow logs sloped through the front area, covered by shale except for a two-foot opening that was chopped out to facilitate water assisted manure removal. Split logs nailed into a grate covered the opening to prevent broken legs, and the tilted log exited into a buried and slightly tipped barrel outside. From there the water moved just off level to spill back and forth through low ditches into next year's garden spot. By a twisted path that returned to the spillway, the water would hopefully leave most of its fertilizer behind? *What happens with winter's solid freeze?* Well, time would tell.

A water trough sloped diagonally toward the bank and dropped half its flow onto a rocky ledge where a small pool built up before emptying into a horse trough, or else tipped into the hollow log. The men had built a privy near the ledge, leaving openings for the water trough to spill through, building it into the wall at head height, with a perpendicular one at chest height that exited back to the horse trough. The cold draft would numb its occupants, but if the water trickled through at all, she'd have a "water closet" of sorts and gravity-fed water sheltered from the wind once she added an enclosed porch. (Thank heavens she didn't need a medical condition to warrant such comfort—how silly!)

The outside privy had both front and back door so visitors to the mill could use it without coming into her longed-for domain. By centering boards across the middle, it would serve from the outside for them and the inside for her cherished privacy. A short section of the barn roof was built for the dual purpose of an open porch overlooking the river. That part only sloped slightly and was heavily tarred and then boarded again.

Thanks to Tim folks heard about the mill. Soon Tim (they never did know where Jeremy traipsed off to) was trading vegetables, meat and hides for boards and planks. The hides Tim traded for her at the post where most of her credit traded for Tim's salary.

Drilling posts and shoveling and picking a food storage cellar behind the fifteen foot barn wall took all January. Despite being only a third the width of the barn, the ground resisted disturbing winter's rest. More joists extended over firewood, mortar was spread on warm days and post reinforcements continued. A tarred root cellar further protected by back filled sandy gravel finally allowed ditches dug for house footings—if and when a thaw came. It was an accomplishment, but she despaired ever finishing. Agonizingly the lumber accumulated.

However, once she had the small home's floor joists laid, she realized the mill wasn't sparing enough planks for her planned home even if the water did flow strongly. People had stopped trading. Without enough to pay Tim beyond early February, without depleting meager resources or tapping her emergency funds, they shut down.

Sadly she told him, "You're still welcome to make your home off the side of the mill."

Instead, he became happily employed carrying mail down the Columbia. Bethany prayed for his safety, threw herself into sawing more firewood for walls and larger logs for supports. Joyfully she stock piled sand found at a nearby erosion spill during the same thaw, and stacked the barn with four barrels full! (The vegetables they'd housed now snuggled under hay.)

How she wished they hadn't been forced to dump her field bureaus in the mountains. All she had now were wooden bandboxes and barrister cases. A cupboard for food and utensils would have been so much neater (and less hay dust.) The small barrels were still in the "shanty" turned tool shed. It would continue to serve as a shed even after her place finished. She intended to use the other single row cupboards as a couch (if tools resisted rust after being left in a barrel.)

Wearily she eyed the skeleton's one room, someday two rooms? For now all it required was filling in with firewood plus a roof. To use less firewood, plus watch a lovely view of sunlight on water, she made plank jambs for a double doorway out onto the porch, and for light put a window opening in the side walls, extending jambs full height, then supports with headers. It'd make it chillier, but by next winter's cold she'd make shutters, Lord willing and health allowing?

In the evenings, when she could no longer see (or barely feel hands and feet,) a pan of heated tallow and a strip of cloth lit on the edge of a tin pan allowed the construction of windows and doors. Thinking it nice to see the river from inside the house as well as warm it up in the morning (due to the southeast position,) she considered glass for the doors. Wearily she located the growing trash pile…maybe held promise after all? The glasscutter that Samuel had wisely included in her tool kit carefully followed a pattern that formed rectangular jugs into small panes of glass (mourning so many pressed advertising discards.)

Small windows emerged between short planks that overlapped with a recessed edge along one side. A shard of glass sanded surfaces smooth. The recess allowed tacks to hold the glass "panes." Bethany mixed up lime, sand and sawdust mortar again and pressed to cover the tacks and keep the wind out. A final tarring, to waterproof the mortar, finished her project. It didn't look too different than windows she'd known previously? Precious nails that Samuel's foresight had provided twisted into hinges or joined panel and sash.

Could she hope someday to afford real glazing, maybe even real windows? Even so, this improved on staying in the dark and using extra candles. Then she tackled doors. Since the windows didn't look half bad with their black edges, she got inspired. By building up planks on either side of the saw, she ran another plank through. And, it grooved an edge. A couple of passes usually sufficed for the heavy glass width. By drilling and stick dowels, she joined perpendicular ends. Ever so slowly a small pointed rock tied to a small branch tapped the inside of more bottles to form desired sizes.

But winter never saw her into it. The walls finished and the back slanting shed type roof went on in March, but she couldn't tar it for the rain and cold, nor could she build a fireplace having exhausted both lime and sand. Canvas pieces overlapped and buried under evergreen boughs. At least she'd keep the rain out.

Still, using her thin reflector oven near an open fire outside and living with the animals wasn't so bad, she reasoned. Adding barn doors made of planks chiseled out to accept bottle bottoms, she was "in residence" on her Indian drum. Sitting in front of the warm east door for breakfast and west door for supper, she only had to move a few feet to feed, water, or move animals. She would have spent most of her time working there with her tools anyway, she consoled. (Many lived with several adults and more than a dozen children, all cramped into one or two rooms and a loft. By comparison, all this barn space probably contrasted as downright commodious? Guess everything is relative?)

Hangnails, splinter wounds, chapped hands, split cuticles, and tied rags indicated the times the logs or sharp glass won. Nails ragged and filthy with dirt or wood pitch, her Sunday "Sabbaths" of devotional readings and prayer were preceded by attending to Saturday bathing and basic hand repair. Animal fat and mittens were worn whenever possible; still, bare hands usually had to poke mortar into small cracks or hold tools.

Well, she wasn't a gracious lady with time to soak and file while Mattie cooked and Heidi cleaned, she grimaced. As predicted, more and more often she indulged in fond remembrance of the gracious life then known. *Thank you, God, I know most women never experience such graciousness. Such a blessing, especially since I was so depressed and destitute. Your provision was far beyond anything I could have imagined!*

A window made by chiseling bottle bottom shapes into two boards, placed high on the south side of the privy, offered both light and a little thawing. (As predicted, the miniature waterfall totally glazed every morning.) Fortunately the refuse system appeared not to be freezing. The removed firewood (to insert the "window" boards) did not come out easily either. Hopefully the mortar would hold well enough until the walls were covered with sufficient waterproofing.

The two skinny cows plus a bag of lime (for which she'd traded the remaining two horses) had surprised her with calves. Mr. Baskin, the gloating farmer who'd traded for them, had her "over a barrel," due to her insufficient feed. However, she'd agreed despite the disparity. After all, the two small Jersey cows required no more feed than one huge horse. And, now, fresh milk, cream, and butter abounded, belated proof of her wisdom.

Tim traded butter for three hens and a rooster during a quick visit. An old one appeared in a nesting frame of mind, so maybe more to come? Timothy also reappeared in early April, having ended up on the coast after taking a short job with a sailing vessel now returned. He looked worn from his travels. Plus his gums bled so easily they both fretted, but he had lost only a few pounds more than the last time she'd seen him. She dosed citric acid in his tea. It at least pacified his mind? But she also worried about him living in such dampness.

"Tell you what, Tim," she declared with a sudden burst of trust. "You help me build a fireplace and I'll move up top side. In the meantime, you move into the back side of the stalls until you can have the place to yourself."

"Won't folks talk?" His furrowed brow evidenced concern. He knew she was overly kind not to demand something for rent after the project was finished. Certainly didn't want her to end up disgraced.

"They probably gossip about us anyway," she stated resentfully. "We might as well be as healthy and comfortable as we can. But," she added quickly, "we'll work fast and hopefully no one will ever know."

"Nah," he finally decided. "I'll add more boughs to the lean-to for now. When you get moved up, I'll move into the barn then. It's getting warmer and a bottle of hot water warms my bedding."

"Well, at least bring your bedding and mattress into the barn during the daytime? You don't have to start out thawing damp and frost!"

Tim smiled, agreed and they set to work. Tim's manly strength managed to shovel up some barely thawed sand and Bethany's horses and a tree root raked flat stones out past ice flows bordering the thawing river. Little by little the northeast corner chimney rose toward an open frame, previously a canvas and bough covered hole. Bethany made sure it had a wide front hearth with a raised edge to prop a "rose" pierced metal fire screen, created from "nail hinges" and three large baking sheets taken in trade. A light metal door, rods and metal pan cover rose into a domed baking oven above the fire pit as Tim mixed real mortar and passed flat stones.

When finished well beyond the roofline, they waited a week before starting a fire. At first, the smoke merely hung in the space. Windows flung open helped it finally draw up the flue. When working well she made vegetable and elk stew. That done she added her previously prepared sour dough bread and later a pie to the oven. Between her soaked few remaining dried berries (that she'd been too tired to bother cooking) and the maple sugar he'd brought her as a donation to her pantry, they managed a fine meal. Biscuits would have been easier, but she lacked essential ingredients.

Moving in became official when Timmy lugged up the Indian drum. A large leggy stump, sawn flat, was covered with two layers of crossed boards to be later rasped smooth into a round. Tim's small upturned nail keg completed their dining room essentials. In honor of the occasion, she swept the place clean, dug out a sheet for a tablecloth and ripped a red flannel rag into two napkins.

"After we celebrate, let's haul my barrister cases up," she smiled with satisfaction. "I should maybe wait for daylight, but I'm just so anxious. Do you mind?"

"No, ma'am," he declared. "I am more than willing to quit that damp lean-to and move in with your warm animals!"

"Thank you, Tim, for coming back." She opened her heart. "Hopefully folks will start wanting a little more lumber so you can work through the spring at least?"

"Been thinking on that," he replied. "Seems to me waiting until willing folks order something makes them lug two long trips out here. If I was to get a little lumber ahead, they could haul it home or float it down the river right off."

"Yes." She brightened at the obvious logic. "They may bring their own wood to ease the cost of trading, but they could just exchange it for our cut stuff, and then theirs would saw ahead for the next customer, seems we'd only have to do it the once, right? I don't see why anyone would mind, do you?"

"Nope, so if you don't mind, I'll start cutting. I noticed bigger stuff higher behind the ridge. Thought I'd start there while the ground still has some slide to it. Clyde and Barb should have an easier time."

"I think…Clyde will have to do it alone, for a bit." Bethany bit her lip hoping it wouldn't change his direction. "I think Barb's new foal arrives any day now. I haven't used her since I noticed."

"Sorry. She's so big anyway, never thought about it." Tim smiled sheepishly. "By the way, that was real nice pie. Most as good as fresh! Ya sure cook good; been missing it bad all winter."

"Thank you. With a fine oven we ought to do very well for ourselves. If you go to Mott's trading post, I'll have you get me some cream of tartar and baking soda. Then I'll prove I can still make biscuits too," she laughed, near giddy having someone to talk to after such a lonely winter.

"I like your sour dough bread just fine," he insisted. He'd heard several suitors (extra land section hungry?) had traipsed out for one-day courtships. During the few warm Sundays in March, Mott said they'd near tripped over each other. That she had not accepted anyone else's dream (or family) was mysterious. Shyly he added: "Too bad somebody doesn't know what a good wife you'd make."

"What," she gushed a nervous laugh, "and stop living this grand independent life?! And, why should I want to wash some man's dirty clothes and kids instead of having an immaculately clean house?"

"I don't know about immaculate." He grinned as he lifted one leather boot to view caked mud and crumbles beneath.

"Well, you see my point right there!" And that was the last time they discussed her marrying.

"Why don't you like to go in to Mott's post?" he asked. "Is it because of Jonathan?"

"No, at least, I don't think so," she answered. "Sure, hard at first, and I miss him of course. But, I threw myself into working to build this place and I think, by now at least, I've adjusted to solitude as well as possible. I'm just not fond of socializing with *male* strangers. His post fills up with idle men having nothing better to do than striking up a conversation. Conversations can easily be misconstrued by one or all (who might also only hear bits and pieces.) If not misconstrued on the spot, it can sometimes be misconstrued by later imagining what was meant. So, if I stay to home, I'm not responsible for any gossip starting. Sound reasonable?"

"So, you've become a hermit, sort of like the old mountain men." Tim assessed the situation pretty correctly.

"I prefer," she exuded triumph and self-satisfied perkiness, "to think of it as 'content with my own company.' Besides, until they get a church built, there's not much need with you willing to fetch and carry!" Silently she admitted to being terribly glad he was back. Just about depleted of all her staples, she couldn't have put off going herself before the end of the month. And, her still gaunt frame showed she hadn't been making good meals like this either, didn't seem much sense for just herself.

"Well," he stood and stretched sore muscles, "I'll move your cases if you'll do kitchen duty."

"Agreed, and readily." She gathered up their few dishes. She cherished the remembrance of the Longs' pretty fine bone china, instead of the silver and pewter taken west, but she was still grateful. So many women had only wooden bowls and spoons. Here she had real dishes, cups and silverware. Suddenly she had a thought. "Tim." She whirled about to catch him before he was out the door."

"Yeah?" He braced himself against the windowed door.

"When you go to Mott's again, look in their trash heap for some small round glass jars or bottles with no imprinting."

"Imprinting?" He frowned.

"Pressed writing in the glass," she explained.

He repeated to make sure, "Just plain, and round."

"And small," she reiterated.

Frowning, he tossed back, "How small?"

She knew exactly. "Small enough to fit easily in a woman's hand."

"How am I supposed to know that?" he asked with a confused shake of his head.

She smiled mischievously. "Maybe you need to find *yourself* a wife?"

"Not now that I have a nice warm barn to sleep in! Wouldn't think marriage necessary at all." He pretended mock belligerence.

"A lot you know!" she retorted arrogantly.

Having given as well as she'd gotten, Tim and Bethany were content to share meals and plan for whatever the future might bring them.

CHAPTER 10:
Nepotism in Charge

On the Panama Pacific coast Mr. Ezra Essem happily caught up with Joseph Bentley Wright III. With identification established, Joe signed a legal document that verified both contact and receipt (the fortunate completion of Mr. Essem's mission.) Untying a saddlebag from his valise and handing the whole thing over, he declared, "You have my condolences, sir, but I'm some glad I didn't have to chase you clear to Oregon Territory like I'd been told. Also glad to get back to Baltimore in half the time. Just wish I'd caught up with you east of those wretched swamps!"

That said, he retreated and left Joe to warily contemplate the contents of the unique package. Why an urgent legal errand from a city Joe avoided like the plague? From it he produced a long packet containing a death certificate, a clipped obituary from the "Baltimore Bugle" (March 3, 1845,) a copy of his grandfather's will, and a letter from Grandfather's Baltimore lawyer, Mr. Noah Simpson. The law firm was still the same one his grandfather had used years ago. In the bottom he found his gold watch (contents validated?)

Having scanned the death certificate quickly, he amazed to sense only fact regarding his grandfather's death. That's because Grandfather was nearly eighty? Or, maybe it's more likely because of long past quarrels? Not quite twenty-two when he'd left home, determined never to see or speak to the old man since? (How's that for hollow success?) But, because the death notice was seven weeks old, emotional mourning should be rather anti-climatic for anyone? Nevertheless, it certainly was not his style to turn maudlin, then or now.

He stuffed everything back inside, left the crowded campsite to instruct the local stevedores how to transport his cargo, and went aboard ship to give instructions to the crew for its careful storage. When all appeared well understood, he returned to shore to keep a watchful eye on his merchandise. Relaxed under a thatched umbrella type shade on the edge of the beach, he figured all progressed well. Finally he had time to read the lawyer's letter. After he read it, he couldn't believe it. So he reread it again, then again. Frustrated with both the heat and the letter, he was in no mood to tolerate even the slightest infraction. "No!" he bellowed and gestured in a negative manner to a dark round faced Panamanian. "Leave that alone! It goes on top!"

He then riffled through the bag for the will, the true document of worth. If a loophole existed, he'd find it there. After all, a lawyer's letter held no clout. However, three readings of the will changed nothing. What the letter said offered no way to disbelieve the intent, and no way to prevent Grandfather's knife twisting from the grave.

Totally frustrated, he abandoned a lost cause and read the obituary. Joseph Bentley Wright's accomplishments via coal mining, steamships and railroads were quite impressive when printed for public consumption. No doubt many convenient omissions guarded how he'd amassed his holdings (protecting the sensitivities of men, women, and children.) He regretted much of the property was the result of his own prior actions or advice the short while in his grandfather's employ. Left behind to mourn, a daughter-in-law, Mrs. Joseph Wright II (ha! what a laugh!) The bereaved also included a granddaughter, Miss Claudia Wright, and a grandson, Mr. Joseph Wright III. As a fit addendum, it stated Grandfather had been "a patron of the arts, and among the original founders of the Baltimore Performing Arts Society."

Patron indeed, Joe fumed. Grandfather spent gallons of money for sensuous entertainment, nothing more. His father, uncles, and cousins had been "chips off the old block," for pleasure as well as internal jostling (to see who could outdo the other's licentious behavior and thus elicit the most gleeful chuckle and patronage out of Grandfather.) If it took a lot of money to buy public acceptance of dalliance, he'd paid it! And more than once he'd exasperatedly evidenced zero tolerance for Joe's nit-combing his obvious lack of morals.

His mother had endured the shame of a husband whose lust was so scandalous that his name "almost" made the papers. It became the local paper's delight to pursue him; his grandfather's duty to pay off the local constable or publisher, and the paper's obligation to find another scapegoat. A chummy club, his relatives!

The aunts decided they could play the same game (more discretely, of course, but just as deliberate.) When they became widows, the aunts quickly remarried. Grandfather immediately cut off their allowances. When they protested, his lawyer informed them their first husbands had been nothing more than supervisors paid to manage Grandfather's business. Previously they enjoyed their father-in-law's generosity. Now that they were married all charity ceased.

Grandfather had lost all but one male heir (Joe's first year away at collage) when a Hudson River pleasure boat exploded. Five had immediately died; three died later of extensive burns, his father among them. His mother had rushed Joe off to his father's bedside while she arranged elaborate funeral preparations. She enjoyed the remembered glory. Joe recalled the agonizing screams of torment, horrid hospital smells, the bloating and oozing of charred flesh and the lonely ride home with a coffin.

Grandfather Wright had expected a lot out of his lone heir. Oh, he was allowed to finish college. After all, making contacts with pampered young men of his acquaintance was part of the master plan. Each classmate was analyzed, summarized, and catered to in every way possible. (Within good taste, even Grandfather knew better than make enemies of powerful and influential parents.)

Summers involved learning, managing, and discovering all there was to know about mines, ships, and railroads. Joe had immediately recognized their superiority over the canals. "Get out now," he'd advised at only eighteen, long before the wisdom was apparent, "but wait and let others sweat the costs. Sit back and wait for signs of trouble. Otherwise, you mortgage a whole lifetime's accumulations."

His prediction proved worthwhile. After his departure, his grandfather purchased thousands of shares on the cheap just before the railroads started their show of money. He recouped magnificently when the eastern ones stopped spending and started reaping. Joe had studied with a purpose, shared planning how soon to advance behind the railroads' costs, and he had a zest for business that still consumed him. However, he was always unhappy with his grandfather's lack of concern for employees, especially the coal miners.

Several cave-ins during his first post-college summer provoked a serious family rift. Joe sulked furiously when his grandfather suggested he cool his heels and go with some of his recently hired supervisors to the ballet. It turned out to be just a bunch of showgirls lounging around in skimpy costumes flirting with men who flattered themselves thinking they were businessmen.

When he told Carl, the oldest, that he was leaving, the man had caught him by surprise, physically spun him by his coat tails through a doorway, and yelled for all to hear, "Don't come out until you're a man!" The cosmetically altered half-dressed girl sitting on the side of the fainting couch had smiled willingly. He, instead, strode to an open window, climbed onto the porch, and fled down the side stairs. After hailing a carriage, he went home, packed a bag, kissed his wailing mother and frightened sister goodbye, and headed west—with fifty-seven dollars in his pocket. At the age of twenty-one, he had hoped never to see any of them ever again.

Even Mother was a hard case. She complained, whined, and generally disagreed with him and anyone else within hearing. His sister, Claudia, was a milk toast doing whatever mother said. What Mother mostly said was, "Men are beasts, Claudia, never marry unless forced to do so by abject poverty!" And he'd decided if women only wanted men for meal tickets, party dresses and new furnishings, he could do without women. (That is, he could until an hour ago.)

Grandfather Wright's will intended to maintain his mother and sister's allowance for only two years past the date he had signed on the receipt. Had he known the contents and the reason, he never would have signed it. Legally they could have been taken care of indefinitely. Now, he only had two years to claim his inheritance and prevent their otherwise over ninety percent reduction. If Mother did not have her own income (which he doubted due to her spendthrift ways) they'd be near paupers.

But, to save them from that fate (as the lawyer had so succinctly pointed out,) he had to:

1) Marry within two years,
2) Operate the family business for one year within the next four, and
3) Maintain a permanent residence in Baltimore or Pittsburgh six months of that year.

Now, he could happily forgo the inheritance. And, he could easily become responsible for his female relatives' maintenance.

But, neither his funds nor his mother's intact income would maintain them in the Wright mansion. Nor in the manner to which Mother insisted society demanded. Grandfather Wright knew the score. On the few visits east that he had felt obligated to arrange a meeting, mother had informed him that his business acumen was followed raptly by Grandfather who had eyes and ears in most corners of the commercial world. Hence, Grandfather twisted this cheap knife into an old scarred wound. That meant two years at most to make a claim.

Failing that,

4) A meager stipulated sum would allow a hotel or boarding house existence for them and

5) A fabulous trust fund established for the Baltimore Performing Arts Society.

"You will burn a hole in my ropes with that glare of yours; then how will my sails stay up?" queried Captain Jules Hanson.

"Hi, Capt'n," Joe guardedly welcomed the seasoned mariner.

"You receive bad news from that fellow?" the captain asked kindly.

"Sort of, sir." Joe knew there were few secrets aboard a ship. "I'm not in trouble with the law, if that's what's worrying you?"

The captain's clenched unlit pipe bobbed agreement. "I should not think so, Joe, but...I am always ready to listen if you have troubles."

"Thanks, but no thanks, sir, not for the moment anyway."

"Well, you think long and hard, but...you should not scare my men. They don't need much reason to jump ship these days." The captain gave him a fatherly pat on his burdened shoulder.

Joe was disappointed they would not be stopping off in California. He'd try to buy hides on the way back, presuming he could find some way to do it? His cargo included several boxes of regular goods he'd have to sell elsewhere or find someone to take overland south from Oregon. But, if indeed the harbor made it hard to unload, he couldn't fault the skipper for not wanting to scrap the bottom of his old Baltimore clipper.

How much of the "healthful" advertising was deliberate ploy? (Government fostered to speed immigration?) And he had more pressing matters to worry about so he tossed and turned for two nights on end. By morning of day three he tired of indecision. Regretfully, it was probably how the "old goat" presumed he'd force Joe's hand! (He'd be dead first before he'd allow a fortune to end up in the laps of painted shameless actresses and foppish corseted actors.) He also was not going to give away his own hard earned dollars when his grandfather's dollars were right there for the taking. (Otherwise he'd be guilty of a blatant case of poor stewardship?) And, improving mine conditions was something that needed doing for years.

His mother may not have been the supportive wife like he'd seen some of the western women support and share their husband's burdens. But she'd experienced more than just cause. And she deserved her due for sticking with her marriage vows, even if only as a public sham. He could easily place his current business in the hands of good men, good friends most of them, just as he'd been intending ever since the fur trade was being ruined by cheaper textiles. And, he could run this business from Baltimore as well as any other.

To eliminate options three and four, requirements two and three he could easily accomplish. The only "fly in the ointment" was marriage. How did a man, who had diligently avoided women fastidiously, up to this point in his life, suddenly become a Romeo? No clue; maybe he *should* have a talk with Captain Jules after all?

He knocked on the captain's door and heard an immediate, "Come in!" The captain instantly hustled his cabin boy to bring tea, cheese and fruitcake and insisted Joe sit in his intricately carved and stuffed Oriental chair. Uncomfortable with the captain making such a fuss over him, he got right to the point. "Captain, I need educating about proposing to a woman."

"You mean you want to know how I proposed to *my* wife," the captain repeated with a laugh. "Ah, I think I see the cause of your troubles. A woman to marry is a serious matter. But, you are getting older so you *should* marry. You should not have children when you are really old like me. My head swims with the screams and yelling of my children! Luckily my ship and the sea rescue me. Most men are not so lucky."

"You wish you hadn't married?" Joe's twenty-nine-year-"old" brain responded.

"Certainly not!" Captain Jules denied emphatically. "Just the opposite; I wish I had married years younger. I might be a contented landlubber by now bouncing grandchildren, and that only occasionally," he laughed. "No, I married much too late. My wife was a widow with four young children. It is a responsibility I take seriously to care for our now seven children. But, they are also my greatest joy…so bright, so bubbly, they bring back my lost youth when I'm with them. And, sorry I married my young Myra, never!"

"She feel just as fond of you?" Joe knew the question was subjective and impertinent, but the captain was usually talkative regardless of the subject.

"I am never sorry to come home, that I know for sure." The captain's eyes twinkled in the midst of a broad grin.

"So, how did you ask her?" Joe prodded.

"Well, first I knew her awhile. She ran a clean Boston boarding house I had come to depend on—still do, for that matter. She called my sailing too risky and my not marrying good, too lonesome and hard for a woman to do all that waiting. Then, she fed me so well I got slow and sluggish. Later, I looked at her and my insides started flopping. Pretty soon, I'm in the net and landed at her feet!"

Joe wasn't inquiring in the right direction. Captain Jules was talking about love. He knew love had nothing to do with his quest for a wife. And forget the Romeo bit, he couldn't pull it off even if he wanted to (which he didn't.) His need of a wife simply meant going shopping for one. Moreover, how to get one handed over the counter? "I was more concerned with the exact words you used, sir." Joe flushed embarrassment over the captain's obvious zeal for his wife's charms.

"Oh, well, I said to her 'we've been walking out together off and on for a couple of years, don't you think that maybe it's time we get married?'" The captain's emphatic chomp bobbed his unlit pipe stem.

That seemed fairly easy, so he prompted, "And she replied?"

The captain hauled back in his stiff chair with fond remembrance. "She said 'I was wondering if you were ever going to get around to asking.' Then we walked over to the rectory and were married the following Sunday. Her sister cared for the boardinghouse and children. I took Myra on a sail down to St. Augustine and back to Boston. There was a full moon when we arrived in Florida. Ah!" he sighed. "If you want to honeymoon in a pretty place, I completely recommend March, St. Augustine and a full moon!"

Joseph returned to the deck more dejected than informed. Obviously there were people in this world who married and liked each other afterwards. He had met few that compared to the captain's love for Myra. Since he had met Sam and Heidi, he figured there were at least two more in the world. He also was delighted and impressed with the genuineness of Samuel's conversion. In one year it appeared Sam had exceeded his own Christian progress of over ten years. (That simultaneously cheered and depressed.) Heidi obviously adored him, they were absolutely ecstatic about a baby coming, and both were dismayed to hear he knew so little about Beth and

Jonathan. All he could tell them was that Jonathan loved his cousin Lois and was calling her "mama" and Ernest "dada" when he left.

That Heidi could so easily and freely talk about Samuel's attempt to marry Bethany was to him an amazing example of selfless love. When she even admitted to eavesdropping on his proposal, something stirred, maybe a deep need to find a love that honest? Now such thoughts, to find a "happy home" oasis, with a timetable to meet, was ludicrous. There were only a few months to manage it (and he was going in the wrong direction. The women who would fit into Mother and Claudia's world lived on the opposite side of his world.)

Then he made a contrary decision: he *would* marry someone from Oregon! That's if he could find someone to talk into it. The closer he got, the more he mentally ticked off all the eligible girls he could remember. The more he thought, the more convinced he was of it being "right." Such a woman could appreciate the rigors of his work, and the hardness in a man wouldn't be anything new. Also, women often were left alone while the men hunted, trapped, sought work elsewhere or traipsed off for supplies.

Trouble was, he kept remembering females by their father's name or occupation. His penciled list read, "Ft. Vancouver blacksmith's daughter, brown hair, dimpled chin." More interest earlier would have helped; he'd already forgotten most women's names that went overland with him just last year! Well, most were married anyway. But new immigrants were flooding the Territory both by land and sea. Over nine hundred survived the trail in forty-three, some more the year after, more coming this year. Surely a young girl for a wife could be found somewhere among all those?

Each stop in Oregon, though, he was struck by some reason to stall. If they weren't sullen, discouraged, or almost skin and bones sickly, then they prattled mindlessly or were so uneducated as to be nearly dumb or obnoxious. He needed a women who could at least converse intelligently. He didn't imagine romance, but these he resisted for being ashamed of introducing them. (*Was that a sign of sinful pride or an excuse to forget the whole idea?*)

Suddenly his steady paddle reverie was broken hearing, "Joe! Joe Wright!"

He barely made out the hat-waving figure. Finally he recognized the skinny guy's funny hop, skip and jump. "Timmy!" He waved back wildly in recognition of a young man whose rambunctious ambition he'd come to admire.

"How you doing, Timmy?" yelled Joe as his light canoe headed ashore. "Was sure you'd be frozen to death by now. How'd you come to survive winter?"

"Just the good Lord looking after me, I guess," the young man admitted humbly. "Both the sea and elements tried their best to do me in though; I'll hope to tell ya so!"

"By the way," Joe grinned and struck his forehead, "I've got three letters for you!"

"Three! You have?" beamed Timmy. "Wow, I haven't had mail since last fall."

"I've also got a letter for the widow from Samuel and Heidi." Afraid of the answer, he inquired respectfully, "Did she survive the winter too?"

"She sure did! Better than most, I'd say. In fact, I'm her hired man, last fall and this spring. Can't have a prettier boss, huh, Mr. Joe?"

"Guess not," Joe reluctantly agreed, more stunned than affirming. He knew the widow was more than a pretty face; she'd proven that aplenty, but hiring men? "What's she got you doing?"

"Milling lumber," Timmy informed with significant pride over his newly developed skill.

Joe frowned. "How'd she buy a lumber mill?"

"Didn't buy one; brought saws, shafts and such with her. Saws were in bags in the bottoms of barrels and connections formed the wagon, tools under the seat. Shafts were what held up her wagon top. You should see her place! Jeremy and I helped some with milling her floor and roof. But, just last month she bought some tar, then shingled over and painted it. That place shines like a new penny! Not another like it. Traded lumber for a plasterer to go over the inside and whitewashed that too. Sorry to admit it, but most folk say she's too stuck up and high toned. I don't though; she just likes nice things like she's used to."

Joe knew that was why too. "So, it wasn't a husband hunt that produced all that?"

"Nope," Timmy grinned.

Joe grunted both as a response to his answer and the heft of the canoe he was dragging with Tim's help. "Men hereabouts must be real busy! I'd have presumed she'd be among the first to find one!"

"Oh, she's had lots of offers," Joe confirmed, "just doesn't have no interest. You gonna have time to come see her? Or do you want me to deliver her letter?"

"Hmm, well now," he slapped an arm over the boy's shoulder, "that might depend on how the Motts treat me. I guess if I don't get too royal a treatment, I'll just turn 'em down and trot home with you, how'd that be?"

"Great! But, I guess I should warn ya; we'd be sleeping in the barn if you do. I'll give up my feather bed, though, and Widow Beth will put on some fresh sheets. She changes them for me every other week, but she won't mind. She has water coming almost right into the house. You've really got to see her place…water even washes away the stable waste. It's the cleanest barn you ever seen, not a bug or a fly anywhere. Course, with the animals outside most of the summer, I guess a lot of barns might be clean right now? I'm rattling on, aren't I? But, wow, Joe, I'm just so glad to see a new face. Well, I mean, one I remember, but not someone here all the time!"

"I'm glad to see you too. I was just about to add 'kid,' but you're getting a little beyond that, I suppose." Joe had rightly observed the beard's shadow and small creases starting around the eyes.

"Widow Beth calls me 'Tim' now," he confirmed with pleasure. "Ernest, though, calls me the 'The Cat' 'cause I always have to be put out when he closes up. But, Joe, this situation with the British is getting downright dangerous one minute and then nary a worry the next. How's a person to protect himself proper if ya don't know the full story? And, if ya only hear one story, who's to say you've heard the right one?"

"You become a trader, Tim. And, just sell whatever to whoever needs it." Joe's wink was not as well received as he'd hoped. Obviously Tim believed in Manifest Destiny a little too strong for his own peace of mind.

The Motts were as generous as always and invited Tim to stay after closing. Their personal quarters centered on little Jonathan talking up a storm. Remembering him as a toddler, falling down as quick as he stood up, was a huge contrast to the small gentleman she mothered. Lois was flattered by Joe's bragging on what a good job she'd done.

When she heard Joe intended to deliver the widow's letter in person, she took him aside for a small pantry powwow. "Joe, please ask Bethany to come in and see Jonathan. I know it's hard for her, but she's the first one I'd go running to if I needed help with him—have already, by passing messages back and forth through Tim. She lugged our dear boy clear across a whole continent! And I'd like him to know the woman who nursed him, protected him, and killed a buffalo that was charging straight for them. By the way," she smiled encouragingly, "I don't think Ernest was here to hear Tim tell about that. Maybe you'd like to do the small honor? I hear you were a lot closer!"

Joe merely nodded an affirmation before adding, "Just not close enough to do anything about it. Sam did right teaching her to shoot. He deserves as much credit as I do for getting the boy through, but Bethany more than both of us together."

"I realize that now, belatedly, once I saw how much work a child creates. But Tim comes in so often, he does all her errands. So, tell her for me what I said, and say I'd also like to see another 'lady' once in awhile. Please?"

"Sure, but hasn't she been in at all?" Joe remembered the widow chaffing under his often mandated lack of female companionship. Consternation now included the possibility of cabin fever?

"She came twice, early on, to have Ernest sell four of her horses. The last time was to swap with Ed Baskin—or haul the horses back. Ernest gets the biggest kick out of telling about that swap, com'on, I'm sure he's dying to relate how a little widow lady bested that old pirate!"

At this request Tim excused himself (having heard it several times before.) He wanted to give the widow warning about Joe's impending visit.

"But don't make her change sheets," Joe called after him. "I'll come early enough to find my way back here by nightfall."

"See ya tomorrow then!" Tim waved his hat before he'd skip hopped out the door. Joe wagged his head at the surplus energy. If that ever got channeled into a proper business pursuit, watch out Oregon!

Ernest took near fifteen minutes, dragging out the details, the suspense of haggling and final negotiations. "Would the little widow lady take Ed Baskins' outrageous offer? He demanded a swap of *two small* Jersey yearlings for *two huge* draft horses!" Ernest finally concluded with, "And those three big hay maws near e't his barn down, to the bark off the stalls and kept going. How'd the little widow lady make out? Well, she still had hay and *two* calves in the spring plus milk, butter, and rich cream. Tim says one of those calves just made the best mouth smacking Independence Day veal you ever laid a lip over! And, she has a new foal so they've got the extra horse coming along she was worried about. Tim says she's breaking him to the harness a little already helping around the garden."

"So she's doing okay, right?" Joe rejoiced both from vicarious joy and amusement.

"Alright?" Ernest exploded. "She's got credit enough stacked up over this spring, I may have to just sign the post over to her in a few years. Or, I've got to charge her rent for all the skins I've got to store on account of her mill. You'd think if folks got along for over ten years without one, they'd be mighty slow to fork over good pelts, wouldn't you? You mark my words, they'll be sorry they bought boards when the flour, salt and sugar are exhausted."

Joe figured it was about time Ernest expected a little business, so he explained why he had come on ahead. "My goods will sail up in a few days,

Ernest. I came early to get you to organize your storeroom ahead of time due to my tight schedule; I've got to catch the same boat back.

"I'm also forced into taking time to visit the widow because my friend Samuel married a pretty Norwegian girl. They both near condemned me to the pit for not knowing what became of her. If I can't tell them I saw her and she was doing fine, with my own two eyes, they'll probably tar and feather me—that's presuming I'd dare show up!"

Lois returned from depositing sleepy Jonathan into bed. "You go see the widow first light, lov'; Ernest and me will see what needs moving. You come back, help us with the heavy stuff, and we're done."

Joe was actually up long before light. Unaccustomed to the rustle of husks beneath him, he blamed it on getting used to "that soft ship life." He quietly grabbed a couple of biscuits and combined it with a hank of jerky from his saddlebags. In one fluid motion he threw himself and his breakfast onto the Mott's old plow horse. He followed the trail, west to a ridge, then down beside the wide river. From the looks of it, should be good fishing? Maybe he'd ask Tim to borrow a hook and line and surprise the Motts with supper? No, he shook himself, no leisure today. His morning imaginings had suggested a woman who was both suitable and educated. She was a natural for the very top of his "marriage list." In fact, if he'd known all things, she should have occurred first, she'd make a perfect choice! However, he rued, perfect was asking too much. In fact, he had little hope, just vain wishing.

Bethany had arisen at Tim's late knock and then dashed about to clean, scrub, and polish. Bathing and shaping her nails preceded going to bed still wet headed, but she was clean from head to toe, including fresh linens. Just as the sun hit her east window, she sat bolt upright overwhelmed with dismay. Her homemade windows looked stark, no curtains! Quickly she threw new linen (intended to become embroidered tea towels) into hastily basted ruffled curtains. For rods she used branches, glass shard planed of bark, and nailed through thread spools for hanging them over.

She was making biscuits and veal pie along with baby carrots in between sewing plain tie backs. No time to do a great job, she mostly regretted no time to hem ruffles and promised to find the time to do it soon. How to attach them to the walls? Making windows and doors had exhausted her small supply of tacks. All she could think of (that was quick) was sewing them to the curtains themselves. She pulled and fluffed until they hung better. The three pair maybe looked a little strange, but she admitted it was better than the severe barrenness. Did it look as though she had completely forgotten her domestic skills? It was amazing how much she had. Dirt, cobwebs, and laundry had been evidence enough. Would she, one of these days, forget every domestic skill entirely?

Lord Jesus, help and forgive me. I'm mostly only in danger of forgetting to be grateful! The work is unending, but you have blessed me above expectations. Please, guard my thoughts and mind. You do indeed look after widows and orphans, but I have been more fortunate than most, and have Tim to help me besides. I totally am undeserving of provision of Sam, Tim and a host of others, and for You always being kind to me and the love you bestow on us all, amen.

Hopefully she hadn't forgotten anything in the meat pie due to distractions. Why did she care anyway? Was Joe's approval worth all this effort? Or, would it be his disapproval that she couldn't tolerate? She had worked too hard too long. He wouldn't even state approval, just nod his head and purse his hard-line mouth in that "it'll do" manner he had. But that would be enough; maybe more than she deserved. With only a second to stick a quick stitch in the last one, she saw him passing the noisy mill. He dismounted fluidly then towed the Motts' horse to the overflowing water trough. She checked her pie. Luckily he took his time tending the slow animal then released it through the gate into the raw post-fenced side hill pasture. "Hello." She met him outside the open doors, her hands smoothing folds of her just exchanged lace trimmed apron.

Joe crossed over the logs and planks that bridged porch to the bank, removed his hat and leaned back against the rail. She was fine all right; couldn't look better. Filled out cheeks had a healthy glow, her coloring great, a whole lot better than many folks he'd seen coming up river. "How have you been?" he inquired politely.

"Fine," she responded, moving out further onto the bright white porch, "and you?"

"Oh, I'm fine and dandy, moving more goods all the time. New settlers down in California too; guess Jed's going to set up a mercantile there. After this year I won't need anyone else to deal with down south."

Tim had related hearing how San Francisco's harbor filled with settler ships. He also said a few men had abandoned their families to go west. In light of recent tensions, she considered it scandalous presumption. Worse, it was probably just real estate promotion. When the prospect of a healthful climate hadn't worked, they'd suggested wealth by farming? She held them in the utmost contempt; you'd think the outrageous claims they'd heard about Oregon would have sufficed to teach only the Bible's plan for success (hard work, frugal diligence and lots of it.)

She looked about, pressed her rose lips tight and then licked them before apologizing. "I'd invite you to sit on the porch, but I haven't gotten around to much furniture yet. Maybe you'd like to find me some cheap Shaker rocking chairs on your next voyage?"

"Sure," he promised with a distracted nod.

Her Providence brown attire featured a fitted over bodice with dipped points front and back, and crochet covered buttons. Dark trim made the yoke stand out below a simple crocheted collar. Wider wrist trim emphasized the sleeves flaring out from the elbow. The bell skirt rustled with starched petticoats, as did her white lace trimmed apron (a parting gift from dear Mattie.) Her feet, usually in boots, were today wearing light black slippers. She *almost* felt like a lady again; that alone made the day lovely. "Well, it's more eating time than porch time anyway, so come on in." The sudden quiet denoted Tim had shut down the mill and would soon be half stripped in the midst of a horse trough wash.

She indicated Joe should sit in the large chair she had made from a curved slash made halfway through a barrel. She had filled the seat with two large cracker tins surrounded by a lot of leaves and then packed rabbit fur to further pad the laboriously tanned elk hide. This she had attached by pulling rawhide through small drilled holes. It looked rustic but was quite comfortable and double padded all the way around the edges.

Joe made it look like it was made for him. Tim, bless him, took the upended barrel so she could have her normal Indian drum. Tim was a good man; she hoped he would get ahead and not always work for others; but until he found his own place, she hoped he'd stay here. What she coveted most was never worrying about him near at hand. Although, to be honest, his constant work at the mill or off visiting left her much on her own. Had it been sharing the Oregon Trail? Had they become like little brother and big sister due to the close confines and shared dangers, made them almost like family?

As the men renewed acquaintances, Bethany quickly heaped fried elk, veal pie, peas in cream, buttered baby carrots, and fresh hot biscuits to the rough table covered with linen and napkins. A pitcher of milk out of a pan of cold water came from the set of shelves that centered across the back wall. Crocheted white lace edgings on each linen strip lined the five shelf boards. They'd fortunately been completed the month prior. She scolded herself for waiting so long to dress the place up. (Good thing to have company once in awhile, forces making a home presentable!)

Just as she was about to sit down, Tim jumped up, "Want to see the barn and mill, Joe?" Looking at Beth's consternation, he added contritely, "It'll just take a minute or two."

"See that it does," she warned, but with a smile instead of sternness. Their pride was equally shared. It took longer, of course, but not terribly so. Since she put the food back in the open oven, and the milk in cold water, there was little danger in the small delay. It also gave her time to remember a forgotten sugar caster, the salt cellar, and a wax sealed jar of pickled beets.

Just as they finished grace, Mr. Everett and son arrived poling a raft full of logs. Bethany offered Mr. Everett her seat and his son took a plate to the old "cupboard" backless couch. She sat on the covered barrister cases "bed" along the opposite wall. (Tim had luckily insisted, when he moved to the barn, that a feather mattress on top of the hay was all he needed.) Having a plate in her lap made her a little slow, but…maybe it was more the men's stories of Territorial unrest (enlarging throat lump hindering?)

After a custard dessert with fresh berries and tea had been served, she felt the meal had gone well enough. Tim and his customer disappeared to transfer loads. Bethany began to move dishes to the wider shelf that extended below the others. Farm paint on canvas covered her dishwashing and meal preparation domain. She refilled the water bucket and hearth kettle and set about washing the larger than usual load of dishes.

Joe seemed content to mull over something as he stood leaning with one hand braced against the top sill of the open doorway. It was a nice warm day, a boon to her thriving garden, and she smiled to remember last year when she'd wondered if it rained as much in summer as it had in winter.

Since she had seen his "it will do" look, she really wasn't paying too much attention to him. In fact, she wondered why he hadn't gone with the men or back to the Motts. She had to admit to feeling a smug 'old tabby cat' contentment, not that she would let his silent approval go to her head. It was only when she was placing the last dish on the shelf that he offered her his cup. "Another?" she asked.

He really wanted to get on with the onerous task but procrastinated by replying, "If you don't mind, I would."

"Not at all, but, if you're waiting for Tim, it probably will take him most of the afternoon to get Mr. Everett unloaded and loaded again." Bethany's information was what she supposed he must know to consider his time schedule. "If you're worried about you and Tim talking some more, he'd be glad to go into Mott's instead."

"Oh, he doesn't need to do that. I mean," he shrugged, "he can if he wants, but he doesn't need to on account of me."

She remembered her manners and hoped he didn't think she was trying to get rid of him. "You're most welcome to stay for supper if you'd prefer?"

"Then maybe," he smiled, "Tim and I could ride in together?"

"He'd be pleased, I'm sure," she added with a bit of embarrassment, "I'm afraid you've always been his hero."

"And how am I to you?" His distressed expression came totally unexpected.

The barest of smiles just froze in place. Only the eyes moved. She knew the wheels were turning, but no thoughts churned out.

"Have I shocked you?" He coughed to cover both his and her discomfort.

"No. I'm just at a loss as to what you expect for an answer. You've been my leader, instructor, taskmaster, and have done a fine job as a minister from time to time. I don't know as you've been exactly my hero, but you've been well respected. I can assure you of that."

He merely exhaled. "Guess I should be glad you didn't say you wished me dead for all I put you through coming out here."

"Joe!" She threw her tea towel on the table. "As a good Christian, I do not intend to wish anyone dead! And, I think you're a fine Christian man who needs to know the world does not rest on *your* shoulders alone. Just because Oregon is in a constant uproar is no reason for you to blame yourself. You are well liked by all the community—and many other communities you visit, as well. And, I will not have you down in the mouth just because you've been traveling for months on end. In fact," she offered, "why don't you finish that tea and then lie down for a nap? I'll be quiet as a church mouse and take my drum and mending outside. A good sleep should let you look at the world with fresh vision."

He looked at the lace covered bedding off to his left. "You mean," his blue-gray eyes rolled in mock horror, "on the Longs' Wedding Coverlet?"

"Suit yourself!" Bethany resisted grinning, barely. His remembrance and mention of the rebuff she had handed him, for roughly assessing her under mattress contents when they'd first joined up with the other wagons, indicated he was more sensitive than he'd let on. "But you *should* get some rest. I can tell you haven't been sleeping much despite your looking generally fit. I tend to let war rumors rob me of sleep much the same way. Just let me grab my mending."

With that, he carried her drum outside and she was soon basking in the reprieve she'd gained from having to gather hay and enjoyed the comfort of a lady like pursuit.

The wildflowers and insect world clamored a chorus of energy and industry. With a little imagination, compared to a Lowell, Massachusetts, mill ladies' parade day!

CHAPTER 11:
The Tummy Tilts East

Reclined upon the elegant satin covered mattress, his feet dangled slightly over the end. But sleep was not his goal. Tossing out one idea after another, he imagined himself saying stupid things and kept trying to make them noble. Only one thing appeared right. If forced to propose, he probably couldn't do better than the widow. There wasn't another marriageable female better at keeping her bees in her own bonnet. Problem was, if she'd refused others, why accept a no-nothing marriage?

Disgusted, he arose and came out to lean slim hips back against her rail and his tall wide-shouldered frame against the post of her porch.

She stated, "You didn't sleep at all, did you?"

"Nope," he admitted. "Not much for lolling about in the daytime, I guess."

"Me either, unless extremely tired, or climbing mountains, or walking through a desert," she recalled her heat exhausted jostled naps. "My father used to be able to take a fifteen-minute nap and be right as rain. Never could figure how he fell asleep so fast, or especially how he woke up so soon." Inspecting the repaired sock heel, she decided it would have to do.

"By the way," he procrastinated, "I told Mrs. Motts I'd relay a message. Says she'd love to have you visit. She's now much more aware of how hard you worked. Also Jonathan's talking up a storm, whole sentences, big words, even Indian ones. Says she'd love to have Jonathan get to know you. Also would like 'a lady' to visit with too."

Bethany nodded silently, rose and turned to stash her finished mending in the first case to the right. Entertaining Joe was time wasted; but, she guessed he deserved it so she oozed back to appear sociable. "You can tell her I'm planning to come in, now that you've come with fresh trade goods. Meaning to get a new bonnet and dress pattern."

"You still miss him, don't you?" he surmised.

"Jonathan?" she asked hesitantly. "Why, he was never really mine, Joe. I knew almost from the start that he would go to relatives. I still miss having a child, my own child, Josiah, and my husband, Jacob. But, then I also miss Tilly, Sam, Heidi, Mattie, and James, even Charles in a way."

"I'm sure Charles would be pleased—if he only knew." He rolled blue-gray eyes suggestively.

"*Be ye kind one to another,*" she chided gently. Knowing full well the Bible declared she was not to teach men, she explained softly, "Charles never had your advantages."

Slowly he assumed a sober expression. "Good point. Guess if we looked at folks that way, we'd give them a bit more credit?"

"Especially if we remember Phil. 2:3, '*in lowliness of mind let each esteem other better than themselves.*'"

Hastening lest she appear preaching, and finally unable to resist blurting it out she added, "Did you see Sam on your last trip?" At first, she doubted she'd get a chance to ask him without Mr. Everett nearby, now she just had to know how they were, that is, if *he* knew.

"Yes, in fact I almost forgot to deliver your letter from them." He retrieved it out of his red shirt pocket to watch her sit and gracefully arrange her full skirt after politely tucking the letter away in her apron.

"He and Heidi are married—as you predicted. In fact, the wedding was only about two months after you left. Sam said he couldn't wait since he was 'getting past his prime.' I guess that's a family joke because they both keep hilariously laughing." He surmised, "Guess you know the joke too?"

"Yes, Heidi's comment long before they became a couple. And I used it to shame him. Well, more to urge him, so he'd speak to her about being courted."

"They're expecting a child this September." His announcement produced a glorious beaming face. In fact, he couldn't remember her *ever* looking that cheerful.

Absolutely enraptured by the news, she lowered her head slightly to choke back her happiness. "Oh, Joe," her blue eyes misted as her smile returned to look him full in the face, "that's such wonderful news. And," she grinned delight, "how is Sam reacting to becoming a father?"

"Like a lawyer, I guess." He resumed his normal gruffness. "He's already talking about which college the kid should go to. Of course it *must* be a boy." Joe shook his handsome head. "I don't know what he'll do if it's a girl!"

At this she clasped her hands on top of her apron and threw back her waves and curls to choke down misty remembrance. "He will love her just like he did me!"

He frowned, suspiciously asking, "What do you mean by that?"

"Think, Joe," she asked. "What kind of girls did Sam like, when you were in college?"

"You want the *real* truth? Mostly Sam liked *any* girl!" Joe regretted the opposite being true of himself, but of course only lately, due to the nature of his ominous task.

Bethany grinned again. "But didn't he mostly like…'pretty' girls?"

"Well, of course," he agreed with a shrugged fluster, "what's so strange about that? Don't most men?"

"Have you met his wife, Heidi?" Her gleeful confidence indicated she knew perfectly well when she had the upper hand.

His response was the anticipated, "Yes."

"And?" Bethany prompted triumphantly.

He caught on but wasn't any too anxious to compliment another man's wife. Shouldn't let her box him in like this either. Finally he said, "And she is *very, very pretty*; that's what I am supposed to say?"

"Exactly, and isn't Sam pretty too?" She giggled at the asking.

At this he shifted position to cross sturdy leather boots. "You hold on, I'm not going around calling Sam Roberts 'pretty,' not even a half world away, and not for you, nor anyone else!"

"But he is, of course," she insisted. "And do you really think that pretty Heidi and pretty Sam will have a baby that's ugly, boy or girl?"

"And, if he or she is pretty, Sam won't care?" Clipped tones added, "That what you're saying?"

"Exactly!" she summarized with an emphatic handclasp under her smile wreathed chin.

Although he agreed with the assessment, he defended his friend with, "Kind of makes Sam sound a bit shallow, doesn't it?"

"Well, he *is* in many ways." Her eyes turned serious. "But, he will never remember himself as such, nor will anyone else soon enough. Children have a way of making handsome, romantic men into *very* responsible citizens!"

His arms crossed defiantly. "The way you say it, you'd think all men should be married and fathers. Else they'll never amount to anything? Is that the *real* message you're delivering?"

"Why, Mr. Wright," she fluttered long eyelashes outrageously and drawled, "ya do carry on. And, ah was just telling Timmy what a tremendous responsibility it must be fer ya all ta manage all that trading 'n' traveling, and ya all so industrious 'n' efficient, 'n' at yer young tender age too!"

He rose to neither the bait of his age nor the southern belle image she was magnificently portraying. He'd been down that lane before; but he wasn't about to insult any hard working widow. Retaliating he asked instead, "Was Josiah a pretty baby?"

The immediate silence turned deafening. She wasn't looking at him anymore either. In fact, she had turned her dark head down so much the curled hair in back showed a neat row of hairpins. Finally she raised her head and managed a low, "Yes, very."

"I'm sorry," he apologized, knowing he had trespassed far beyond good manners.

"No, don't be." She gulped before returning a lovely serene face with her naturally upturned lips. "It's actually good to talk about him. It's so rare that anyone asks me about Josiah, that's all, took me by surprise."

For a second the fairy tale *Snow White* made Joe's comparison to Bethany Clark. Again the silence hung heavy. One big tear coursed down her rosy cheek. He wished he could hand her a clean handkerchief, but he didn't have one. Needed to reverse her thinking of him as totally unfeeling too; hadn't intended to get on her wrong side at all. Why was it the southern belle always brought out the worst in him? That last disaster should have taught him to remain a gentleman forever! Just when he thought he'd better interject something to keep the conversation from dying, she rose to view the sparking river and opposite bank's cascading forest.

She spoke in subdued tones, almost as though the rail were an altar. "Josiah had curly brown hair, like his father, thick long eyelashes and high coloring like me." She gulped, turned back toward him, and took a deep breath. "His long skinny feet reminded me of my dad's; dimpled knees reminded me of my maternal grandmother, but probably only because they b-both were fat."

"I'm so sorry, Beth, really, that was an unthinkable question to ask," he pleaded for forgiveness with a longing that made her more sorry for him than for her.

Probably it was memories of Jacob had helped her turn down all suitors. Until she found a Christian man who was just as nice, she wasn't budging an inch toward matrimony? "It's okay." She mopped up tears with a lacy white hanky retrieved from her dress pocket. "I really never expect to get over losing them. I'm sure I'll still cry many long years down the road."

"Sure you will," he agreed. "Need to ask you something that, unfortunately, will likely bring back more painful memories. You don't need to answer me, though. Feel free to say, 'go see Tim,' or 'go to the Motts.' But, maybe, you should sit back down first?" Not sure to be pleased or irritated, when she immediately did so, it reminded of the one thing about her that always amazed. For a woman to do as she was told was, in his mind, the last thing to expect. To have her do so immediately, without question, seemed incomprehensible.

"Alright, for personal reasons, I need to ask about…you and your husband. Like to know how you and he got along. Did you disagree much? I'll tell you why I need to know right afterwards." She nodded suspiciously and took her time composing an answer. When she did, he wished he hadn't asked another prying question.

"I should never have married my husband. Jacob held no regard for religion. And, yes, I knowingly disobeyed God's Word. Jacob adored me from the first moment he laid eyes on me. Sometimes I thought he just needed someone to love. Other times, I felt he was an adorable man with a heart that needed more filling up than life had allowed. He was basically gentle, warm, caring." Bethany produced a sad smile before continuing. "I initially used his kindness and attentions as protection, to keep other men at bay. When that didn't work any longer, I accepted his proposal for the safety of marriage. In that regard, he never disappointed (I always felt protected and safe.)

"We were good to each other. Over time I learned to love him in ways I never dreamed possible." She paused as though overcome with the wonder of it. "On the other hand," she recollected, "he could make me feel naughty when I hadn't been, sometimes he acted like he wished I would be, and when I wouldn't, well then I felt guilty both ways."

"I'm afraid I don't understand." Joe's wide forehead squished up into one massive frown.

Bethany blushed and choked slightly before admitting, "Wouldn't expect you to. And, quite frankly, I have no idea why that came out. But, there was one other major issue: his parents totally despised and hated me, his mother especially, irreconcilable."

"Please." His weary eyes kept looking for what? "Try, this is really important to me, try to explain to me what made you feel guilty with your husband."

"I'll do no such thing!" she protested with firm resolve. "You'd know things only a husband should know." Vividly she remembered the Greek styled nightgown he had bought her for her December 29 birthday shortly after their quick honeymoon trip. The crossed gathering provocatively accentuated the already noticeable bust line. Jacob would grab for her and kiss her passionately; so much it would leave them both breathless. Finally he had relented and given in to her discomfort. Revamping it into a more decorous one became finality one day later. To make amends for her fuss, she'd trimmed it with ribbon and a satin bow. He'd later whispered he planned to get her another one some day. It could still make her blush, just as then. The heat in her face prompted a slender groomed hand to rise to an equally inflamed neck. His "look" finally made her add, "It wasn't anything, exactly, Jacob was just a bit mischievous, that's all."

"So," he concluded, "you wanted him to be what, more prudish, proper?"

"Certainly not." Her laugh pealed delightedly, as much as his news of Sam and Heidi.

Not encouraging. "You're not going to tell me, right?" He looked pacified yet one dark neat eyebrow raised hopefully.

"I see no reason for any of this." Devastating lashes lowered over sincere mortification.

Wasn't sure he could be around her too long; what might life be like seeing her day in and day out? Joe's thoughts shifted. "If I gave you reason enough, would you tell me then?"

"Mr. Wright," she protested, her eyes seeking the rough boards that seemed not to have changed all that much despite her arduous smoothing with sand, "I'm out of mending; unless you have a need for some, I am at wits' end to know how else to pass the time of day. You're being most uncharacteristic. Let's change the subject, shall we?"

"Wish I could," he muttered darkly. The tone and ominous gritted teeth turned handsome features into grim foreboding. He uncurled his body from the post and sauntered off toward the water trough. She thought he must be going on to the mill and had already read most of Heidi's letter. It conveyed her happiness with Sam plus a description of their lovely wedding that Sam had made into a grand event for the sake of introducing her to his prestigious friends.

Instead Joe returned with his saddlebags. Reluctantly Sam's thin stationary was tucked back. As Joe sunk cross-legged onto the floor just off to one side, he rested massive shoulders against the rail post, heaved a sigh, and then bowed to dig through the contents. Pulling out the lawyer's letter, he held it awhile longer. He was losing his nerve, but he had to approach someone sooner or later. Besides, he'd lost his nerve with every female he'd come across. Finally, he bit his lower lip and stirred up gumption to proceed. "Do I recall correctly you enjoyed a fancy house; would have returned east if it had been feasible?"

"Yes," she nodded.

"Have you changed your mind?" he plunged further.

She shook her head, shrugged and smiled answering, "It isn't an option open for me to consider."

"Well, it might be. I'm going to show you something," he lifted the letter toward her, "and I'm going to ask you something personal again. If I get the right answer, I'll never show this to another living soul. Regardless, please, I beg of you, keep this in *strictest confidence*."

"If it's nothing illegal, I presume you may have my word," she replied primly, not knowing what to expect or why he should care to share confidences with her. Accepting the single sheet of paper, she read rapidly to determine the general contents. She raised her eyes assured he must be the bereft heir addressed. She read it again slowly to digest the exact specifications. The letterhead was embellished and the script neat and professional. But it mystified as to why he would let her read it. "It mentions *your* grandfather's death, I presume?"

"Yes," he confirmed, eyes closed, mouth grim, nostrils flared breathing heavy.

She gently inquired, "And what does this all mean?"

"That my grandfather will leave my mother and sister near penniless," came his flat monotone, "and give his estate to a lot of riffraff if I do not do exactly as it says. That is, I need to 1) get myself a wife in less than two years, 2) return to Baltimore for at least six months of a year's time, and 3) assume management of his estate for a full year. I have exactly two to possibly four years to accomplish these things. After that, I get on with my life. I could very easily expect my mother and sister to live less luxuriously on what I could afford. And, I don't need his business or money. It irks me to the teeth to give in, yet otherwise I give it away to a crowd I loath! To leave the bulk of his money to such frivolous scum absolutely galls me! So," his mouth twisted, more severe than even times when Bethany had practically felt like cowering, "I've decided to fulfill my duties, just like the old fox dictated."

Bethany's awareness of spite beneath his carefully modulated tones, made her hold her breath. His suppressed anger and bitterness were too intense to be contrived. If she knew anything about the man, who had both intrigued and frightened her on the trip west, she knew he was brutally honest. Whenever he had come near, afraid of discovery, she had immediately done whatever he said. At times it chaffed to be such a lamb in the face of his threatening bluster, but she had never wanted anything but for him to leave her in peace. So, he'd commanded, she'd obeyed. Yet, when he'd ridden away, he always appeared more confused than pleased. He was a difficult man to understand and she pitied whoever he coerced into marriage.

"And," her mixed emotions prompted, "what's this got to do with whatever you said you wanted to ask me?" He evidenced similar intensity and confusion as exhibited on the trail. It unnerved her as usual. Like Jacob, she could feel guilty without even knowing what she'd done.

But Jacob always embraced her and kissed away troubling thoughts. Joe…well, was he even capable of loving a woman, let alone caring what one thought?

Charles had once voiced that Joe "was likely a eunuch." And then, of course, went on to suggest worse.

Timmy defended his hero saying, "Charles, you just can't abide men who're above thinking your low-down lustful imaginations."

Joe interrupted her reverie. "There's only one glitch in fulfilling my decision. I need a wife to claim my inheritance and start serving my 'one year sentence.' I've decided to ask *you* to be that wife."

There, he'd proposed. And she'd reply as she pleased. As long as his affairs were kept quiet, not much worry. If turned down, he'd proceed from here, although his list of potentials looked shorter than a bobcat's tail.

She almost didn't believe she'd heard right. Acting as though it were nothing unusual, she inquired, "Would I stay here? Or, are you asking about *my* returning east? Had you meant going *with* you?"

Not a flat "no," he perked up. "Yes. I'd think you should. My word or a mere piece of paper might not be sufficient proof, don't you agree?"

"Probably not," she surmised, "I learned from Sam what sticklers lawyers can be."

He arose, disappeared into the room and retrieved his hat. When he returned, he swung it round and round. Held on tenterhooks, he preferred to leave and quickly. Finally he blurted, "I'll return to the Motts; give you some time to think. Need to have an answer by tomorrow night though. I'll come back here. If you say 'yes,' I'll help you pack up. Timmy could stay on until you got a buyer for your place and the Motts could transfer the sale for you. We'd be gone in a couple of days, married in Astoria. The clipper I came up on is going back by mid July. I'd like to be on it, bound for home. You say, 'no,' then nothing changes."

That said, he strode away to recapture the plow horse. In three minutes he was gone.

Bethany retrieved another cup of tea, and returned to her drum. The battered silly thing had been the only constant in her life. Endlessly it had amused Jonathan, so it was worth far more than the few coins paid.

Okay, first, admit he had her pegged right on wanting to leave Oregon. Joe was sharp at sizing up people. But, was Joe Wright "right" inside? If so, what was she to think of this totally bizarre and *enforced* "proposal"? And, what exactly did the term "wife" mean to him?

When Tim came in, he helped himself to the just past warm leftovers, but Bethany refused to apologize for not having his supper ready or offering to heat it up. She was thinking, praying, worrying, and dreaming all at the same time. She sat staring off into the trees, the same trees that usually suggested skulking hostiles, red *and* white. The fear she'd known in the factory was physically real. Fear in Oregon pervaded eerily, based on hearsay, rumor, half-truths and supposition. While men relentlessly pursued Eminent Domain, Bethany cringed over the potential for *wars and rumors of wars*. She had married for safety once before. Less than honorable, but what might have happened had she not left that Lowell mill, something a lot worse? Dying of lint disease was a real risk too. Had it been God who provided escape? Or, was it the devil's own stumbling block? Hadn't she beaten herself up sufficiently over the years since? Face it, the past was dead. Her regrets should be too, dead and buried in God's forgetfulness. More precise and to the point, was *this* offer God's provision of safety?

With Jacob, he presumed she gave her heart, which in a very short time became true. But, with Joe, wasn't he suggesting a mere business partnership? Surely not love! *I mean, even a normal man would have a problem finding a wife on such short notice.*

Honestly, she longed for safety. And, with admiration born of knowledge of his care and concern enough, she considered Joe a well respected Christian man, although impossible to figure out emotionally. Well, the most important part was right.

If he *didn't* marry, his mother and sister wound up disinherited. Wasn't he asking her to join him on a mission of mercy? Where was the shame in that for either of them? But, could she just throw away Sam's thoughtful provision? She'd become a respected business owner, employer and a woman of some means in less than a year. This home and barn were built with her own two hands. Throw all that energy away? Would she regret it for the rest of her life thereafter? And, if Joe scared her as a detached trail boss, think what he'd be like as a husband! (No gentle Yankee there!)

But, on the other hand, Oregon had turned her into a drudge; more and more she wore that Indian man's leggings. Lately, she didn't even bother wearing a skirt over, just let a long shirt flow down like some "bloomer" suffragette. Days filled with backbreaking labor in fields and woods. And how she longed for the gentler world she'd once known.

She went to bed almost the minute Tim left for the post. However, sleep eluded long after Clyde returned. The next morning Tim relayed a hair-raising tale of violence against American settlers at the hands of disgruntled British deserters, now apparently turned marauders. And, he continued, "The trappers are as mad about the new settlers as the Indians are about more new trappers." Another straw in her mental accounting balance, an incidence that tipped the scale decidedly east.

"You okay?" His voice registered concern.

"Yes," she assured, brightening deliberately, "no doubt overdid the cleaning and sewing."

"Joe sure took note, though." He shifted into a grin.

Bethany's too obvious pleasure undid her indifference. "He did?"

"Yup," he pronounced proudly, "and when the Motts and I explained how you'd near built the whole house by yourself, he told us you were one of the few women he knew who could take care of herself. Then he told them about you downing the buffalo just yards out from your wagon. Made it 'the tale of the evening,' he did! Finished up saying he had no idea why men worked lugging meat so far back to camp. Said, 'all you have to do is chase one in to the ladies for shooting, and they conveniently do the butchering right next to the fire and water!"

She cringed in remembrance. "I trust he didn't embellish it any more than that."

"Nope," Tim continued. "You can't embellish a true heroine, Widow Beth."

Strange name, the West frightened even by its familiarity. You had no say about what you were called unless you wanted to be considered offish (or some other more descriptive term.) Since they'd crossed the Mississippi River, it seemed her last name had never been used.

Would Mrs. Joseph Wright become her new "handle" IF she had the option of staying here? Or, would Oregon acquaintances call her, "Joe's widow woman"? The future was scary any way you looked at it, east or west. But, truthfully, to stay meant she'd daily anticipate death's nasty possibilities. To head east would include the risk of "death at sea." And the east meant trembling over an uncertain future. After all, an ancient grandfather could have neglected his business; employees could have absconded with profits? Who knew what Joe would find when he returned home? And, there's always the possibly of dying of plague en route. Wouldn't that be a cruel joke?

When Joe arrived, as dusk settled into shadows, she'd convinced no further either way.

Met by Timmy, Joe explained he'd "come for a few moments alone with 'Widow Beth' about 'her hides' and how many rocking chairs she wanted." He left him watering Mott's horse adding, "Don't expect to be long." He strode straight up to cross over by her plank bridge, stood in the open doorway and announced without any pretense at social graces, "Come for my answer."

His down to business approach shouldn't have hurt Bethany so, but it did. Honorable men usually treated her as a great beauty, a desirable prize to claim. Did it concern him little one way or the other? Men of base passions flattered her more? He sounds like he's buying a side of beef? But, she figured many a woman would jump at the chance to go back east, impersonal or not. Sudden realization admitted to being similarly inclined. Did she value her safety enough to swallow her pride? But, was this accepting nothing but a ticket? Was safety valued more than self-esteem? Give up her home and livelihood? What had less than a year in Oregon done to her? "I have some concerns," she hedged.

His stance grew taunt and a left mouth muscle twitched. "Which are?"

"Well, first," she gulped, "do you plan to sail 'round the Horn' or shortcut through Panama?"

He shifted into explanation mode. "I planned on crossing over Panama in swamp season…to save time and get this over with."

"Either way has its perils," she acknowledged. "I inquire because I would need to know how to dress."

"Anything else?" He relaxed by a hair's breath.

"Well," she continued, "where will we live? And, especially, what do you expect of me?"

"My grandfather left a home in Baltimore, also one in Pittsburgh. There are more than enough rooms for all of my family. As to what I expect, I ask no more than a legal wife."

This was exactly as she'd expected, but what of their day-to-day routine? She was aghast as to what "legal wife" meant. Maybe staying in Oregon was preferable? She had to have more details. "Perhaps you should sit for a few moments, Mr. Wright?" she suggested. It sounded stiff and formal, but so did the whole deal (whatever it was!) Composing her thoughts, she twisted the corner of her apron into a wad. Finally she offered the question that had plagued her. "Am I," her eyes shifted, "the first woman you asked…since you knew of your grandfather's will stipulations?"

He nodded over reluctant remembrance. "Yes. Nor have I ever asked another at any time. So you'd be my one and only ever. You say 'no,' I'm condemned to try another. Probably should have rehearsed some? Might not have botched it so bad?"

"Why do you say 'botched'?" she wondered.

He frowned over embellishing his faults further. "Are you asking why I never wanted to marry before?"

"No, but if you wish to explain that, it might help." She grasped for any glimmer of knowledge.

"Ever hear of the term, nepotism?"

"I'm afraid not." It wasn't often that a word stumped her, but this one most certainly did.

"It means someone who runs a business, politics, a nation, or any group of people by granting only his closest relatives any positions of power, authority and especially wealth. My grandfather was such a man. He had four sons. When his wife died, he preferred casual dalliance to creating a second class dynasty. Each of his four legal sons, unfortunately, emulated his casual morality, so *their* wives produced very few heirs.

"I'm one of what used to be five grandsons. On one of their own steamship cruises, the male Wrights were celebrating my cousin Albert's formal entry into the family fortunes, on the very boat that he was to own. It exploded. That killed my grandfather's chance of being the head of a great clan, except for Joseph Wright III, me! I was finishing my first year of college. Although my father was the oldest son, he married last so I was the youngest grandchild. In one fell swoop, Grandfather's egg basket splattered, leaving me his only live hatchling.

Summers thereafter he drilled me like a sergeant major. When I wasn't with him, I was alone with men I was expected to command. He demanded a say in what I studied. He removed me from a school he thought not prestigious enough. Oh, it was fine when he had other choices and a long stretch of time to bring me along. But, when I was all he had, he rigged all the ropes at once. And, he had to depend on strangers for the first time in his life. If something went wrong, he had to send me or an employee, or else rush to its aid himself. He hadn't done that for years. In his eagerness, he made the mistake of depending on strangers to introduce his grandson to the ways of blatantly promiscuous women, a family heritage you might call it.

That proved the final straw! I walked out, never looked back. By threatening to toss it all to his pack of strumpets, it's a final attempt to either justify himself or drag me back to his envisioned legacy. He knows I cherish honor above all else, that I'd rather walk on live coals than one thin dime go to some scantily clad public display dancer!"

Moments crept by before bilious anger slowly subsided from the room, crawling and slinking across the porch floor to roll fitfully off the barn roof.

"The real question is," she managed in a near hush, "why ask me? You must know many women. Why wait all this time? You've passed dozens of other women."

He wasn't sure of any reason except: "Couldn't think of another woman I'd trust."

Her eyes widened perceptibly. "Trust in marriage? I assure you there are a great many virtuous women in the world, Mr. Joseph Wright III!"

"No, well, yes, that's part of it I suppose. Just meant…you'd keep your mouth closed if you turned me down. Most women make a really big deal of a proposal. Tell everyone they meet every small detail."

"Oh," she acknowledged. "Your public honesty must be guaranteed no private embarrassment, that's it?"

"Guess so." Both statements fell as flat as his hat brim.

Bethany thought the severe hat style suited him. He was a strict man, lived by a strict code, and strictly disciplined himself. But could she abide such a man? Or would she be able to share herself enough to temper his claim to justice with Godly tolerance? He claimed to be a Christian. But he hardly evidenced a will to forgive, others or himself. (Much as she had struggled to forgive herself for so many months?) But he'd had it worse than she. Not by strangers' evil intentions, of course, but by close family.

And, she appreciated his loathing of lust; would that all men avoided such. Well, she'd give honesty and bluntness their due. "Joe, if I agreed to marry you, you should realize my only reason would be to get away from these dangers plaguing Oregon.

I shudder to have come all this way just to be slaughtered, or worse. Whether because an Indian visited Motts' post and came down with a white man's disease, or because some British trapper caught more beaver or got a better pelt price than an American trapper, or because some king in far off Europe decides to declare war, I despise these wretched agitations.

Being a Christian is in your favor, but I must be promised more than transportation. I won't go back east to become a pretty face at tea parties. Nor will I travel that far to face the drudgery of cleaning your house, preparing your meals nor tending laundry! Not after managing to make something of myself here. I'm scared every day, but I get ahead. I value my independence and what I've accomplished. It may not look like much, but I paid for it by mighty hard doing! I'd insist on something of my own because I won't risk winding up like your mother and sister. Nor will I be dependent on you to take care of me under a marriage that offers nothing but a ticket.

I'm being honest, but you shouldn't take it personal, it's my own peculiarity. I won't be stranded again. Such fears are brought on no doubt by my own, not so long ago, similar dire circumstances."

Why should she so want to smooth out his wrinkled forehead? Was it the thought that they might legally become man and wife? Surely he wasn't scowling because she wanted to go back east? Did it represent male disapproval of female independence?

"You'll get a third of everything," he surprised, promising after some hesitation. "I can't guarantee selling it all quickly after a year, but I can promise a healthy allowance until then. I'll give my mother and sister another third with the stipulation that any remainder is to pass to Claudia, and I'll keep a third. Mother and Claudia's share I'll entrust to their lawyer, but I'll hand yours over to do with as you please." There weren't many he'd feel comfortable handing over a fortune, male or female, but she'd already proven her remarkable capabilities.

"Joe," she sighed, "your offer sounds very noble and generous, but I haven't a clue what you've inherited; a third of what?!"

"Oh," he exclaimed. "No wonder you've got questions. Knowing what it entailed all my life, it never dawned on me to elaborate. Well, let's see, a third of what I remember is a couple of steamship lines, four coal mines, stock in eastern and Canadian railroads. You could take your share in railroad stock and live off dividends if that's what you wish."

"Hey! Joe!" yelled a tenor bellow from far below. "If you're visiting, I'm not going to hold this horse's hand all night, you know!"

It was a perfect excuse for a good laugh to clear the air. "Tell him to come on up, I made a squash pie with the sugar you gave him last night."

"No, Bethany." He held up a right hand to object. She hesitated. "Could it be," he amended more politely, "just for the two of us for now? Please?"

Joe pleading presented an entirely new prospect. "Sure, he can have his tomorrow."

Almost in a single bound, he returned the yell, "Turn the horse into the pasture. It's almost too dark to see my way back tonight anyway; think I'll bunk with you if that's okay?"

"Sure," Timmy shouted back. "But, give me an hour to get myself straightened up?"

"Is he that messy?" Joe chuckled softly.

"Just disorganized." Her eyes rolled. "He never knows where he leaves anything. And, I don't know why he'll bother. His 'straightened up' looks just as disorganized as before."

"Seems I remember," he stroked imaginary chin whiskers, "letting him pack back in Missouri. I vowed then he'd stick to the horse detail."

"He wondered why he always got the same jobs," she revealed from her sideboard shelf. Slicing each a wide piece, she was pleased to see a flaky crust on the bottom. A nibbled crumb of filling convinced that the pie made from her last squash was indeed edible. A couple of pewter mugs of tea completed the array when she realized he might not have had his evening meal. "I forgot to ask; have you eaten supper?"

"Sort of, enough to make do." He shrugged as though it didn't matter.

"No need to make do!" she exclaimed, rushing boiling water into a pewter beefsteak dish. Loading it up with roast chicken, dumplings, sage stuffing and a glass bowl of tiny onions and new peas in creamy butter, she admitted, "I was in such a state that I worked in the garden in the morning and cooked most of the afternoon. It's my way of dealing with mental meandering."

When he'd had a good taste of everything, he remarked, "Never known anyone so productive when musing."

Both high praise and cynicism, how typically Joe Wright! If she kept a journal, she'd make note of it. Did he feel like she did? When you planned to marry someone, did you take note of things you never had before? She lingered long enough over her slice of pie that they finished eating simultaneously. "Another slice?" she suggested.

"Yes, and thank you." He handed back his dish. "One of the best squash pies I've tasted."

She deferred quickly. "The thanks should more properly go to the sugar you provided."

When she'd reseated herself he added, "And, now that we've been ever so polite. Do I get your answer tonight or wait until morning?"

"I don't think I'd sleep for another night if we waited until morning," she admitted.

He nodded wry agreement. "You figured right about me being tired. Afraid I slept like the dead last night, too worn out, too many nights contemplating proposing."

"And did it go like you'd imagined?" She arched a delicate brow.

"No." He evidenced lip curling disdain. "Ten times worse than any disaster I've ever supposed!"

The dejected face created a chuckle as well as a protest. "But, you didn't do so badly; after all, I *am* considering it."

"I've given more elaborate pitches to buy salted herring!" he blurted. "Honestly, Beth, you deserved far better!"

He'd deliberately dropped the "widow" prefix. He didn't need her remembering a man that loved her. "I couldn't do anything but spit out misery! I've chastised myself twenty ways from Sunday. Don't know how I'd feel worse without being keel hauled. Told myself to expect a 'no' answer. Don't fret thinking you need to spare my feelings."

She marveled at both apology and rare lack of confidence. "So what have I already said in your imagination?"

"To take my wretched proposal and bury myself in Alaska, or any place else where the world would be well rid of me!" His hunched stance reminded her of a dejected little boy.

"How uncharitable!" She also marveled because she considered it such an opportunistic possibility.

"Look, Beth, the suspense is making me nervous," he admitted. "When I get nervous, I eat. If I get any more anxious, Tim won't get any pie."

"A little more information, please, Joe? When you asked me yesterday about my husband, was it really wondering how we got along? Or, if I liked being married?"

"The latter," wary eyes conveyed nothing more than bare facts.

"But how I loved Jacob would have nothing to do with this marriage to you," she stressed.

He shoved the barrel chair away from the table with a thud. "Probably not, just searching for clues, but it's not important any more, is it?"

"Don't know," she confessed. "You come armed with considerable baggage."

"Baggage?" His brow creased frown displayed smoky eyes filled with utter confusion.

"Yes, funny, weird ideas," he noticed her New England accent by the "idear" pronunciation, "like me being the only one who wouldn't run off at the mouth. You seem detached from your mother; never speak of her with any particular fondness. And, I haven't heard kindness expressed for your sister either. Their welfare doesn't even appear your strongest reason for complying with the will. Folks on the trail—and your friend Sam—thought you disliked women in general. In fact, I used the term 'woman hater,' and Sam never defended you—not what a lawyer, nor a friend, usually does. Hooking up with you appears doomed from the start. How can I live up to your expectations?"

"If you can't, no one can." His firm jaw and steely eye brokered no argument.

"Well, now, that may be the crux of the issue." She grasped and massaged her shoulders and neck. "In a round about way, you've complimented me. Another man would have made it sound like high praise. In your mouth, it's another task added to an already long list!"

He stood and shoved fists into front pants pockets. The lightweight black wool was tired at the knees from too many times between pressings. He viewed fringed buckskin shirt, faded loose red bandana, and dust caked boots. Why was she prolonging this ordeal? "I'm sorry, Beth, I've no talent for romance and no patience with females, and well you know that's the truth of it. Guess you and Sam hit the nail on the head."

"Patience and romance are worlds apart, Joe." Solemn eyes softened.

"How so?" He turned toward her.

"Well, romance is trying to please a woman. During courting you find things out about one another. We already know what we do or do not like, I'm sure. But, I need assurance about a lot more before I'd marry you. Marriage, of any kind, is a bigger life responsibility than almost anything patience can imagine."

"You've told me about how you—and others—think I'm strange, but I assure you I do not hate women personally, just generally. Haven't met too many that inspired confidence, but I believe I can say that you have been quite the exception. However, you also have things I never thought right about you." He suddenly turned defensive.

"Well, perhaps it's best we follow Proverbs 27:6, '*Faithful are the wounds of a friend but the kisses of an enemy are deceitful,*' alright?"

"Well, any time I told you to lighten a load, tighten harness, keep closer to the wagons, throw out stuff, nap, whatever…well, you always immediately did as told. Not only that, you kept at it. Thought it abnormal, it's not natural to be so submissive. Didn't Jacob find you too passive also?"

"Joe." One hand clasped her mouth to cover a wide smirk. "I never wanted you to inspect my load. Afraid you'd make me leave my sawmill blades and shafts behind on the desert, or throw them down a ravine. Immediate obedience was my ploy to get rid of you!"

In astonishment he suggested, "Then, you're not always so amenable?"

"Hardly, there was a good Irish temper counting way past ten on dozens of occasions!"

"Thank God!" he rejoiced, glancing heavenward.

"I Thessalonians 5:18 does recommend, '*In everything give thanks,*'" she interjected as he reseated himself, "but thanks for my Irish temper is as unlikely on my list as making me England's queen!"

"Then I trust to see some evidence I'm not the only *rouge Christian?*" He pronounced it with such deep sorrow that she couldn't help sense his heavy guilt.

"Rouge Christian, that's a terrible phrase, corrupt doctrinally I'd suspect too! You should be ashamed to even suggest such a thing." She could have scowled, but remembered Sam's admonition about not making him mad. To cover the silence she offered, "More tea?"

"No," he glared. "I'd just like an answer, 'yes' or 'no'? I apologize for not making it fancy. I'll work to provide for your independence, that's my promise. And, within reason, you should be safe once we make Baltimore. I can't promise you the sea's cooperation; but anything in my power, I will happily oblige."

"Is this a marriage in every respect, Joe?" She finally summoned the courage to ask what really nagged at her conscience.

"You're smart enough to figure out that's my problem." His anger rekindled. "To have Grandfather's demands go that far, controlling my life that far, I can't accept. And, I won't tolerate you expecting it either. If that's not acceptable, then 'no' is your answer."

Rejected totally, she steeled herself. "So, name only, right?"

"Marriage means children," he explained. "If I had a child, Grandfather's nepotism starts all over again, generation to generation. I resent the old man dictating my life to model his. On the other hand, I can't expect you to readily wish to deceive. I suppose, in a sense, God as well as man, right? But, my resistance doesn't mock the institution of marriage. I was just born into and brought up by the wrong family."

"Yes, but that bothers me. I've sensed your animosity, versus marriage. And I also wondered why you proposed to me, since I'd dearly love to have another child."

This had turned hopeless for certain. "I wasn't sure. Since you'd lost one and hadn't remarried, guessed you thought the potential pain too bad to risk again."

Her eyes glued to her teacup. "So you chose me, thinking abstinence was a safe topic?"

He nodded into the table where his tense splayed hands gripped the solid edge for support.

"Excuse my pushing," she continued, "probably I'm vain to ask. But are there any particular qualities I possess besides abstinence and keeping my mouth shut?"

"Sure, you never flirted or made flighty comments. Remembered you didn't try to catch men's attentions, kept to yourself, so I just concluded—apparently in error—that you didn't want to remarry. When I found you still single, figured you found marriage distasteful."

"Aha! There's the real reason. Thus you concluded I had the right affliction for the right marriage!"

He winced at the blunt assessment. "Sorry, yes."

Some time elapsed before she interjected, "Do you remember Lottie Modine?"

"Blonde, big boned, three kids?" memory responded.

"Yes," Beth verified, "she never got pregnant the whole trip, remember?"

He might become more uncomfortable yet. "Can't say as it was on the top of my observations, why?"

"I asked her about it one day," she revealed. "She said she and her husband had an abstinence pact. Said she usually got sick as a dog when she got in the family way, sick every day throughout an entire pregnancy, and there was no way she could endure that plus wilderness and rough traveling. It therefore is certainly possible to live celibate married. A man as self-disciplined as you are should have no problem, I'm sure.

So, here's both an answer and deal: promise to take me back east and allow me—in time—the resources to take care of myself, and I will agree to become your wife as you wish. I say that having one very BIG objection.

No Christian should live a lie. And you know now that I would dearly love to have a child. However, I will vow before God and you to resign myself to live other than as God intended, and as I would desire, provided you agree we can do so *without conflict* until you: 1) Fulfill your business obligations, 2) Allow me to build a new life away from the threat of war, 3) See that your relatives are provided for, and 4) Prevent your inheritance from falling into undesired hands.

If you fail, we annul the marriage. If not, per your wishes, I will also promise never to *legally* adopt a child, IF you promise that you will accept my 'rescue' of a child that needs someone to care for them. But I'll wait until your terms are fulfilled and after I am living on my own. Does this sound reasonable?"

By his silence Bethany experienced the worst rejection of her life but managed to choke out, "Is there a problem with my 'yes'?"

"I won't fail. So decide now I'm not easy to live with, at any time," he reminded her grimly. "Living closely with a man who doesn't even pretend to love you, are YOU *really sure* you can endure this? And I'll accept no change of heart later. Once married, I'll give you no out except distance. It's 'til death us do part' regardless of celibacy, I'll offer no annulment ever!"

(Probably she'd never find anyone like Jacob again anyways.) That clinched her nodding. "Alright, my word to a legal marriage in name only. But I expect both of us, as Christians, will at least show Christian love and respect for each other? Philippians 4:13 assures us, '*I can do all things through Christ which strengtheneth me*,' agreed?"

"Don't approve of folks using Scripture like peaveys and pulleys, Beth," he mildly chastised. "Apostle Paul never had marriage, and especially not this kind, in mind when he said that."

"But do you agree we should get along well enough, at a minimum, as Christians who should have basic concern for one another?" she demanded. "I've feared your temper more than once. I'll not stay married if you scare or browbeat me after I'm your legally married wife!"

He begrudgingly admitted, "I do, doctrinally anyway. You're offering me more than I expected; guess I ought to graciously accept." He stood, as though to leave, negotiations finalized.

She needed one more reassurance. She stood and took two steps toward him. Aware of his height and immense strength, she breathed in saddle soap, hair tonic and admired manly torso and rippling biceps. Thinking she had better prepare him, she whispered, "I'm not being romantic, Joe, but I need physical assurance that *you* can handle a pretense marriage. Your legal situation demands we not act like monk or nun. Nor will it validate your claim living apart. Lawyers can hire detectives to discredit your past. Remember, you have a very motivated competitor." With a tentative motion, she raised her hands to his buckskin shirt, then his muscular shoulders and drew herself up on tiptoe to plant a kiss on his tense mouth.

At first it just lay there. Suddenly, callused hands slid behind her shoulder blades. Her gentle kiss returned with a strength that shocked her. Renewed awakening (of what it meant to be married) caused her to press back against his hard chest and stare into anguished eyes, astonished to find her emotions "tummy tilted!" Was there hope he could someday become as soft and vulnerable as she felt?!

He stared momentarily but could no longer endure the sensation of lovely blue eyes probing conscience. Firm muscular arms restrained her, his heart pounding, wanting instead to rest his chin in the center of her center part. "We'll find a way to be civil, Beth," his husky voice quavered. "I can't accomplish alone what I've tried to avoid like the plague. But, don't try that again unless we're getting married."

Once stated, he abruptly left.

Her impetuous "test" answered nothing. Instead it added pounds of regret. Her promise committed her, this time to the "wrong" Christian, one she'd instantly wished to be much more than a legal husband. *One more selfish choice,* demons accused and bile rose dissuading she knew her own mind. Leave it to her, matrimony mess!

CHAPTER 12:
Three Weddings to Go

"I'm sure going to miss you, Widow Beth," Timmy's thin lips quivered. "And you know I'm especially going to miss your good cooking."

"You need a wife, Tim," she softly violated their unspoken impasse.

He nodded in agreement but added, "Don't have much to offer a woman right now, but…maybe someday?"

"New plans?" she queried, hope rising.

"Yeah, a few, I've been thinking why not clear a spot for a cabin and garden right across the river? Figured if I registered a claim close to my job, slow but sure I'd get me something f'r myself. Guess you've inspired me; figured if a lone woman could accomplish all this, I should be able to get ahead too."

She rejoiced to hear something that sounded real and practical. "That's a great idea, Tim. Maybe the best you've had so far."

"Sure gonna try to make it work; or maybe better yet, I'm gonna work at it almighty hard."

"Look," she urged, "as soon as possible clear out anything I've left. I want you to have it. Anything that isn't nailed down, you grab hard onto it. Most of it came from the Long family so you don't owe me any thanks. Whisk it across the river right away, okay? Take the shed too, and the animals you can rent out to the new owner or go to your place as soon as you can get them some pasture. I've left a bill of sale in your name that says 'For services rendered,' left it on the table. You don't want anyone seeing stuff they'd expect to be part of buying this place, okay?"

Tim was momentarily overwhelmed. "More than I ever expected!"

"Well, you make sure those big horses get paid like they deserve if this lumber mill keeps going, you hear?" she near sobbed.

"Yes, I will!" he agreed. "Honest."

Blue eyes misted. "I'm going to miss you terribly!"

They both couldn't bear to watch each other depart. In the Lord, she loved Tim with her whole heart, and it was more than just gratitude or motherly instincts. And, she would just *hate* it if she heard he attained heaven too soon. Too good a man to waste on this evil wilderness, she fretted. Two barrister cases, personal clothing, two sets of silverware, two beefsteak dishes and the old drum were all she took. Joe said everything would be taken care of on ship and they'd be there in a few days.

"Beth," Joe whispered. She turned from packaging up the cotton, flannel, crochet thread and embroidery floss she'd purchase.

"Yes?" She glanced up expectantly.

"Fellow just came up river." He inclined his dark curls. "He and the family look pretty prosperous; wants to start a grist mill."

Anticipation mixed with regret. "And my place might do?"

"Might, want an introduction?" he volunteered.

"No," she resisted his taking over, "just point him out." They'd barely exchanged a dozen words the whole trip in to Mott's place. Mostly she still felt out of sorts for constantly buckling under to fear.

They left the dim interior's coal oil and animal hide smells to adjust to bright mid-morning sun. Thurston Bridges could not be mistaken. He, his blond wife and children lined up like a golden staircase. The immediate opportunity presented was followed by their family's on-site inspection.

Her place sold by nightfall for five thousand two hundred dollars. Considering that her investment had been mostly labor and Sam's provided emergency fund still remained largely intact, it'd shown a huge profit. But, now, there was no turning back, her bridge was burning behind her. She prayed the man would stand by his agreement to keep Tim on. She also hoped the nineteen-year-old blond daughter, who'd been forced to leave her fiancé in Tennessee (because the family needed her efficient and organized labor to help with the younger children,) might someday favor Tim Martin. (Had she detected a slight smitten look on Tim's face already?) Shy and reticent, she was hardly a "match," for Tim, but they could very well compliment each other's strengths, talents and balance out weaknesses.

Contentedly she sewed, sat on her drum beside Mrs. Mott and Jonathan, and enjoyed a cookie after a lovely evening picnic. His questions and antics endeared. Now that she was leaving, she regretted her lack of visiting more often. Wasn't that always the way? You never appreciated what you had until you lost it. That evening, alone on a pallet in their storeroom, she pulled an encased string of gold coins into the plackets sewn behind her petticoat's ruffles. Afterwards, she stuffed the bottom one with horsehair. In the morning, it seemed a bit awkward but cooler in the heat. Well, hurrah for progress! The trip went smoothly; campouts were scenic and trouble free with the exception of mosquitoes (occasionally worrisome to the extreme.) Bethany slept with a sheet tightly clasped over her head since she did not share male enthusiasm for camp smoke.

Joe had thought at one time to ask her mummified form not to sleep on her side, the silhouetted curves proved extremely provocative. However, when she flopped over on her back it was worse. Waiting to see if she slept on her stomach too, he wondered how many of the other men watched likewise. She did; not much better as she moved into curls and curves when turning and she proved a fretful sleeper, never seen such femaleness.

Had he made a mistake on that score? Too late! The dye's in the batch. Not about to propose to anyone else, what other choice? If he weren't such a penny pincher, he'd have brought along more canvas so she'd have her own tent. Where was his brain? She didn't even have privacy for dressing, his men either. Joe acknowledged (this once for sure) pure ignoramus stupidity! But, as usual, there wasn't a peep of complaint from any of them. She went her way; they went the other.

His "provision for a bride" was nothing but a canvas sheet, mere protection from rain, roped between trees. Reflecting, he questioned his priorities. He could afford nice tents, folding camp chairs and table or a tin reflector, why hoard the money? His father had stated Grandfather had been a terrible skinflint in his early days. And he didn't care for the similarity. Well, he'd learn to do differently! If he sold and keep the money from all the pelts he'd collected, he could likely rest easy right now. What was money for but to provide a little comfort? What other motivation possessed him? It wasn't as though he'd accumulate enormous wealth by his frugal ways. Probably he should get into the wholesale end of the business, settle down and let someone else do this? (Sure easy to hire someone with more social skills!)

He knew, in his heart, Grandfather's business had really been more his line. Dealing with tough men with a grievance, handling a bunch of ruffians who were trying to horn in, or outsmarting tycoons trying to defraud, dishing out what bankers wanted to hear, those he could handle well. Maybe God was working his life out for the best after all? And, he could still run this business from the east. If he had too many irons in the fire, he'd just hire some good men to supervise. He'd done it for Grandfather; he'd do the same for himself.

"Joe?" Bethany's dainty pointed toed shoes were inches away from his kneeling form hunched over an Indian pack basket.

He managed to calmly answer, "Yuh?"

"You plan to get married in Astoria," she whispered, "but by an American or British minister?"

"You mean," he guessed her worry, "which way the territory will eventually go?"

She nodded her answered "yes."

"You thinking," he presumed, "maybe one might not be as legal if the opposite side wins?"

"Not exactly," she admitted. "Not that the marriage would be cancelled out religiously, but if the territory changes hands, it might not be exactly legal government wise. Not only that but there's the rare chance a government may have already given or granted claims Oregon folks don't even know about yet."

"Well, can't have that," he agreed. "You suppose the smart move might be to get married by both?"

"And present two marriage certificates in Baltimore?"

"Well, I'd present the American one—that's who I think will win—but have the British one as a back up in case of trouble. Sound sensible?"

Silent agreement assented.

His chin outline had the slightest concave center. A probing thumb rubbed that same chin area. "Three pieces of paper might be irrefutable."

She shrugged shoulders into her shovel bonnet, no idea where a third choice might originate.

"Bethany, do you take this man to be your lawfully wedded husband?" asked Captain Jules about halfway through the short ceremony.

BRIDE OF PROMISE

"I do," she vowed for the third time today.

The captain's intoned, "And do you promise to love, cherish him, obey and forsake all others for him alone?" seemed far away.

"I do." Even children, she resolved with incredulous consternation at the enormity of her promise.

The captain asked softly, "Joe, do you have a ring?"

"Here, one for each of us." Joe laid the plain gold bands in the captain's weather roughened hands. He had bought them back from Ernest after having just delivered them. Amused that Ernest had demanded a profit, just on principle (that a man should be willing to spend money on his bride) he had obliged with only a once grumbled objection. Only Ernest and Lois knew of his plans but they had not known until they were about ready to shove off on a log barge. Ernest had called it, "the coup of the Cascades!" Lois appeared a little hesitant with the congratulations, even perplexed.

The American and British ceremonies had been witnessed by his crew of six and the last had included the British minister's wife. He guessed Chicky Greene, Jed Stone, and Mike "Moose" McDowell had connived to let the rumor slip, but how? Their great shared mystery apparently would be known only to them because he hadn't stayed long enough to find out. When they'd exited the British ceremony, they were met with a clamorous "Hurrah!" Fiddles, a guitar, a wash tub bass, a musical washboard and miscellaneous mouth organs hit up a rousing rendition of "Yankee Doodle" around the slanted walkway. He guessed it was a tribute to his merchant profession. Course, unlikely anyone knew he came from Maryland.

His wide bow tie, new long tailed suit and starched shirt and high collar (that Bethany had pressed over a padded sheet covered tree stump) seemed too confining at that moment.

Bethany's dotted lace wedding hat trimmed with pleated net ruffles and tucked white satin ribbons and bows could have graced an eastern ballroom, and it made him more aware of how fragile she seemed. And the scoop neckline on the mauve gown, with scrolls and flowers on a net overlay enhanced her femininity. The Blond lace trimmed scalloped collar dipped deep over her bust, the princess waist emphasizing her full skirt below lacy short cuffs. She had gingerly lifted her gathered side skirts and train loop to descend the granite steps after Joe had motioned to the crowd, repeatedly, to halt the music.

"What is this?" he recalled his belligerent bellow. Shouldn't have been so rough, but he was afraid for them both. Some of the British used any excuse for a ruckus; and an excuse for a charivari constituted a sure recipe for mischief against a too ambitious American. Nor would they mind making them miss the ship.

Ed Morrow, owner of the local general mercantile, grinned and offered, "We couldn't have ya git married and no one glad clap ya now, could we?"

"No!" rang in unison from the wanting to be hilarious group of immigrants and trappers.

"'Sides," grumbled "Moose" in his loud bear growl voice, "don't git much chance to kiss a purty bride ever' day neither!"

"You had *your* chance," Joe managed to good-naturedly badger the aged mountain man. "Seen her and you traipsing off every chance we hit a settlement. See what you get for courting too slow?!"

This tickled the crowd immensely and instantaneous joyful bantering of the old mountain man ensued with enthusiastic noise making. Bethany couldn't help teasing along. Held tight by Joe's big right hand, she leaned over to plant a solid kiss on Moose's one-step-lower whiskered cheek.

His speaking Sioux and translating for her to discover local herbs, medicine plants, and native food sources had been marvelous help, and she remained deeply grateful. And, she'd also relied on the giant handy whenever Indians wanted to touch Jonathan's soft blond curls. Her wisdom gained was one of the few things she was able to pass along to the other women without rude comments. Although, it never prevented receiving funny looks.

"Hurrah, Moose!" Chicky yipped with a great thumping on his broad buckskinned back. A general hoot and holler, accompanied by wild applause and tossed hats, was interrupted by Joe's suddenly scooping Bethany up in his arms. Charging through the right side of the crowd, Jed immediately bolted into the driver's seat of the American pastor's carriage they'd borrowed. The reduced wedding party slapped reins for a mad dash for port, the crowd dashing close behind. Luckily their riotous clamor generally added to the horse's speed.

They made it to the dock safely but with little time to spare. A waiting rowboat soon held a very surprised sailor. Joe had near thrown Bethany into his arms (a fact he rectified quickly enough) but then had to angrily order an overly apologetic sailor, "Row!"

Joe's attention swung back to the present and Bethany's mauve and lace presence. The captain fumbled with the rings that seemed to have been off as much as they were on. He finally got the right one in each of his prescribed hands.

BRIDE OF PROMISE

"This one's for you, lass; and this, for you, Joe. Now," he cleared his throat before the open air assembled sailors, hide and fur buyers, "you first, Joe, you repeat after me, 'With this ring, I thee wed'..."

"With this ring, I thee wed, and with all my worldly goods I thee endow." Joe had by this time memorized the hateful (lying?) lines.

The ring ceremony concluded with the familiar: "I now pronounce you man and wife!" Captain Jules Hanson beamed so brightly, you'd think he'd managed it all himself. Well, Joe smiled in retrospect, maybe he thought he had? "Mr. and Mrs. Joseph Wright, please lead us below! We shall all celebrate around this ship's humble table!" And a feast it was by ships' standards. Fried pork, gravy, yeast bread, new peas, cream, and new potatoes accompanied fresh butter, jellies, and pickles. He hoped to see something similar for at least a week or two. They'd loath hardtack and thin soup for soaking it soon enough.

Unbeknown to Joe and Bethany, the crew in alternating errands that most thought were ship tasks, had prepared a "honeymoon cabin" in the top deck's carpenter shop. Emptied, the portholes had oilcloth shades to tie up or drop down. The "double bed" was merely two bunk mattresses laid on a high rough platform (workbench) with open area for storage below. Joe knew the crew meant kindness but separate bunks would have suited them so much better.

He had warned Beth not to eat fat or oily things, but noted she had *not* followed his advice. Freely discussing her trip west, she also revealed her loss of a husband and child.

Now why did it bother Joe to have her discuss her past? Maybe it's just a protocol thing? He sure couldn't determine any other reason. The captain revealed in turn that his dear wife had been a widow woman. "But, less fortunate than you, dear girl," he had insisted, "she was left with four small children!"

Joe sensed, from the sudden erect posture, that Bethany was not similarly thankful. But, by the time the noisy party escorted them to their honeymoon quarters, he noticed her smiling again albeit with clenched teeth. Was she looking a shade or two less rosy? She was not in as bad shape as the older fur trapper-turned-merchant though (as pale as a frog's belly approximated *his* shade.) From the looks of her, though, Beth would not be worrying about a "honeymoon" night for many days hence. He'd simply prefer the trip over and done. Alone in his own home, no one would question separate rooms, but until then...no hint of anyone testifying to a less than intimate marriage. Maybe this provided a good idea after all?

Leaving her to undress in private, he returned only after Captain Jules had clasped his shoulder like a stern father-in-law. "I'll maroon you in the Easter islands if you aren't good to your beautiful new bride!"

Her stalwart condition worsened upon his return. "Want a cup of tea?"

She nodded with closed eyes. He figured the swaying lantern was the avoided object and fetched the tea promptly. He knelt on his mattress to lift her head. In attempting to help by clasping the tin cup with both hands, she either forgot, or was too sick to care, or figured (after three marriage ceremonies) she was going to act married? Whatever the reason, loosed hair hovered in ringlets around shoulders where beribboned eyelet gapped into remarkable cleavage. After a few sips, only she relaxed when she hoisted covers to her neck. "Any more?" he managed evenly.

"No, thank you," clenched teeth responded, "I think it helped."

In two gulps he drained the remaining warm liquid, blew out the lamp, and hung the tin cup on a wooden spike, proceeding to do the same with his clothing. Disrobing in a honeymoon room with a bride bordered on the lea side of nightmare. Nor was he too sure his self-discipline was as easily celibate as she'd predicted. Cautiously he oozed into bed under the tucked fancy coverlet she'd added.

"You know what?" he whispered into total darkness.

She forced, "What?"

"I should have always known that I'd marry the Wright woman." She smiled at the pun but was too worried about the effect of the sea to do more.

"Joe?" she later moaned into her balled up pillow, "maybe I'm going to get seasick."

"Everyone does at first," he informed, "but all recover. To my knowledge, no one's ever died of it. Although, most wish they did before they get their sea legs. You'll feel better in a few days, I promise."

He sometimes had a queasy stomach for a day or two, but was never really sick. Though, usually he tried to avoid coming close to other sick passengers. He forced himself to get mentally and physically prepared for caring for a wife who likely would need to get up before long.

"Is there a way to stay still somehow?" she fretted.

"Nope," he chuckled but dragged both himself and her up to cradle her head against his bare shoulder. "There, upright any better?" he soothed as though she were a child.

"I think so, maybe." She gulped with a shudder.

Then she latched a desperate bare arm over his stomach so her hand clung to his ribs. Long loose curls tantalized his arm and eyelashes flicking occasionally against his shoulder gave him prickles inside and out. As she slowly slid into relaxed slumber, molded curves conformed against his side. He thought of Song of Solomon's description of *sleeping between his beloved's breast*. But, he rued, that was *very guilty* of misappropriating Scripture. Nor was Bethany's generous breast that of any *young fawn*! Movement even when she walked, even her breathing distracted! Stalwartly he schooled emotions into iron band resolve.

In the morning he found her in a fetal position. He intended to get them a biscuit and tea before she awoke, but she slid cautiously upward almost as soon as he stirred. Immediately nauseous and grimly dismayed to view the far corner commode, she requested with closed eyes if he'd place the top barrister case on his side before he left. When he returned, she was dressed and outside on her Indian drum, a white crochet-edged hanky under a gripped upper lip.

Originally he'd had no clue why she'd insisted on bringing that old drum, but it proved amazingly useful, apparently as great an idea here as the plains. The ship deck really had few seating choices for a lady. Those available would likely be shared with men. Bethany's wisdom and foresight again, he silently saluted.

Captain Jules rejoiced to see their lovely bride up and about so early. Her erect posture, her face gazing intently into the bow's horizon, reminded him of some Viking Queen. Had she been blond, the image would have mesmerized him completely. He discretely half watched the groom emerge from the bulkhead. With pleasure he noted Joe was never deterred by any sailor's greeting. He faithfully proceeded straight to her with biscuits and tea. He smiled again to view the huge fellow often sitting on a keg and feeding her small morsels and sharing his own cup. From the looks of it, he wasn't getting her to eat enough to go hungry himself, but the captain thought the marriage was going marvelously well. In high spirits, he whistled into the wind and the crew responded with full topgallant, royal, skysails and moonrakers (a full "cloud" over his lovely Baltimore clipper.) Captain Jules' happy mood soon had his sailors in top of the lungs singing as well.

Joe, for once, didn't seem to notice how early it was for singing. He patiently explained to Bethany how the sea chants helped the sailors work in unison.

Just when Bethany was sure she'd die from dry heaves, improvement commenced. But, the sea was not willing to give up its victim without another fight. Just when Joe and she were near establishing a friendly routine, he volunteered to help nurse the ship through two days of rough seas and four-hour shifts. The lurching craft, fearsome swells and troughs made their cabin nearly a convent. She clung to her bunk, day and night, her biscuit and tea delivered by either Joe or one of the polite sailors who waited for her to open her door and resolutely receive the meager fare.

A week later, as Joe climbed into his berth in hot sticky weather, she bolstered her courage to inquire details about the next phase of their trip. Joe just shook his head. "Just focus on getting across Panama, Beth. You'll have all you can do to keep your sanity through that."

He flopped over, asleep almost as soon as his head struck the pillow. Her mind reeled for hours with his blasé aloofness. All his kindness and gentle ministrations took on caretaker attributes. No longer was she a woman with a mind and will, merely his ward. He'd care for her, but that was all. After all, he'd told her what to expect and she'd promised to expect aloneness. Why think a *woman's* wants could change a *man's* specific plans? He'd never promised anything more so why increasingly long for him to do so? But, would his other promise be kept? If she held on to her own mill money, could she provide for herself? He hadn't asked about it. What if she had to run away and change her name? Would he hunt her like a fugitive? Serious apprehensions stared into a bleak future. How had she gotten herself into such a fix? *Only yourself to blame!* (Yes, as usual, she was her own worst enemy.) Only God could hear heartbreak, but didn't she deserve it? What if instead, Joe both took the money and traded her? (She had heard of places where white women were highly valued; and Joe traveled enough to know where! And, he could be downright mean! Why hadn't she thought of that in Oregon? *Now, how can I trust him, after having such horrific thoughts?*)

By dawn, she withdrew into a lethargy that matched the tropical clime. Why pretend? (Their marriage was a sham from day one; they'd pretended a honeymoon long enough, why continue?) As time passed, the air cleared but Bethany became distant, almost formal. Bethany quietly requested the captain return them to a cabin below. By bedtime, she was either asleep in her bunk or, at a minimum, her back was turned. By daylight, she merely stayed covered, kept her eyes to the wall, and waited until Joe left to finish his toilet on deck.

Joe chaffed under the tension; he didn't know what had happened or what to do about it. Unfortunately his confusion showed on his countenance, never could he be accused of dissembling. Bethany's, on the other hand, appeared nearly serene. She sat on her drum, embroidering and crocheting, passing the time of day with any passenger who stopped by, like a Baltimore matron holding high tea! She was not embroidering very fast, he noted. She was not a good enough sailor to focus on it for long periods. But crocheting was accomplished without watching; copious amounts of lace therefore accumulated. In unguarded moments he remembered her tiny feet tucked against his calf and his arms drawing her into that first night's seasick embrace. He would not presume to call it anything more. Gradually he gave it a proper sea burial; after all, she was hardly responsible for being indisposed. And, it was his request that they take the sea journey so he had to accept the consequences.

"When you get to St. Augustine, Joe," Captain Jules advised, "I think you need to take Mrs. Wright ashore. You might even want to stay awhile. I know it's warm, but she is not the traveler you are. The Bible talks of women being the weaker vessel, but I think we men confuse that with muscle. It's more than that. I think your little lady needs quiet and rest more than most. My Myra, she just yells, 'Enough, Jules Hanson. You've worn me to a frazzle!' but not all women let you know, understand?"

"I think you're right, Captain, and thank you. My wife never did allow herself to complain; I'll plan only quiet diversions." And, he had. They were staying with an old Louisiana friend of Joe's who'd taken a Spanish wife and accepted managing her inherited sugar plantation and home. They had eaten long leisurely meals of tropical fruits, succulent seafood and fresh vegetables. Walking through whitewashed streets of courtyard-protected homes, their host explained how his wife's place was highly valued, like many older thick walled ones built of tabby, for their cool interiors. Bethany admired the two-foot window ledges and homey garden atmosphere. She especially delighted taking beach strolls and exalting over the strong tropical colors of the unknown flowers. When he couldn't name a flower or tree, she'd remember to ask Maria (who shared her fascination.) Like a child in a sweet shop unable to make up her mind, she remained undecided what to like best. Marveling over the fact there were more than one type of palm was something he'd never even considered. In fact, she could name more plants and trees after just one visit than he could despite several years in the tropics.

He took the ladies shopping and tried not to intrude on Bethany's purchases with the large amount of cash he'd placed in her reticule. Instead, he had remained outside under overhanging balconies to mull over his unknown errors. Resolve stiffened to fulfill their promise to co-exist harmoniously. Browsing at her own pace, she still hadn't found enough to fill more than a hatbox. The blue pleated bonnet with it's dyed to match front falling plumage was lovely, but it saddened him to have it often hide her expressive lovely eyes. A little extra embroidery floss and crochet thread were all she bought. Mostly they both helped effervescent Maria with packages for her children.

It grieved him when she tried to return the large unused portion of money. Instead of insisting gently that he wished her to keep it, he'd snapped and growled at her. He was sorry about it but didn't know how to undo the damage. Must he constantly stir up like an old grizzly?

After a couple of days he wandered the streets alone, leaving her in Maria and Charlie's shady courtyard contentedly reading. Gradually it dawned that maybe getting back east was her sole motive. Could she have utilized feminine wiles suggesting she wanted a child? If so, "back east" might be considered accomplished? Did she not need him anymore? She had more than enough money to "get by." If she became totally fascinated with St. Augustine might she prefer to stay here? Could he agree? No, he had to insist that she continue to Baltimore. That was the deal. He intended she carry through and would see that she finished that thorny task, like it or not. More likely though, she'd play along until she got more cash out of him? So be it; and good luck to all the women in his life.

Mental consternation made him ornerier than cat droppings! Charlie Morrison had just reprimanded him for scaring his little girl so badly she'd cried. She had skipped in, told him that dinner was ready, but being so preoccupied, he'd absently yelled, "What do you want!?" He had apologized profusely both to Charlie and the little girl, but Bethany's horror had been the hardest to bear. She shrank from him, also stiffened with alarm when he'd yanked her chair back too roughly.

The formerly peaceful plantation no doubt sighed with relief when he helped her back aboard ship. A few days later they gradually became their usual civil selves. No one asked if they'd had a nice time, not even affable Captain Mike who'd transported them from Panama. Luckily this crew had no idea how newly married they were; otherwise, they too would be long past suspecting "the honeymoon's over."

CHAPTER 13:
Arrive, Celebrate, Leave

Seven days following their Baltimore arrival, a grand ball was held; one his mother insisted on as befitting the new Wright estate's heir. The brick arched front door evidenced tiered boxwood and white mums attached over wine velvet braided into cording. Similar hall decorations led to a ballroom ablaze with ivy entwined by pink and wine hothouse roses hanging in clusters beneath gas chandeliers. Roses, ivy, and wine satin streamers bedecked both opposing arched windows and fireplace mantles. Cascading beds of roses flared from the short fire screens that protected dozens of candles forming pyramids of flickering light.

Joseph Wright III surveyed his gilt and white marble magnified holdings (fortress or palace?) He could decide only that it was not his idea of "home" and he would have made an even trade for Charlie's place (Maria's place, whatever.) His black swallowtail eveningwear was crisp, his upright collar and shirt starched, and the cravat wound closely enough to half smother the scream he wished he dared utter.

Mother had already ordered a gown for Bethany (in light of his letter earlier sent from Florida) that had only to be stitched at the waist, shoulders and side-seams. The precise fit produced a vision of layered apricot satin that hugged and plunged (perhaps a little more than Mother intended due to her diminutive size?) Twisted strings of seed pearls looped into a round gold filigreed broach that dripped a knot of seed pearls below. Layered sleeves featured strings of pearls below the elbows. The tiny waist hugging lines dipped before alternating puffs swooped and swirled with strings of seed pearls that swaged and cascaded over a bell hemline. On her earlobes dainty clusters of similar pearls enticed. His eyes couldn't help but fix on her slow descent, her hair coifed into high poufs with thick long ringlets that draped over her right shoulder.

Claudia followed behind on marble stairs holding to sculptured rails that were interrupted by massive posts and outlined brass peacocks amid floral panels. Brown hair, pale with a center part, gold ear bobs hid behind thin ringlets that framed both sides of her head. Light green satin rosettes decorated a gown of darker green and more modest gossamer flounces that spilled in ruffles over her off-the-shoulder sleeves. The scoop neckline emphasized a dazzling emerald necklace (one of father's "repentance" gifts to Mother. First time he'd seen it since he was a boy.)

Mother, matronly but elegant silver hair piled high, brought up the rear ridiculous in black silk. That she could pretend to mourn his father forever was the height of ludicrous pretense. Slenderizing lines with frilled neck and iridescent beaded hip hiding jacket with feminine frills at the hem did compliment her normally square figure, he had to admit, but no hiding of tight lip and double chins could conceal years she had barely spoken to his father or grandfather. Everyone knew it, why bother?

She had traded her heavily mortgaged home for a few railroad shares and moved into her father-in-law's house a mere month following father's death. That too was a mystery. They were well known frequent combatants. Had she long ago staked out territory for her son to inherit? Or, did she just refuse to accept responsibility? (If so, Bethany shone by more than stunning physical contrast.)

"I am the master of only one thing for sure," he boldly uttered the carefully rehearsed speech his new secretary had prepared, "the Wright household of beautiful ladies." He then bowed low before grandly proffering his arms for their short glove covered hands. Bethany glanced around hesitantly to make sure she was to have the honor.

Mother quickly informed by ignoring him and charging ahead. "We will stand on the left of the door. I will stand by Joseph's left," she directed, "first in line, and Bethany, you on his right." Bethany obediently glided to Joe's right. "Claudia, you take up the end position; make sure Bethany has been properly introduced. Harold," she beckoned to the head butler, "you gather their coats, put gloves *inside* their hats immediately and place them in the right anteroom. Clarice," the first floor maid's short brown bun, frilly cap and apron curtsied, "you offer punch by first inquiring if they'd *care* for any. George and Paul, direct our guests to the drawing room as a *suggestion only*." An assembled group of newly hired servants and well established slaves scurried to their appointed posts and the assembled receiving line could hear the orchestra tuning up on the covered terrace beyond the open French doorways.

Joe noted with both admiration and sadness that Bethany looked no more comfortable in her new role than Claudia had ever seemed in hers. Luckily there was no need for figuring out what to say; Mother was still busy commandeering, inspecting and preening her troop of already perfect people. He resented her fluffing his cravat and especially adding Grandfather's diamond stickpin. Managing to grit his teeth to endure without comment, not so much for her sake but to fulfill his promise to Bethany, he inhaled for additional patience.

Soon their first guests could be heard rolling from off the crushed oyster shell drive onto the brick pavement. Torch lights would center their descent from an elegant varnished carriage any moment.

Harold opened the door on cue, and the doorway, garden lights and carriage lanterns spilt a path of splendor for the French ambassador and his very young new wife. (How typical, he acknowledged, guests from the furthest away *would* be the first to arrive.) The evening commenced and Joe and Bethany manned their post well after Mother and Claudia had departed to lead their guests to the dining room.

"You look lovely," he offered after what seemed an uncomfortable lapse.

"I feel more exposed," she admitted self-consciously.

"Ah, I should have warned you about the cost to modesty when joining high society. The rule is: men dress up, women dress down, strictly from a neck perspective, of course."

"I suppose I had an inkling suspicion from my time in Boston; or at least I thought I did," she admitted, "but never could have suspected it could take all day to get dressed for a party."

"Well, the leisure rich must have something to do with their dull insipid lives now, don't they?" he growled.

Bethany saddened at his snide assessment. Was this her life now? Better than when she had suspected the worst of Joe's intentions, of course, but it was also worse than becoming "Joe Wright's widow woman." At least in Oregon she'd felt productive. Now she was catered to, served, pampered and urged repeatedly to assert her authority to fulfill her slightest whim. She had been scrubbed, soaked, slathered and soothed. The problem was adjusting. She didn't covet any of this. Oh, the attention and pampering was enjoyable, she silently apologized to God for seeming to complain. But, how could she be comfortable in a *slave* holding household? And was it wrong to miss the company of her husband, no matter how distant? They had been home five days; in that time she'd barely seen him at three meals.

She required more than leisure and admiration. Her life amounted to total solitude, in both her extravagant boudoir and in the midst of a house full of strangers. She knew that was partially due to their recent arrival, but it throbbed into her senses far deeper, a holdover from the journey?

Claudia was sweet, but she'd never become Bethany's ally. They were too different, their backgrounds too opposite. Nor could she ever share a confidence because Claudia would be too easily intimidated into revealing it, even the servants were apt to get information out of her. There was only one thing to do, work towards her independence. Joe likely wouldn't stay in Baltimore much longer than the required six months so she had to know where she was headed before that timeframe expired. More than that, she had to find a church that offered more than stained glass, selected readings and polished pews. Even Joe's methodical Bible readings on the trail west had been more inspiring.

"Might as well join the lynch mob." He glanced down at her décolletage and tiny waist resisting a wish it were for his eyes only. "Mother will be throwing daggers if the soup gets cold."

Bethany nodded, pasted a less than enthusiastic smile on her face, and accepted the offered crook of his arm. He led her through the hall to the far end of the exceedingly long table where he seated her on his right next to an elderly statesman he had carefully selected (and greatly upset Mother's arranged seating.) He stood in front of the head chair and rang the small bell at the center of his plate as instructed. An assembled forty privileged and influential businessmen, politicians, military brass, foreign dignitaries, wives and escorted guests looked up expectantly. "Rev. Shapleigh, would you lead us in grace?" He bowed into his seat.

After a grace that should have been profoundly moving, yet somehow came off superficial, Bethany allowed Joe to do most of the discussing of frontier events. Tired of sympathy and revelations of her past, she meant to go forward and know what to expect from her future in SAFE and gracious Baltimore, Maryland. She also didn't intend to feel inferior or intimidated any more than she felt already. As much as she had enjoyed the Long Mansion, this was different, and a role she had no experience fulfilling. Nor was she sure Joe had made such a wise choice. Obviously he knew many women who would have fit into his world far better than she. Was it her tolerance, her lack of complaint, her ability to endure pain and suffering that fostered this unsought (but agreed to) partnership?

"My dear," enthused the not so early departing French ambassador's wife, "you are totally enchanting! You must come to see me in Washington City. We will promenade and tour the sights, no?"

"I'll see if I can find the time," she promised half-heartedly.

"Good, and bring," she whispered a throaty chortle, "that handsome husband of yours along too!" Proclaimed enthusiastically, it was as though Joe weren't right there beside them.

Joe bowed over the pointedly lifted hand and kissed fingertips in the continental manner he knew she expected. The comely young wife of the forty plus ambassador giggled like a schoolgirl (which she almost was.) "As much as it would be a lovely diversion, I'm afraid my sister and wife will have to comply alone. I have been away far too long not to immediately set myself to inherited tasks."

"So sad about your grandpapa." She pursed full lips into a sad but pretty pout as the ambassador wrapped a generous mink about her dark ringlet enhanced shoulders.

"Thank you for your kind condolences," Joe responded mechanically.

"Bye, cherie, you *must* come soon." She turned to touch Bethany's hand with her fan as a parting gesture (or polite afterthought?)

"Good night, Mrs. Wright," the ambassador addressed Joe's mother. "We can't thank you enough for the gracious and pleasant evening." The wife's playful eyes and fan gesturing obviously included Joe in her husband's description.

"We hope to open our home much more often now that Joseph and his wife are in residence," Mrs. Wright II pointedly promised, both as a threat to Joe not to argue, but also to give Bethany the disapproving message she had not missed the obvious flirtation.

And, so it went. The men adored, admired and flattered the ladies but knew the real reason for the evening. Joseph Bentley Wright III was on the prowl to launch business contacts and establish connections with anyone who had the money and power to play. The ladies adored Joe for feminine preening and posturing before the very handsome 'cock of the walk.' Bethany, distressed by obvious female flirtations, also blushed before the meaningful nodded glances she received. Joe, though, could be in much more control of his dancing partners (to her knowledge, only herself, and that only once.) She had avoided the dancing as much as good taste would allow after the initial first dance with Joe. She thought he felt as awkward as she did, and was relieved when he quickly gestured their guests to join in.

She conveniently "lost" her dance card and stuck to Claudia to pawn single men off on her. After several glasses of punch with male strangers she felt she could legally hide out in her boudoir for at least twenty minutes. It was an uncharitable thought, but she felt almost as unprotected as she had in a Lowell mill. Joe had rescued her on a couple of occasions in the process of introducing her to late arrivals, but he was generally in deep conversation with men he expected to engage in business.

When the clock struck midnight she discretely asked her mother-in-law if she could not be excused from the small ladies parlor versus staying to bid good night to the few men who had absconded with Joe into the library. "The smell of cigar smoke, reeking into the hall from under the double doors, has given me a frightful headache." Mrs. Wright II nodded affirmatively and (after bidding adieu to the other patient ladies) she did not glance back to see if she gained her mother-in-law's 'Wright look of disapproval' or not.

"What do you mean you do not care to attend our church?" Joe's mother demanded during a November's Saturday evening meal.

"I didn't say that. I said I've accustomed to less formality, more simplicity in my worship," she explained patiently, "and I've found a small group near the dock that appeals to me."

"Bleeding hearts trying to save the riffraff that clutters up the docks, no doubt. Well, you've no need to participate, and it's no place for a cultured woman. Leave the do-gooders to their charity work and just support them financially," Mrs. Wright staunchly insisted instead. "Mind you, the docks are no place for a woman with any sense or good breeding."

"It isn't right on the dock," Bethany had insisted, "it's near the lovely walk that skirts along the shore."

"It's quite alright," Joe unexpectedly came to her assistance. "Paul, our tallest and broadest driver, will see that nothing happens to her. I will stress upon him his responsibility," he turned to inform Mother. "And," he captured Bethany's attention again, "I will inform him that he is to be your driver on a regular basis." Beth had flashed him that delightful radiance he had seen on only rare occasions. He basked in its reflection, blissfully ignoring his mother's ominous glare.

He wondered what Bethany had found interesting while escorting his fur coated and muffed relatives to the church that his father, and grandfather before him, had considered the "proper" church to belong to. Although, he had attended more in not quite two months than either might have done in their lifetimes, maybe the two combined? It was their well-established Wright rule: women tended to religion, men tended to business. He desired to establish a much different reputation, but was it spiritual fervor or just distancing himself from any familial similarity?

For Christmas, he gave his mother a list of influential men he wanted to attend a post Christmas dinner. He hired a large choral group that came complete with musicians. He couldn't bear the thought of Bethany being subjected to another ball. The few frequent invitations they'd accepted had been dismal failures. He had picked up on her dread almost immediately and usually offered to take her home about an hour after the meal was served. She had accepted his offered escape mostly too gratefully. More than once she had said, "Good night," with tears misting deep blue eyes. He often turned away to spend time alone in the library, as he knew she often did in the daytime, knowing otherwise he would only stay awake tossing and turning. Unfortunately he often found himself surrounded in the scent of her perfume, doing little to lift his spirits and make him forget ambivalent sensations.

He regretted the gaudy two-carat diamond he'd presented for a combined twenty-fifth birthday and Christmas gift. The purpose, of course, was to impress their important guests the following day. On her slender finger it screamed "opulence!" She, on the other hand, had quietly presented him with a magnificent English saddle via a card that said "I hope you like what's in front of Sugar's stall." He smiled over the docile name for his rambunctious stallion.

He chuckled again over a recent revelation of her rare thrift. His mother presumed Bethany had bought two dresses of a similar style. Instead she was shocked to learn Beth had simply allowed the same dress to be dyed, not just once but three times, from light colors to dark, and then changed trimmings to avoid detection. If Mother's slaves had held their tongues, it would never have been noticed, nor any source of complaint.

Much against his mother's wishes he had insisted on entertainments of simple musical ensembles, invited lecturers, or renowned soloists. If people wanted more fast-paced entertainment, there were plenty of other choices. Bethany picked out her own clothing now and he noted the necklines rose by several inches. Mother complained about that too. He relished conveying, "Bostonians are more concerned with being properly decorous than flagrantly fashionable." There was little today's styles could do to hide her gender, but at least he was delighted with her Christian desire for modesty.

Her recent trips with Claudia to see the aunts were mother's latest complaint and current puzzle. They always came back happy and he was glad to see his sister getting out with someone her own age. In fact, at times lately Claudia seemed almost glowing. Beth was good medicine for most of the household. Clearly, one by one, she was winning over some of Mother's most loyal servants. Mother Wright complained about that too, to say the least. As usual, nothing pleased her. She went so far as to suggest he needed to keep an eye on Bethany's sojourns.

Before Christmas, Joe easily dismissed it as shopping expeditions. After Christmas was over, her long afternoons of solitary rug hooking in the solarium produced insistent protests. "She's deliberately avoiding returning necessary social obligations!" After that, it was about solitary journeys that returned Beth barely in time for their late evening meal. Feast or famine, the hubbub was more than he had patience. But then, he'd informed his mother of that more than once also.

CHAPTER 14:
Detectives to the Rescue

His mother arrived at his office just when he was leaving for a late lunch. As Mother had never cared to visit the office before, he didn't anticipate it was for a tour of the building. He begrudgingly invited her to join him for lunch instead of the solitary break normally afforded his hectic routine. She clearly had something on her mind, most likely it involved Beth? Her severe black hat, the grim mouth and vigorous tugging of her black gloves proved he could expect double portions of grief. As soon as they'd ordered, received their food, and served tea, she pierced him eye to eye.

"Joseph the Third, I am the last person in the world to interfere with your marriage, and the last person to give marriage advice, but it is obvious even to me you and Bethany are estranged to where your father and I were only after two children and many long years of unpleasantness. You have little to no knowledge of your wife's wanderings about the countryside. She leaves as soon as you're out of the house, sometimes not even stopping to eat. She used to take Claudia, but no more.

And, she returns almost exactly one half-hour before you're expected home. When you leave the city she does too. She vanishes without a word to anyone as to her destination or expected return. You cannot expect me to remain silent. I don't have to tell you what I endured with your father. But, as a woman I had no legal rights. *You* are a man who has both a legal right *and* a moral duty to *insist on her propriety!*"

"Sounds ominous," he growled over a mouthful of oyster stew.

"Well, what would *you* call it?" she demanded in a huff.

"Boredom?" he suggested, using a rather bored tone himself. "She's always had something to do; she's no doubt finding it hard to adjust. She was running a business in Oregon, built a house even! You really ought to take more of an interest in her and explain how the filthy rich are supposed to fill up their idle hours."

Mother's frosted voice nearly hissed her retort. "Hard, my foot! Doing exactly what she darn well pleases and caring little if it pleases anyone else."

"Well," he countered, "she's a great hand to meet a challenge with enthusiasm; shall we leave it at that?" His jaw set equally firm as hers.

"If that's all the concern you have, I suggest you consider instead a woman's intuition often knows such things by instinct. Men ignorantly refuse the possibility of a problem until it's far too late to resolve." Her spoon clattered with indignant wisdom.

"I *trust* Bethany implicitly," he assured her with great emphasis. "I will *not* subject her to an inquisition about her daily outings. Nor is her schedule any of your business, or mine!"

That at least managed completing their meal in silence and got her back into her waiting carriage.

"You mark my words, Joseph," she gave one last feeble attempt, "you and Bethany are not getting along now," she held up her hand to silence his protest, "and it will get progressively worse the longer you ignore it. It's ludicrous you both claiming to be God-fearing Christians. What your domestic problems are, I predict emphatically, cannot be cured by mere prayer." She yanked down the shade on the door and rapped the back of the front upholstered seat with her walking stick. Joe watched the carriage depart and decided maybe it was time for a talk with someone who knew Bethany as a friend.

"Joe Wright!" Samuel clasped his hand and then swung an arm around his increasingly bulky shoulders. Three abundant meals a day plus frequent snacks fed both his appetite and frustrations. "What on earth are you doing here in February?!"

"Nothing to do with business, just a quick social call for a change." He grinned at the enthusiastic greeting and shrugged out of his long winter coat.

"Wonderful! But, quick," Sam ordered, "close the door. Heidi will skin us both alive if Danny catches so much as a sniffle."

"Hello, Mr. Wright." Heidi wagged her blond braid crowned head at Sam's dire pronouncement.

"Hello, Heidi." He turned from his completed task. "You are looking exceeding well. I trust Daniel is well enough too?"

"Indeed, ve are proud to say, jus put down for a nap, vould yo like ta peek of him?"

"Sure." He agreed more out of politeness than anything, and they all went trooping up the arched Federal stairway, past the Palladian windows to a small hallway created by rose topped columns that lead to the south-facing nursery. The cast iron and mica fireplace insert reflected both firelight and a sunny location that evidenced a blue blanketed darling. He viewed strawberry blond curls, Heidi's light coloring and Sam's prominent chin and dimples. Joe smiled approvingly at Heidi and Sam and they all tiptoed out, retracing the grand spindled staircase to the parlor below.

"So, what great social obligation brings you here?" Sam demanded suspiciously.

"It's personal, I guess," Joe hesitated.

"I vill leave." Heidi rose instantly.

"No, please stay," he invited. "Maybe a woman who knows Bethany can help me more. I know it's trivial but I'm at my wits' end to have peace at home. You both know her well. My mother is convinced I should be checking up on her every outing. I trust her, but I can't get my mother to back off. What am I supposed to do? Mother is making all our lives miserable, especially Bethany's."

"Maybe do what I did," suggested Sam.

Instantly attentive, Joe asked, "What?"

Sam announced with a lopsided grin, "You hire a detective and prove she's a saint."

"Vhat?" Heidi protested in alarm. "Yo didn't!"

"Well, I did too," Sam confessed. "And, I was so confused compared to the low opinion I thought she had of me that it made me curious. But I was too proud to find out why. But I'll do better than that. I'll give you the report and you hand it to your mother. That ought to suffice. Com'on, I've got it in my desk someplace." Heidi and Joe followed and there ensued a total search of

Joe's enormous desk, including several hidden compartments. Finally, from under almost the last pile of legal documents came a long yellowed envelope.

"Can ve all know this?" asked Heidi with hesitant blue eyes.

"You may," Sam beamed and swung around in his wooden high-backed swivel chair, dumping her into his lap and kissing her soundly. He obviously recognized the barest of insecurities.

"Samuel Roberts," she fumed, "ve have guest!"

Sam grinned and winked at Joe. Joe wished he could share in the enjoyment of his friend's delightful teasing. Instead, he was green with envy, not so much the intimate kissing but rather the innate sensitivity. Sam was good with women. He wasn't, never was likely to be if he lived to be a hundred. This obvious shortcoming irritated his soul more every day.

Sam read the short synopsis of Bethany's life up until they met. Obviously she'd endured more misfortune than her share. Her unselfish provision for her father and brothers struck a nerve. He'd never once considered his mother and sister's needs other than for an occasional visit (and made them travel to see him at an impersonal hotel.) True, their needs would have been of a different nature, but he determined to be more considerate just the same. It was high time to turn over a new leaf. He really must do different, think different; not only that, he needed to more adequately show he was a Christian by deed as well as by name.

"If this doesn't do it, would you suggest hiring a detective now?" asked Joe, unwilling to disturb the delicate balance he knew existed between him and Bethany.

"Sure," Sam replied.

"I do not believe yo two!" stormed Heidi. "She is good, always, no body to vorry, for you it vhould be shame!"

"It's not for me," Joe protested weakly. "It's my mother. She chastises Beth every time she comes home! Mother's such a chronic complainer she's even starting gossip by complaining to her friends. Beth's staying away longer and longer, sometimes for days. Probably because she doesn't want to face a browbeating judge and jury, and I wouldn't blame her for a minute."

"Vell, that's not so good." Heidi looked them both over and shrugged. "If it vill help her, then guess yo must do this?"

Joe rose. "Thank you both."

Sam demanded indignantly, "You're not leaving so soon?"

"I'm afraid so, I squeezed this visit in 'on my way' to Harrisburg, Pennsylvania. I should have taken the Cumberland railroad instead of a clipper. As you can imagine, my arrival will be a bit delayed. There is a train leaving at three, though, and the driver outside is waiting because I intend to be on it."

"Well, Joe, let us know how it turns out," Sam insisted brightly. "We hear from Bethany every once in awhile. She has such a marvelous descriptive writing style we feel like we've attended the same parties, soirees, and outings. She sure tickled us with the tale about the magistrate who lost his wig in the punch and the hostess ordered the whole thing removed, neither to be seen again!"

"Yes," he laughed, "I'm afraid the old judge still misses that ratty headpiece." What he didn't mention was his surprise that Bethany had never let on she had any mother-in-law problems. And, she could have mentioned husband...what? Well, at least perpetual to intermittent grump?

He showed his mother the pitiful description of Bethany's early life. It unfortunately did not suffice. "Yesterday's newspaper is only good to wrap fish," she'd sneered. So, he hired a detective to discretely follow Bethany's movements on a weekly basis. Each week there was another objection. Finally he asked for a *monthly* report; firmly out of patience with weekly confrontations with mother.

When March's report indicated an inordinate amount of time spent at the small church, sewing Easter angel costumes, that was the last straw. "I am not doing this any more, Mother, if this doesn't suffice, you're impossible to satisfy!"

"That doesn't explain her running over the east shore with real estate agents. Doesn't that strike you as unusual?"

"No!" he'd shouted back. "I'm about ready to do the same myself!" He had stormed out of the study to stumble and near topple over Claudia.

"I'm sorry, Joseph," she apologized, both helping each other up.

"No, little sister," he refuted, grabbing her by her terribly thin shoulders, "you have nothing to be sorry for. It's my fault; I'm the one to apologize. I'm also terribly sorry you've been terrified by either of our strong words. You need to know you've never given us any cause for apology."

"Oh, Joe." Her head bowed to cry into his shoulder as he propelled her down to the library. "I love you all so much; I'd do anything to help!"

"I know." He handed her his valet's provided clean "second" handkerchief to muffle her piteous sobs. "But Bethany and Mother are both too strong-willed for you to handle. So, don't you worry about it, you hear?" Her lopsided smile ate at his heart. *Why didn't some painter or poet come and carry her away to Italy or some lovely romantic spot like Venice, or the Rhine in springtime? She was beautiful, soft hearted and accomplished. Any man should adore her.* How could she possibly be a wealthy twenty-five-year-old spinster? Before the same age Beth had been married twice. Did Wright relatives scare every man away?

"And, here, sir," Mr. Andrews, his capable secretary handed him a couple of envelopes, "is the past two detective's reports."

"The new U.S. Naval Academy at Annapolis' supply need prospects?" asked Mr. Wright brightening, albeit absently.

"No, sir," he corrected, "that's on your left, under the steamship's retrofit contract that requires your signature."

"Then, report on what?" Joe stopped rummaging for an apple he knew he'd tucked away, but couldn't remember where.

"Your wife, sir," answered Mr. Andrews, evidencing embarrassment. His brown eyes peered over reading spectacles and Joe viewed the immaculate suit, thin bow tie, and neatly slicked down center part. His own appearance could never be that neat, no matter how he tried. His curly hair was always on his forehead, his tie usually twisted to one side or the other, his vest wrinkled, or he spilled his coffee or something else on some item of clothing. *Shouldn't he head back west when this year was over?*

"I meant to cancel that," he exploded. "Don't bother writing the letter tonight, but leave yourself a note to do so in the morning. It was a stupid idea in the first place, and let that be a lesson to us all. Never think you can appease a mother-in-law or that a lawyer will give away good advice for free!"

"Yes, sir, I'll do it first thing!" Mr. Andrews bowed backwards before scurrying away.

"And send word to fetch my carriage." his voice carried beyond the closed door. At times the guy was a lifesaver. Other times, like today, he bothered Joe with his overly contrived neatness. Over two weeks since he'd seen his own bed. He'd planned to use today and tomorrow to catch up on mail and paperwork. Then he intended to spend at least three quiet days at home and tackle his grandfather's 'empire' next Monday.

Though now he needed to find that apple; he was starved! Giving up finally, he surmised the tidy Mr. Andrews must have thrown it out.

"Good to see you back, Mr. Wright." Seth opened the carriage door for him.

"Thank you. Everyone all right at home?" he conversed easily with the lanky driver as he climbed in.

"I believe so, sir," Seth hedged.

"Good, but let's leave before I perish or eat one of these horses, down to hooves, hide and bit to bout!"

"Right, sir," Seth laughed with good humor as he jumped to comply.

When they pulled into the front of the huge baroque mansion, his mother was waiting. He could see her foot agitatedly tapping as Seth managed the turn. She'd obviously been waiting and watching for his arrival; he certainly hoped it had not been for any protracted length of time.

"Hello, Mother," he kissed her smooth and fragrant cheek, "how nice of you to greet me. But, you would have been warmer inside, wouldn't you?"

"I'm out here to inform you your wife has just arrived. She left the minute you did and never returned until just moments ago. If you have no curiosity about a wife that gads about for sixteen days, with no explanation to anyone of her whereabouts, then I question your sanity!" So saying, she turned abruptly, slammed the door, and left him standing alone on the front steps.

The virulent welcome contrasted brutally in the midst of spring's splendor and the calmness of the neatly manicured lawn and gardens. Great cascading beds of tulips praised heaven, urging him to forget instant depression and *rejoice in the Lord always*.

Joe turned to follow Seth into the carriage shed. Beside his phaeton sat the one Paul usually drove. He pulled out a small whalebone covered straight-edged razor from his pants pocket. Next he pulled his handkerchief out to receive a hastily dug soil sample from between a couple of spokes.

"Forget something?" Seth returned from the stable.

Instead of answering, he retrieved his flat brimmed hat from the other carriage and waved it for Seth to see. Seth thought it strange just the same. Mr. Wright always left his hat in the carriage until he went out again. *Must be going for a walk?* was Seth's eventual summation.

Joe disappeared into the library and got out a magnifying glass. The soil sample evidenced sand mixed with mud and strands of coarse grass. That could be found most anywhere, especially in Baltimore. However, hunger all but forgotten, he pulled the reports from his inner pocket that he'd formerly intended to throw into his desk and forget. He read the usual drivel: church attendance, church supper, helped with a charity bazaar, church attendance, went with Claudia to see Aunt Bernice in Annapolis, prayer meeting, shopping for fabrics, dressmaker, on and on.

Then he noted a distinct change. She'd attended an animal auction?! Afterwards she visited eight different horse farms, some of the best around.

Surely she wasn't considering buying him another horse for his delayed birthday, was she? Sugar was still a young animal, and the high-jumping stallion's response to "call to hounds," was really quite remarkable, excellent in fact. It had become one of the few types of invitations he readily accepted. Beth, Claudia and Mother seemed to enjoy the company of the more sedate ladies who chose to stay behind and await their return. Plus he didn't have to worry about male-female interactions making any of them uncomfortable. He also could whisk them away either before or soon after the morning meal, pleading business concerns. Everyone seemed satisfied, even his social climbing, status conscious mother.

Suddenly his musing stopped. He sat bolt upright, then scrunched his shoulders to peer more intently. The detective's missive contained one huge GLARING GRABBER! It said she bought a farm at the Delaware shore, four hundred and four acres (four acres on the ocean side, four hundred on the opposite side of the road.) The Rehoboth Beach property became hers in early March. But the heart stopper for Joe was in what name she'd bought it: *Mrs. Joshua Clark, widow!* He transcribed the address to the back of one of his business cards and slowly added it to his vest pocket. How was he supposed to react to this?

The evening's belated birthday meal was a great success on the surface. Bethany inquired about Joe's contracts for the new Naval Academy. Claudia asked Bethany how her new crochet pattern was progressing. She admitted to initial difficulty, but had now become quite adept at the detailed center flower. Mother requested their attendance at the christening of a returned Virginian, now a Countess (with a penniless noble husband in tow.) This produced a veritable barrage of opinions between Sam, his mother, and Claudia concerning wealthy Americans' yen for European titles. Mother and Claudia gave him a new suit. Bethany gave him gold monogrammed cufflinks.

Later, in the library, he and Bethany had quite a spirited discussion on the finer points of desirable horseflesh. But, she also departed early. Only her fancywork remained in a basket beside the outrageously ornate Baroque chair. The carved pierced back, sides and skirt ended in stuck out casters. Only the padded seat and back had any value as far as he was concerned?

Gradually he stopped scowling at the ostentatious drapes that gathered high into their corners. The drapes, clasped in the talons of a Federal eagle, drew the curtain up toward the wide cornices and ornate painted ceiling. He knew the drapery style was an aberration of the original ornate lavish Rococo architecture, but presumed its real purpose was to make Mother happy spending fresh money.

Accepting responsibility for his irritability made for a difficult Scripture reading and prayer session. He climbed the ornate staircase only after several wick trimmings, his tie and coat cast viciously into Bethany's no longer occupied chair. His undone neck and vest buttons added to his emotional disarray. Passing Bethany's door in the hallway late at night created both a desire to leave home and an urge to kick open her door and loudly demand why she'd apparently forgotten her married name. Worst of all, he didn't know whether to blame her, himself or his grandfather for the raging conflict that tormented his equilibrium. Instead, he ultimately pled defeat and wearily trudged off to his own quarters to pray, concluding with, *Please, God, let us all find Your peace as only Your perfect will allows, amen.*

CHAPTER 15:
Confrontation or Duel?

Joe anxiously contemplated his options, personally and religiously. As much as he loathed deceit, he abhorred driving his beautiful and peaceful wife Bethany away from him even more. As rejection ate at him, he hunted for a Biblical solution. Finding none quite appropriate for their unusual circumstances, he had Seth drive him through the darkened streets for hours on end. Both of them soon evidenced dark shadowed eyes wreathed in anguish. Delay involved weeks of soul searching and miserable hours of agonizing hesitation.

In desperation to understand what had happened between them, or between her and his mother, he decided to have Seth drive him along the shore to glimpse the small church Bethany attended. Was it there they taught wives to become independent to the extent of deceiving their husbands and in-laws? Was that why she preferred attending there? It presented quite the opportunity to find out when he noted they were open, but at four in the morning?! That alone raised tremendous questions.

The small prayer meeting he joined, though, held no secret inklings of instigating wife revolts. And, the more he learned about them, the more it became obvious nothing could be further from the truth. If anything, this church interpreted the Scriptures much more literally than most other churches he'd visited. And, they expected more holiness of their members, men as well as women. In fact, Bethany's fancy frocks might be a source of embarrassment for her in the midst of these mostly plain hardworking folks.

He prayed frequently alongside men who would be shortly off to low paying jobs along the docks. It gnawed at him to hear their fervent prayers for enough to feed their families, that work would be plentiful enough until the cold weather ended. He knew he could have easily answered their prayers, but also knew they would have been mortified if resolved by the public asking. As he investigated skills, he secretly asked the pastor to steer men to jobs his own company needed filled. In very short order his company benefited much more than they did. But, the more he prayed with them, the more he realized his own problem was harder to fix than mere physical supply of food and shelter.

Finally, he accepted the true crux of the issue. *He* was more of a problem to God than his wife ever was to him, or his mother. On a mist shrouded morning after most of the men disappeared, in heart wrenching sobs he poured out his heartache and pleaded for forgiveness, for all the years of bitterness against his family, and for ruining beautiful Bethany's life by expecting her to be content with a loveless marriage. *Oh, Lord, let me find a way out of this misery, for all of us. Let me be the son, brother and husband I should be! At least, with Bethany, let me gain the courage and honesty to want to understand why she needs to use…his name.*

Still, he resisted instigating a confrontation within the walls of the Wright home. There could always be someone within sight or hearing. Disconsolate and bordering on fatalism, he threw himself into upgrading the long neglected mines. Almost three months later, at his welcome home supper, Bethany informed the family that she would be taking a trip to the shore and would be gone for two to three weeks. Mother's eyes, he knew, demanded he ask where and why.

"Would you mind having Seth drive you?" Joe asked as if nothing were strange about the lack of details announcement. "I plan to take a trip myself and I'd like Paul to drive me. I believe he's more familiar with my destination; I trust you don't mind?"

"Not at all." She appeared to lose some of her effervescence but regained her composure enough to spare a more or less normal sweet smile. Just the same, she retired early. And since he spent most of the night praying and pacing in his study, she left even earlier than he did.

He returned to his office as usual but had no intention of staying long. As he arrived, Mr. Andrews handed him a newspaper wrapped package. "A present from a Captain Jules Hansen," he was informed. "A small craft sailed in with it last night and the first mate left it here first thing this morning." Joe's peeking yielded the assumption it was more a gift for Bethany (or at least for them both.) Since she would not return in time to view it at its best, he silently assented to deliver it for his sentimental old naval friend.

Joe turned his signed paperwork over to Mr. Andrews and informed him (and his surprised staff of four) that he would not return until next Wednesday and perhaps even Monday. Unfortunately one thing after another occurred until he had dawdled away more than an hour. Quickly grabbing up the captain's gift by its small wooden box, he nodded to his hard at work employees, returned to the carriage and placed it on the floor beside the far door. In the process of travel and jostling the box a small note attached fluttered onto the floor. The captain's note revealed only that he had made his last voyage, returned to his Myra and children. (No doubt beat by increasing steamship competition.)

Paul showed no surprise at his Rehoboth Beach, Delaware, requested destination (perhaps expected? Well, he shouldn't be; likely the whole household knew he had a detective following his wife's movements.) After a smooth sun drenched ferry ride across the Chesapeake Bay they headed for the Delaware shore. Eventually they were rewarded with bedazzling glimpses of open Atlantic waves. The rhythmic undulations reminded him of his travels and how contented in some ways he now felt, at least soul-wise, compared to then. But, like the entangled weed inflicted foam sliding back to rejoin watery depths, how complicated and tangled life had become. He eyed the package with somber far away thoughts. Would he ever want to sail "around the horn" again? And what would happen to "their life" after the end of this day's journey? If he could choose, he'd prefer hiding in an animal burrow avoiding Sioux? Nothing could prepare him to endure this vexingly unwelcome and long overdue confrontation.

When the small carriage turned into a sandy lane, Joe noticed freshly painted crossed fencing. With the exception of several clumps of woods (deliberately left for shade?) the pasture was freshly cleared of young saplings, brush and a few larger trees. There was evidence of brush and grass burning and earth raked over roughly with new grass seed sown. Since the grass was already sprouting fresh green shoots, perhaps it had been done in the early spring? Was this Beth's first improvement project?

Some fine looking Arabian riding mares raised their heads to stare at the approach of the familiar Cleveland bay horses. As they climbed up a low crest, he noticed a windmill and water tank recessed into a squared off section of the fence. Below hid a barn backed up to a clump of mature trees. As the carriage wound around them, he viewed both ocean and a secluded white cottage with rustic gray shutters and a tall slate "Dutch" roof intersected by three triangular paned "eyebrow" dormers. The ground level evidenced large square windows of small panes facing south, one small one plus a projecting larger one front. The ocean side's round pillars supported a large shed dormer, as though someone had cut off, or forgotten to finish a third of the downstairs? A sloping dune slid languidly towards beckoning curled finger waves. Unfortunately he determined to tend to sticky business.

Paul had quickly jumped down from off the driver's seat. "Shall I leave your card, sir?" He risked his employer's ire with rare bravado.

Joe near clipped syllables muttering, "No, thank you, Paul, I shall attend to this myself!" He wasn't even sorry for dripping sarcasm; the situation was just too audacious to bear. He detested disloyalty as much as dishonesty. Paul opened the door wide as though whipped to attention and Joe glanced around with mild trepidation. Slowly he placed his hat on the seat and picked up the box off the floor.

His tentative knock before the half opened gray Dutch door was answered by Bethany's happy voice ringing out, "Come on in, John; it's open!"

Instantly his spine stiffened, jaw clenched, teeth meshed with each mate and nostrils flared like some ancient dragon. Obviously the overly detail conscientious detective was more verbal than thorough? One obvious slip up glared like a bonfire! Should he presume the lack of Seth and carriage was due to retrieving "John" (probably from a train station or nearby residence?)

His tightened arms endangered ruining Captain's Jules' gift. In fact, if not wanting to be rid of his obligation to a man who exhibited more loyalty than his "wife by law," he might never have crossed the threshold? Loveless or not, she'd promised!

Inside he met an assortment of small armless old wicker with new rose floral puff padding and deep crocheted edges. One glance recognized the center flower pattern as the one his wife and sister had discussed. The white background and crocheting matched the long white tablecloth with similar edging. It gave small comfort it couldn't quite hide a rough barrel base. The top bore an expensive cloisonné vase filled with wild flowers and sea oats (John's gift?) Depositing the note and newspaper wrapped gift box on one side of the table, he viewed French doors and a flagstone terrace. Pink petunias flanked a set of stair steps offering a center egress almost buried in the drifted sand dune. To the right, cornered window seats showed off similar white edged puffy padding. The comfortable light-filled living room was simply furnished with a fruit wood Biedermeier couch and deep rose velvet covered Martha Washington chairs. Their simpler lines were well suited to the humble cottage. (Or, might it more appropriately be called, the "cozy love nest"?)

If he were not so disappointed in her, and trying his best to maintain some semblance of detachment, he'd be mad enough to fly from the fat to the fire. And with no regards as to who got singed! As it was, he complemented himself in remaining unmoved by her obvious feminine charms for almost a year. Another Wright trait, too busy with business encouraged unfaithfulness in wives!?

He turned to the left. Rows of cherry cupboard doors lined up under a set of stairs. Small brass fixtures suggested the recently sanded and varnished doors were labeled at one time. In his overactive mind's eye he entitled them: "adulteress," "conniver," "deceiver," "manipulator"...only to reign in escalating animosity for the sake of his own sanity. The freshly painted horse hair plaster, farm painted white walls rudely contrasted his wife's pretense of purity. The open railed lofts on both sides above caused similar walls and ceilings to reflect dormer light. Large window seats and French doors also flooded reflected light off sand and ocean. A small ledge and railing over the French doors connected the stair's two open lofts with an open door's center room that exuded light from the shed dormer over the terrace. *Everything open and above board?* he fumed. *Well, for "John" maybe, but most certainly not for me!*

Just as he questioned whether to confront "John" and Bethany or leave, he heard a heavier conveyance approaching at some speed. With full knowledge that he could be facing the eventual challenge of a duel, or another more imminent danger, he moved so he could peer resolutely through the doorway he had purposely left open. A rickety draught cart and huge white horses carrying an elderly man and an older teenager in fisherman gear appeared to be quickly bearing down on his carriage.

"Hey, mister, move up!" yelled the barely slowing burly driver.

Paul was already in motion from the looks of it. Another motion to his right, beyond the stair and hall with cherry built in drawers on the bottom and small doors on the top, caused him to spy Bethany Anne Brooker Clark Wright, masquerading as Widow Bethany Clark. She was kneeling into a wine velvet cushioned window seat to peer out at the replaced carriage. Her wine dress, the one she'd appeared in to deliver Jonathan to Lois Mott, was covered almost to the hem with a huge white apron. A three-cornered cotton rag wound over her hair secured with a hatpin versus tied in a knot.

As though realizing it had to be Joe's eyes upon her, she revolved with appropriate consternation. She gulped at the thunderhead expression, reached for the hatpin, carefully became erect to remove the improvised scarf and apron. She folded them carefully onto the velvet seat and carefully wove the hatpin into the tieback for safe keeping. Now with her back to him, she slowly moved to a column framed wide gilt chimney mirror and stroked a few stray hairs back into place.

As he marveled at their calm acceptance of the outrageous situation, she solemnly broke the silence with, "If you'd open the door a bit wider for John and his grandson, it would be a big help."

Joseph Wright III considered this request as "new" and "nice" information. About them, and her, and found it more pleasant and conformable than any he'd encountered in months. His mouth smothered a sudden tumultuous upward twitch, and he pulled the door inward to full open.

Suppose "John," the grandfather, would relish being considered such a formidable rival for his young and attractive wife's loyalty? If they ever got to know each other well, they'd likely have a great laugh over his imagined "near duel." *But, that did not explain why I felt like dueling, did it? Why was her name such a big deal anyway? I've hated the Wright name much longer than she has!*

The men trudged slowly and set down their burden: the old stacking barrister cases Bethany had brought from Rhode Island to Oregon and back east again, plus the Indian drum dangling from the boy's shoulder. They carefully shucked off high rubber boots on the wide outside granite step. She emerged to introduce him as they entered. "This is my husband, Joseph. This," she gestured, "is Mr. John Stoultz and his grandson, Henry." After their polite acknowledgement, she pointed the way she had come. "Just set them in there, two high, under the mirror with the chariot scene over it." When they returned, she paid John and gangly Henry from her dress pocket.

They responded in unison, "Thank you, Mrs. Wright," and eventually departed by traveling around the back of the barn, then circling back to the road that brought them.

Well, they'd used his name, but he still had the original "bone of contention" to chew. But he was so relieved about John that it had rather unfurled his sails.

As though nothing were amiss, she offered, "Would you like some lemonade?"

"Yes, I would." He despised his instant relief over delayed unpleasantness. Despite recognition of the long thirsty drive, the subject had to be broached, and this was the occasion he'd chosen to do the thorny deed. He'd delayed far too many months already.

"I'll be right back," she vowed, disappearing between two bookcases that centered on an airy swinging door. Light filtered between its lattice construction and he noticed it partially hid a tiny galley kitchen and the small front gingham framed window. Several loud bangs later, she reappeared with two goblets of icy drink. "I'll just be a moment finishing," she said as he gulped his first big swallow and handed him a second drink, "if you'd give Paul this, I'll join you shortly." She instantly rushed back to the bedroom.

A large chunk of ice prevented either an ill-tempered refusal or a mannerly response; and, his full hands kept him from physically detaining her. He silently fumed to be so easily manipulated. Still, he delivered the fancy glass to his driver. Paul, tough of face and muscular of body, now lounged a short distance beyond the house in the shade of his carriage's open doorway. Good, less likely to overhear and pass on what he wanted off his chest.

Upon his return, he proceeded down the short hall to gaze upon her smoothing the 'Long's Wedding coverlet' (white satin diamond shapes quilted with stitched lace woven through with white ribbon; small white ribbon bows decorating each band at the ruffled edge.) He'd seen it a few times before, even slept under it on the Pacific side voyage, but this was the first time he'd viewed it to full sun-lit advantage. A high four-poster Sheraton feather bed hung bedecked with diamond pointed crochet netting. The recent brass handles, that replaced worn straps, and rose stenciled stacking barrister cases appeared to be a wise selection in light of the small room's size. The old damaged cedar panels had been replaced with formal marquetry panels; the decorative woods lent a small air of elegance to the seaside bedroom.

She placed tatted edged satin pillowcases over feather pillows that had lain on a wide shelf to the far side of the headboard. (Was this a gift from Claudia? He knew Bethany decreed she had no patience for learning the tedious art. Was Claudia also in on this deception?)

When the shelf emptied of pillows, it revealed a portable box of stationary supplies. Her Indian drum resided in front, ready to serve a mistress that was sentimental over a child's toy. (Did it remind her of the poor bargain she'd made that deprived her of both a proper marriage and children?)

A large hooked oval rug of rose and wine flowers stretched in front of the bed. A wine velvet cushion covered a Shaker rocker and wine velvet padded cast iron footstool sat in front of an opposing window seat. Swags of loosely overlapped crochet edged netting, held by braided velvet cords filled with large satin rosettes, hung in cascades around the cross ventilating windows. He recognized the long winter's labor that had gone into them. The overall effect was that of pleasing cottage opulence. Tim's comment, about her "liking nice things," rolled into recall.

Joe leaned two hands over the doorway's plain molding. He made no effort to make it easy for her to squeeze past after finishing with the bedding. Instead he took a similar pose in the imported English closet's doorway. A strong "whoosh," when she pulled the chain attached to the high wooden box, dispensed with the pail of scrub water. Obviously, the new windmill operated well.

He had offered no assistance and made no comment. She washed her hands slowly, furtively gazing at his somber reflection in the black wooden "book" hinged triple round shaving mirror that hung from a brass cup hook. Also original to the house was the copper tub with its new cherry surround and replaced plumbing. The revamped chair commode whose tin base connected to the long pipe and wooden box was the first thing she'd made operational. Thank heavens for Paul's local contacts. How amazing to find a driver that knew everyone where she wanted to vacation. (And perhaps where she'd eventually stay through her old age.)

Not a word passed as she applied rose scented lotion from a white bottle on the pierced wood shelf above the new porcelain sink. Why couldn't he have stayed away just a few more days? (By then more improvements would have been delivered.) She put the hand lotion back and replaced the huge cushion diamond on her ring finger from the safety of a small flower covered porcelain dish. The light custard walls were an attempt to dignify the ancient cherry wainscoting. Paul's efforts to restore its luster managed at least partially successful. Why was Joe here? Was Paul the informant? But why would Paul no longer be her ally, surely he wouldn't?

Again Joe forced them to touch as she passed. To be visibly shaken, as much by his physical contact as the emotion charged atmosphere, she clutched the sink edge at the end of the galley's tiny kitchen. Safe behind the latticed small doors, at least for a moment, she deliberately calmed enough to hammer off chunks from the ice block, took a slow sip of lemonade and slowly replaced the heavy wooden cover of the tin lined box that drained drip by drip into her consequently often rusted cast iron sink. She must prepare herself for much more than the normal "Wright look" of disapproval. Sam's remembered warning haunted. Controlling her expression finally into a normal placid façade, she returned to the entry area. "Want another?" She indicated his empty glass resting on the table.

"Yes," he nodded evenly, "thank you."

She filled a monogrammed crystal goblet Aunt Bernice had insisted was a sad reminder of being married to a Wright but was "too nice to throw out." The narrow shelves behind her shone with lovely china and silver that had accompanied the crystal goblets. Returning she suggested, "Want to sit outside? There's usually a lovely breeze." His nod preceeded her quick exit.

Intricate carved wood surrounded a lone love seat with button tufted upright round cushioned arms and similar padded bench. Offering the only seating available, there was no need to make decisions about sitting together or not. Joe and Claudia's other aunt had surprised her only this morning with its delivery. Her note had merely read:

> A small thank-you for bringing "The Light" to these old dull eyes.
> May God bless you!
> Love and affection, Aunt Doris

The carved bench was too nice to stay outside, especially in the salt air, but she had fortunately postponed deciding where to place it. (She intended to use her drum for outdoor seating until she acquired some affordable Shaker rockers. She'd thought she might encounter a rare visitor, possibly the aunts or Claudia, but never had she anticipated or guessed the first one would be Joe!)

Bethany was so glad she had acted on impulse after Claudia had poured out her distress over her mother's alienation toward the aunts. "Even if they're not related by blood, they're the only living relatives we have!" the poor girl had wailed.

Although they were almost the same age, she couldn't somehow help thinking of Claudia as a child. "You should feel free to have your own opinion," she had encouraged the lonely distraught girl on frequent occasions. And their visits had been more marvelous than either could have dreamed. Both aunts had long ago been ostracized, mostly due to the influence of Claudia's mother and grandfather, by their social peers. But more exactly they were guilt ridden by having made their own lives miserable by immoral actions in their younger years. Each visit produced a sharing of faith that made them more and more open to the Gospel.

She'd commiserated with the aunts over how ostracized she had felt on the trip west, and they had shared their pain and sorrows that had embittered them toward the Wrights. Claudia had opened up by releasing some of her emotional scars and sorrows. As she further related how her mother made life miserable for Bethany, the aunts rallied to her defense and became her devout stout champions and generous benefactors.

Now Claudia had opened into a delicate rosebud herself, accepting the Lord and repenting along with the second aunt. Bethany slightly wished she could have opened to someone how ostracized she felt toward Joe. However, Claudia need not think less of a brother she obviously adored. Any considered plight was of Bethany's own making. (Nor would she ever complain about what she had allowed—and gone into with full knowledge. Pining for what might have been was only an exercise in frustration. In addition, she would not pretend they would ever have more than a verbal promise to be peaceful co-conspirators. Yes, that was the exact phrase for it. Were Joe not the rightful heir, and he likely could have legally challenged his grandfather's will anyways, she might have felt more like a criminal than his assistant. Nevertheless, she would be glad when she had only herself to consider.)

He was more than kind and generous to her. How many poverty-stricken desperate women would gladly trade places? Never had she resented him personally, just the loneliness in the huge ostentatious house. But, in Oregon, she'd faced more than just loneliness. Except for the geography advantage, she must do for herself as always. In retrospect, why had she ever thought a man like Joe would desire a woman's friendship? It bordered on the ridiculous. Silly schoolgirl stuff, she chastised herself. She was productive again and had the support of wonderful Christian women friends. She would not dwell on any thoughts other than making her future more comfortable.

Even the aunts' husbands were now receptive and 'not far from the kingdom.' Now that this place was nearly 'shipshape,' and would be more so by the end of the week, she must take Claudia to visit again (presuming the girl would be allowed to associate with her still?) It was not idle neglect, but rather giving needed space for Claudia to overcome being so timid. Nor did she enjoy being Claudia's only excuse to "get away from Mother." That only threw Bethany and Mother Wright at loggerheads more than ever. Besides, when Bethany was away, Claudia devoured huge passages of God's Word and would near radiate her rapid spiritual growth. Sometimes it rankled that the girl didn't stiffen her backbone enough to speak her mind. Especially she'd get so much more out of the smaller church, but Bethany hadn't the heart to press it.

"Comfortable looking place," Joe broke the silence with casual social observation.

"I like it," Bethany admitted. After another lengthy silence she wondered aloud, "Suppose Paul would like another glass of lemonade?"

"Paul can fry!" He glared immediate stiffened profile.

"Joe!" she exclaimed at his uncharacteristic vehemence. "What a horrid thing to say!"

He surveyed her righteous indignation with amazement. "But I suppose it's fine for him to scheme against his employer?"

His hardened eyes brought a tight lump to her throat. Her hands slid back to back between her knees for support. "He has not schemed against you or anyone else. He knows your mother is upset with me. He's merely protecting your interests, trying to preserve what little calm your household can maintain."

"So, maybe instead, we should be discussing *your* disloyalty?" he suggested.

"What disloyalty?" She feigned more disdain than she knew he deserved.

"Oh, how about buying this place as Mrs. *Jacob Clark, widow?!*"

So he knew that too? But how could he? Oh, yes, the detective, a better sleuth than anticipated. Well, good enough, she'd had enough of pretense for a lifetime. Softly she questioned, "*Is that such a deception, Joe? Or, do I not deceive more as Mrs. Joseph Wright III?*"

"Touché," he acknowledged, "but, is bearing my name such an awful high price to pay?"

"You mean, in light of payments received?" She acknowledged his lavish habit of throwing enormous sums of money at her almost every time they met.

Averting his eyes, knowing he had pushed her beyond that fine edge, he tried to soften the accusation. "I'm sorry, Beth, I'm sure there was a more tactful way to express my exasperation. As usual, my lack of social graces makes *me* the scapegoat!"

"I have not betrayed you, Joe, and no one is at fault." Although her back was as stiff as a board, she added, "I simply am carrying out my original plan, plainly stated, to be self-sufficient."

"So I'm not providing well enough for that?" His tense jaw tightened his mouth into a thin line. He had provided the same allowance for Bethany alone that had kept both his spendthrift mother and Claudia quite happy. He considered the deception a breach of proper gratitude, if nothing else.

Bethany thought instead of how overwhelmed she was with his annoying fits of temper. Didn't *the peace that passes all understanding* matter to him? It was becoming a daily chore to be light hearted in his presence; her nerves couldn't stand much more? If it has to end sometime, why not stop now and by her decision (versus his?) "I don't need another dime, Joe. In addition, I also relinquish you from your promise to give me a third of your inheritance. I've been more than well paid for services rendered, which I consider as practically nothing but showing up at social functions."

She calmed herself before continuing in the face of his darkening countenance. "Lest you suppose I am making some enormous sacrifice, let me inform you that Jacob's parents died within a month of Jacob—cholera, I'm told. They died so fast, they had no time to put their affairs in order and an old will left everything to their son. I thus became their heiress, albeit by default. Sam learned of the search for an heir, applied on my behalf, and the inheritance became mine as their legal daughter-in-law. I never expected this, but there was no one else to accept it except distant cousins in Europe. The house has already sold and, when the shop sells, I shall be more than adequately wealthy. Beyond that, I still have some funds from Oregon. I intend to live here modestly, with no desire to attract attention, so I shall have more than sufficient for my small personal needs."

He blazed back, "What you mean is, Jacob provides for you, Sam comes to your rescue and you don't need me any more, that it?"

"No, Joe, that isn't it at all." She denied his rage as well as the presumed accusation. "Really it's more *you* don't need *me* any more. *If* you have some important social engagement that really requires my presence, I shall be glad to oblige with sufficient notification. But you don't enjoy balls and outings any more than I do, so why don't we both stop pretending any desire to attend? Certainly no one is going to miss me. Or, your mother would be even more delighted if you took Claudia instead; she does require a certain amount of social interaction with young men. And your female admirers would adore having you all to themselves. And, especially, your mother will be relieved and stop chaffing over my threatening her rule over the Wright domain? But, if you must have my presence, I insist your mother not interfere with what I wear. Also, if I must attend a ball, I refuse to be preyed upon by the landed gentry. I will stand patiently by your side while you conduct business, or go to the ladies parlor. But, I simply refuse to dance or be left with anyone else. I'll be as agreeable as possible otherwise, but I insist on at least that much consideration."

He nodded, but a lump in his throat prevented any audible answer. Obviously her discomfort had far exceeded his suspicions.

"However," she continued, "it's apparent you *do* enjoy your business interests, so why break it up and encumber your mother and sister? They enjoy having you take care of them; and you never know what the future may hold for either, although for now you should make a will leaving it all to Claudia. She would need help, but I'm sure you know that. I think keeping everything together may be your best route. I'm merely relieving you of a promise you made under duress. Had you not been in such a bind to find someone willing to legally accept the role of a wife, we'd never have entertained this farce in the first place. I'm letting you off the hook, Joe; you're a free man."

Aghast to realize she felt an imposition in his life instead of the key to his success, he sat stunned speechless. Further horrifying was thinking that Sam had been working on the Clark estate even when he'd poured out his heart to him and Heidi. Betrayal was all around it seemed; had he no right to expect more of his sister, friends or servants? Familiarity with attorney confidentiality did nothing to dissuade experienced abandonment. Rejection and loneliness forced fresh anger into the salty air (despite months ago promising to bury his quick temper within God's sanctifying forgiveness.)

"I could take you to court and confiscate everything you own. A married woman has *no* property rights!" *Oh, that's great*, he fumed over his lashing out at her; *that ought to set things straight.*

"Yes, I know. That's exactly why I legally registered as a widow. But you'd do well to remember this, Joe. You have more to lose in a legal battle than I do. If push comes to shove, *I'd* win, not you. That is, unless you're willing to lie in court under oath. I don't think you'd want to besmirch your Christianity *that* much, right?"

He stared at the insolent carefree waves, knowing he'd been less honest every day since he'd married her, but shook his head in a negative response.

"Thus, you can't afford a lawsuit. And I *did* purchase this as Jacob's widow for more than just legality. Because, I truly feel *Jacob* did give this to me, and he would be thrilled to know he'd provided for me despite his vitriolic parents verbally disowning responsibility for us both."

He sadly acknowledged she had the upper hand totally. Even he knew better than to attempt a hostile takeover in the face of ironclad constraints and the risk of greater financial loss than what could be gained. Unfortunately he'd miss just seeing her, more than all the real estate or profit in the world. A spider could not have spun a more complex web. "So," he let out his held breath, admitted defeat and held out a flag of truce, "do you revert completely to Bethany Clark?"

"No, I never did. The locals know me by 'Wright,' I merely used Clark when signing for the property at the county court house. I'll maintain your name and wear your ring. When anyone asks, I always say you travel a lot. Surely that will be increasingly accurate; you've been doing it more already, now that you've fulfilled your six months in Baltimore requirement."

"Suppose folks will marvel how a mature widow could be so foolish as to marry a man who materializes every other Christmas, if that?"

Resolutely she replied, "What others think will hardly constrain how I run my life."

"And," he conceded, "what will that be like now?"

"Oh, quite a quiet life: church, sewing, crocheting, sell a few horses at the port auction, read, write…and repent at my leisure of all my many sins."

"Like marrying me?" he stated it as a fact, his elbows on his knees, head bowed, and hands clasped.

"Joe, I'm more than relieved not to be physically battling the Oregon wilderness. And, the conflicts we hear about now confirm my wisdom in leaving. There were more *real* dangers than imagined. Mistakes I've made in marriage, whether to Jacob or you, are due only to my own personality flaws. They bear no reflection on you. My fears and insecurities have always forced me to flee to safety. Or, if you prefer, they stir my resourcefulness to take advantage of opportunities. I thank Sam, of course, and am grateful for the unexpected largess from Jacob's family, but I also thank you, profusely. I lay no blame at anyone's doorstep but my own."

Since last spring he'd desired something entirely different. If she was going to be kind, it was entirely too painful in light of how badly he had torched his recent iron clad determination to be calm, gentle, and understanding. Not knowing how to respond, he asked, "Where's Seth?"

"I left him home. He'll meet me on Saturday."

"Why?" he dreaded to ask.

"I wasn't planning to return until then. John offered to bring me over on his boat so Seth delivered me and my belongings down to the dock. John takes seafood to Baltimore twice a week. And, I really need some separate quarters before I'd feel comfortable housing a hired man. We usually come by boat and I have Paul go shopping for me or help fix things to fill in his time. He luckily has parents who live near here; otherwise housing him would have presented quite a problem too. Actually, it's worked out very nicely for us both."

To fill in the ensuing silence he asked, "How is it John and you became acquainted?"

"His grandson lives one cove over and looks out for my horses, clears land when his grandfather can spare him—or the sea's too rough. John sells seafood to the shore folks off his boat. I ordered some fish, and one conversation led to another, and I hired Henry to look after my animals." A small sailboat drifted nearer. As it passed, two of its occupants started to wave. "Wave back," she prompted while doing the same, "it's a local boating custom. They all like to think the shore folks are one big happy family."

Joe flicked a small gesture but didn't smile nor want to consider his wife being part of anyone else's family but his own. Near pea green with envy and half livid with jealousy, he chaffed at the thought that he and the Wright fortune could lose her to a small seaside cottage. With the exception of a few new things, the house wasn't even finished, and the downstairs was only half a house.

When he thought of the mansion she'd give up for it, the house his own mother had endured repeated verbal abuse in order to attain its grandeur, he remembered his own recent comparisons. He would have traded his grandfather's mansion in a minute for Charlie's sturdy plantation house and cotton fields. And, he'd trade a dozen businesses for Charlie's simple sugar cane chores too. He therefore couldn't too readily fault her choice. Even an unfinished home was better than living with snitches and inspectors in a cold museum, regardless of grandeur.

CHAPTER 16:
Olive Branch Picnic

"What's wrapped in the newspaper?" she inquired pleasantly.

"A gift from Captain Jules," he regretted to admit. "From what I could peek, it's quite spectacular. You really ought to open it."

When they approached the French doors, she propped a small tree limb between the door bottom and an old indentation in the terrace's mortar. Then she opened the windows on the ocean side and south end of the living room. He waited patiently for her to get around to opening the gift of which he'd at least been the bearer.

"Oh!" she breathlessly exclaimed. "How beautiful!" Several white and lavender orchids hung from an umbrella type wire support. The simple low pink glazed bowl blended with the room. Captain Jules could not have succeeded much better. Only one showed any sign of brown aging and that was quite slight. Glad to have spared it an unappreciated demise, he regretfully realized he had *never once* thought to bring her flowers, not even on her birthday. "Well, it appears the captain knows how to please a lady. Wish I had the same knack, but I suppose that'd be like trying to change a leopard's spots, right?"

"No." She folded the newspaper and neatly tucked it into a cupboard. She added, "You don't realize how sometimes you are really very sweet and dear. If our lives were planted in the same bowl like these, I might have mentioned your romantic tendencies before."

"Me, romantic?" he sneered. "That's a joke!"

She reseated herself to admire the lovely arrangement. "Remember how I said romance was trying to please someone? You have pleased me well on *many* occasions."

"Must have really impressed you in light of never wanting to see me again!" he quipped.

"Joe, that isn't what I said and you know it!" she emphasized with equal vehemence. "Please, let's not attempt melodrama!" Her heart froze over saying such words to a man who'd been more than kind to her.

"Well, I'm real sorry," he replied with acidic tartness, "but I think it's a little one-sided. I'm not quite so anxious to become a bachelor again. In fact, I don't want to at all."

"You won't." She seemed confused. "I mean, unless you'd want...a divorce?" Her heart constricted as she stood to ask, "Do you?"

"No, I don't," he near shouted, then inquired with gentler consternation, "do you?"

"No," was her only reply, her clutched hands mangling her skirt folds.

He hated himself for asking, "Why not?" (*Fool! Why ask? Keep your mouth shut!*)

"Maybe I'm just hedging for a Saturday night berth," she teased to turn the conversation into a lighter vein. She turned away to marvel again over the radiant tropical gift and the captain's unexpected kindness. *Had God known she'd need reminding of a special friend today?*

He rose to face her. "I don't understand what you're talking about."

"Church, I can't seem to find one I like as well as Dockside Chapel. There is a colored pastor here that's interesting, but since I abhor separation by race, it's hard to make it permanent. Course, I suppose if I did, the church wouldn't be all one race any more. However, I got the impression none were too comfortable with me attending."

In a flash, he realized he knew far too little of her persuasions. "Are we discussing abolitionist leanings?"

"Oh, my, yes! As were my parents, and both sets of grandparents before them I'm afraid!" Solemnly they reseated themselves.

"Then," he offered regretfully, "Mother's plantation slaves must be quite a trial for you. I presume you made quite a stir hereabouts too. Was it a large congregation?" He was having a hard time suppressing a grin.

"Just fifty or so, mostly they're local freed slaves." How she wished the matter approached less controversial.

Did she realize the possible danger? Quietly he asked, "Had any visitors because of it?"

"Just one, well, more a small delegation, a couple of well-bred ladies—moral support, I suppose. They presented their well-intentioned cause quickly enough; there was nothing ominous in it. I doubt you need fear any repercussions, at least if I don't return."

"I can't believe I'm almost laughing," he marveled. "My wife has just told me, first, that she prefers to live alone, and then, that she may have potentially incurred the wrath of some local lynch mob!"

"You're looking at it backwards." She was delighted by his humorous response. "I've just told you I want to stay married and want to attend church from your home in Baltimore." Were he to really know the truth, would he laugh more? Why *did* he mind? Embarrassed male pride? Or, maybe more fear of what important people might think? Although, somehow she didn't believe that quite fit Joe's image.

He crossed his arms. "True. But can you pardon me if I see a saw toothed edge to our blissful separation?"

"Would you *mind* if I showed up on Saturdays?" She asked partly to stay connected with Claudia and partly because she knew his magnetism drew her so much she *wasn't sure she could stay away.*

He wanted her there more than life, but he also wanted to protect her (and himself?) from unpleasantness. "I'd love to see you," he admitted honestly, "but why would you want to face my mother ever again?"

"Maybe Claudia needs me more than I need peace and independence?" she suggested shyly.

"Claudia needs a husband who can fill her life with love and allow her to become a mother herself."

She rejoiced over him thinking like that. "Maybe you should find her a gentle Yankee husband?"

"Maybe, but I was thinking more of a gentle poet, painter or musician—someone with similar interests in life?"

"Yes, although for now, she only wants to go to church with me. But she doesn't have the courage to ask your mother's permission. Before she finds a husband, she needs to find her own strength. When she's at peace with God *and* your mother, then she can manage to handle other battles and goals, also by her own initiative."

"Too right," he agreed, "I've been attending Dockside Chapel myself, going to the early prayer services. Pastor Hughes is very special, but God has the real answers for us, if we allow the time to search for them."

"Yes." Her heart leaped at the news. Praying for a long time that he would find peace, she hoped his frustrated soul-searching was finally over. "But it also helps to find others of similar persuasion. Perhaps you could take Claudia with you? Mother sleeps too late to miss her at that hour. Sharing church together grants special closeness, don't you think?"

"I'm afraid I've been too distressed over your purchase to think much of anyone else, a bad habit being so self-centered, I'm afraid. I'll speak to her about it; I'm sure I can convince her to go. Especially she'll find the courage if I promise to stand up to Mother when she finds out (as I'm sure she will.) If you don't object, I'd also like to start attending regular worship services there too."

"I'm delighted. But, I'd also like to sit with you? We make a handsome couple, I'm told." She glanced to view his reaction.

"Thank you." His eyes were near mesmerized by her increasingly glowing smile.

Beginning to blush, she asked, "What caused you to first attend?"

"My carriage was roaming through dark streets—afraid poor Seth hasn't had much sleep lately; it's a good thing you gave him some time off—and the prayer service was about the only respectable place open that early in the morning. At the end a few men prayed for me, really loud I thought at the time. But it made me feel better, so I returned. I've been back every time they've had it since. Last week I stayed late, requested the pastor pray for me, us, my marriage. When he asked to direct his prayer in some specific direction, my totally honest reply was, 'Not without making you a felon, Pastor Hughes.' Guess that's the closest I've ever come to confessing *criminal deception*. Might have admitted it fully, but I doubted he'd be 'encouraged in the Lord' by vicarious guilt. My audacious statement made the poor man pray with some real serious vigor!

He stared at the wide cracks in the hardwood floors, years of neglect unalterable despite the shine. With bated breath, he admitted, "I'd like to tell him God answered that prayer."

She stared at the orchids, hardly daring to glimpse a ray of hope. "How would you like God to answer his prayer for your marriage, Joe?"

How he wanted to admit his longing heart, but he had no right. "Guess it's best if I don't say."

"Might be best," this faraway look took over as she caressed an orchid petal, "if you told Paul to go on home?"

Barely able to grasp her meaning, he asked, "Alone?" Could he have continued breathing if he'd received the wrong answer? Her nod was so slight it might have been missed if his watching hadn't been so intent. He pushed the light chair back so quickly he nearly tipped it over. "I'll be right back," he grabbed to steady it.

When he returned, he could hear pots and pans rattling in the galley kitchen. He sat down in a high back Martha Washington chair to drink in the rich salt air and marveled that he dared stay. He closed his eyes to silently petition every guardian angel available to wave a breeze over his fevered brain. It seemed forever before she rejoined him.

"Would you like supper here or a beach picnic?"

"Picnic okay with you?" He feared making the wrong choice.

"Love it," she smiled. "Just inside the barn door—there's a path through the trees," she pointed out the now open upper part of the Dutch door, "you'll find an old blue quilt. If you'd retrieve it in a bit, you can also share lifting the basket."

"Sure." That some dramatic turn of events could occur on this day, of all days, became more joyous by the second. *Was it only...and she'd said...and now...now what?*

"Would another glass of lemonade appeal?" She sat on the edge of the couch as though she'd flee at a moment's notice.

He didn't want her disappearing. "I'll wait for the picnic, thanks."

Tongue-tied and unsure of herself, she didn't know what else to say so conveyed simple information about the house. "Your Aunt Bernice knew the older couple who owned this. She'd spent time here as a girl; their daughter was a neighbor and they often invited her to the shore, along with her parents, during the hot summer heat waves. When I told her what I was looking for, she thought of it immediately, but didn't know if they still had it. I guess it's been neglected for years, only known about by family, friends or locals."

"Wonder why? It seems a perfect vacation place and Rehoboth Beach is a popular enough spot."

"You didn't see it!" Her shaking head suggested a lot of effort had gone into making it this presentable.

He wished he'd thought to buy her a fancy beachfront home but asked, "How rough was it?"

"Oh, to start with, the lane was nonexistent. To find the house we had to come in by a neighbor's path and walk down the beach. If Aunt Bernice hadn't known the neighbors, I'd never have found it. There were tiny, tiny windows, missing slate so lots of water damage, especially ocean side. Missing foundation stones let in assorted spiders, mice and rats. Mold covered over almost every doorframe and window; the upstairs was a shredded maze of old blankets. Actually they may have helped soak up some of the water; the damage was less than it might have been otherwise. At least, that's John's explanation."

"And you accomplished all this from early March to August?"

She nodded. "If I'd believed your mother would have accepted my project, I might have explained myself. But, solitude was more assured than any reluctant acceptance. Rude therapy, I suppose. I'm so very sorry that you've borne the brunt of her suspicions concerning my disappearances."

"And totally inconsiderate rug hooking!" His sad disbelief, so full of regret that he'd not protected her more, reinforced renewed determination to honor her gentle pursuits.

"Umm, that," she tried to look guilty, "and requiring the detective too; I'm sorry I've been such a controversial wife, Joe. Seems strange, do you know Sam hired a detective too? Is that another thing the very wealthy do to fill up their idle leisure hours?"

"Don't be sorry, Beth, please; I apologize instead. I should have bought my own place. My mother was never easy to get along with. I could blame myself for being engrossed in my grandfather's estate, but that wouldn't actually be the truth of it. I…I just didn't know what to say to you any more. Thought others around might make it…less awkward…and, that Claudia needed a friend. But I should have known better, pacifying Mother is like trying to mix oil and water."

He got absolutely no response. The silence stretched and stretched and she just stared into space. Finally he could stand the quiet no longer and rose asking, "Mind if I take a look at your horses? Looked like some fine animals." She blinked and nodded but still seemed like she was hundreds of miles away. "I'll bring the blanket back," he added on his way out, wondering if he'd blown this chance to made amends. She at least nodded, but not by much.

The barn loft was full of hay, must have bought it as he didn't think the newly cleared acreage spared much feed. A ladies saddle indicated she must ride at least one of the horses. Was that how she got to the train? Again his lack of sensitivity smote his heart. He hadn't even thought to ask her to go riding despite the fact he knew she did (she'd done so on the way west, hadn't she?) Regret built up like a lumber mill produces sawdust. He left his gray frock coat on the blanket and headed up the road. The acreage across was even more overgrown along the road, but showed significant evidence of clearing within. A few large trees remained in the opened areas. Would she harvest them later? He was sure she had plans, but could he wedge himself somewhere in between? And, what had maliciously taken over his mind for months now haunted his observations. In the distance he heard a train moving through the countryside. If the acreage was near the tracks, the potential could prove advantageous to a horse farm?

He rehearsed again his repentance; he was his own worst enemy. His grandfather hadn't been the problem, he was! Instead of showing his mettle, he'd run away like a kid. In creating his own identity, he'd hauled along bitterness. Both lives were the same because *he*, in trying to wash his past away, had nearly drowned in his own misconceptions. Making Beth his wife constituted one of the few things he hoped not to regret, but he couldn't even take credit for that. She was likely the only woman he'd have ever trusted enough to expose his vulnerability.

Lord, grant me wisdom, let me say something right for a change. If nothing else, give me the courage to blurt out my true feelings. Even if she rejects me, at least she'll know. She's kind, deserves children, and is the sweetest part of my life. Only You know how much I need her strength and firm faith. I even thank you for my grandfather's will. If it hadn't been for that, I'd still be floundering so far from Your perfect will. I'd never have confessed all this without her. Please, help me "plant" myself in her life, with the same goals, the same faith, to hold and raise the same children in Christian faith! With other ladies babes I see how her eyes fill up; I know she longs for one to fill her own arms. Let me be a whole man in Christ for her, with no anger, no deceit!

There was no "amen," but rather a continuing sense of need. By the time he'd returned, it was past seven. From the galley a mistress of the house voice announced, "Socks and shoes in the first cupboard."

He hung up his gray coat, added his vest, removed his tie and sat down to happily comply with the bare feet picnic rule. A few quick movements rolled up his dress pants and they were soon situated just above the high tide line. After fancy china, crystal goblets, and "W" monogrammed silver were assembled, she bowed her head for his normal saying of grace.

Lord, thank you for this time together. Let us rejoice in you and each other. Bless our time, the food and the loving hands that prepared it. Amen.

Soon he asked, cradling a stuffed potato shell in a linen napkin, "What's in this?"

She replied readily, "I call it three cheese potato salad."

"My compliments to the goats!" he enthusiastically enjoyed another fork full.

Her softly returned, "Thank you," cast him a shy glance.

"The stuffed fish is good too; what kind is it?" he complimented her further, sensing it pleased her.

She looked confused and floundered for remembrance; then answered with considerable aplomb. "John's fish."

He swallowed a relished mouthful of flaky mystery fish. "Goes well with the cucumber, watercress, and…" He held up a green filled fork.

She laughed, "I haven't got a clue what to call that!"

Both shared the humor. The meal simply reflected what was in the small kitchen and her skimpy new garden. Had she known, she might have stocked up with more groceries; still, the day had turned out better than she'd ever have envisioned. In fact, was this the most optimistic day of her life? Maybe! And Joe was absolutely magnificent with his hearty laugh! How she wished she had a portrait of him like this, his torso in profile against the sand, sea and sky. It was like remembering him on board ship. He had been so kind and tender when she'd been so seasick. Could she ever manage to think of him as just a distant friend? And what if she couldn't?

Instead, she chose to apologize for the lack of a topping on the plain raspberry cobbler that concluded their meal. "Harold's mother knows I need milk, butter and cream, but it won't come until tomorrow."

He squinted dejectedly into the sea's pulse throbbing waves. "I'm just glad to be invited, Beth."

She quietly ate her dessert, not knowing how to respond or comfort him. He was just as uncomfortable and they soon stacked dishes and such back into the basket. She rose to add hers and he rolled the blanket up under his arm before grabbing the basket as well. "Could we walk?" he added in near panic. When she nodded, he happily informed from a running start, "I'll put this away first and be right back."

When he returned they either watched the sandpipers and gulls or mimicked them intermittently by escaping or wading into the receding gentle waves. She pointed out her boundary as they passed and continued on until threat of sundown made them start heading back. Regaining the terrace they'd viewed the sunset's inland horizon. Now the ocean surface viewed ablaze with promise of a lovely day tomorrow.

As she washed up the kitchen, he picked up a Bible from the far chair to later read a chapter from Psalms that echoed shared praise. Devotions were always a safe shared event? She then closed and locked the doors, both washed up and when she rejoined him, she wore a delicate white mull dressing gown with lacy flounces and a tie waist. He turned his seat away from the orchids to stare at the basking waves. Would she now pronounce that there was a bed for him in the loft? Or worse, say there was none, but he was welcome to the window seat, couch or the barn?

Taking the end large chair, she perched her chin on top of intertwined fingers leaning into the upholstery. "Tomorrow might be the best day of the whole summer," she declared of the blazing sunset's diminishing glow.

"Not if you leave me," Joe pled unable to hide the wistful longing, no room or time left for foolish pride.

Glancing upward, her thick lashes fanned against eyelids. She inquired softly, "What *are* your hopes for tomorrow, Joe?"

Not yet daring to spill his guts entirely, he admitted only, "I hope at least to get better at holding my tongue. I've no plans to deny you your place here, Beth, and I'm sorry if I troubled you. And, I'm miserable I lashed out just because you surprised me by getting yourself settled before my year was up. You did well to stay in Baltimore as long as you did."

"What are you *already* good at?"

It seemed a strange out of synch question so he hesitated to answer. "Uh, I suppose mostly handling business, buying, selling, making decisions or telling people to take some course of action. Why?" Did her eyes hold a secret longing too?

"Do you suppose emotions are so vastly different?"

"You mean," he measured the possibilities, "assess my emotions, make a decision, then plan actions that will bring about what I really want to happen?"

She nodded...afraid she might shed tears otherwise.

Okay, he already knew the too real risk of losing her and acknowledged little room to negotiate. She didn't need him to take care of her. But, he wanted to be her husband (and to forget any resemblance to a tyrant tycoon!) Decision made? Well, him staying alone here with her felt right. It offered the best opportunity to become her husband, away from family. If this wasn't the right time, he wouldn't give up though. In the meantime, find a reason to hope.

Guilt forced the issue too. God's displeasure with deception needed to be appeased as much as his personal heartache. To be right with God he'd also refuse to deceive Bethany any longer. But it was for much more than honesty and forgiveness that he wanted her.

What action *could* he take? At a minimum, he wanted to touch her, at least…hold her hand? With trepidation, he held out his right palm, watching for response. Bethany readily slipped her slender ring enshrined hand into it. Watching her every nuance, he pressed her other hand to his right cheek. At her encouraging smile, he reached out his left hand to raise her from her chair. Tenderly he then pressed intertwined hands against his held breath chest.

"I love you, Beth." His husky voice released his long guarded secret and resistant paranoia. "I know I have no right to ask, but I want you for my wife, before God, before man, and before my heart breaks with longing 'to have and to hold!' I'm sure there's no way you could have known, but you've become the absolute center of my life! If you'll let me, I'll stay here in Jacob's house and fill both these lofts," he tossed damp curls upward, "with your beautiful children!"

She shook her head to ward off his making any commitment he'd regret. "You need not promise children against your will, Joe. I'll always remain your wife."

He shook his head. "You talked of sins and needing forgiveness, well I've had more than almost anyone I can imagine. Even my grandfather was at least consistent, which is more than I can say.

"He wasn't my nemesis; it was my own dumb response. Believe me, I truly now *want* to have children, probably more than you—after all, there's no 'risk of life' involved for me, right? The main reason I've had this change of attitude is because just a short time ago, with pastor's help, I realized nepotism is *my* choice! So, my children—our children—will have to earn their promotions instead of having them handed over to them. If they don't have the talent, then they'll get by the best they can. I don't care if we have a dozen! What I want is Eph. 6:4, to *'bring them up in the nurture and admonition of the Lord.'*"

"Oh, Joe." she hid her bowed head into the open throat of his shirt, her heart too full to properly respond. "How long…have you felt like this?"

"About kids, I'm not too sure. Maybe I was charmed by little Jonathan a couple years ago? Or, it could have been seeing how Sam and Heidi's little Daniel had a little something of both of them? Maybe I'm just so despondent I needed something that was truly mine on which to lavish affection?

Oh, Beth, without you I'll remain *so* desperately lonely; all I've felt otherwise is rejection and estrangement. I can't imagine life without you. You're my only hope for a normal life!"

Her radiant lips whispered, "I love you too."

His head tilted to kiss her expectant lips. *Oh, yes, this had to be living right!*

"Forgive me," she resumed her bowed head, "but I'm having a hard time believing this is really happening."

"I know. Do you realize how long it's been since my heart acknowledged I wanted you? About the time I whisked you away from our uninvited British wedding guests. When I held you in my arms, felt you warm against me, normal desire was almost overwhelming. My head resisted, stupid pride and bitterness got in the way, sure, but the feelings were still there. I've wanted to blurt them out almost every day since!"

"Do you know," she turned her face upward to reveal in turn, "when I knew I loved you?"

He shook his head. "I'd be surprised if you ever did."

"I've loved you ever since you first kissed me, in my one room house in Oregon."

How could he believe that (after all that tension aboard ship?) "Really?" His blue-gray eyes melted and his voice cracked.

"Really." Her dark misty blues sought his.

"Oh, Beth, please forgive me? I've wasted so much time and you've been *so* patient." His anguish enveloped her like he'd never let her go.

She instead kissed his fears away and fulfilled an oft rejected fantasy instead.

"I know my family's been a total trial." He rushed on with his revelations, wanting her to totally know his heart. "If you want to stay here, I will too. We'll never leave this house by the sea until it's so full of children you insist we build a bigger one, boys on one side, girls on the other, and a housekeeper in between, what do you say?"

"Maybe today isn't the time for rash promises?" she cautioned with a chuckle that released both relief and ecstasy.

"Rash, my decision rash, I don't think so!" he proclaimed. "It seems I've been waiting to declare myself to you for simply years!"

"I mean about never leaving here. You *might* want to show off at least the first two or three of your twelve children!" she teased.

Both laughed by turn, but when she pulled away to see his magnificent smile, he'd quickly clasp her back. "Promise me you'll never mention leaving me again?" he held her closer and pleaded for reassurance, his chin weaving into her fat side curls.

"I promise, dear Joe. Oh, how I've longed to call you that!" she exalted.

"Even when I thought, well, oh, Joe, I do love you, as completely as I know how!" Throwing all caution to the wind, she threw her arms tight around his neck and clasped herself to him, believing with all her being that God had created both a soft heart for Him and a gentle husband for her, a gift so great she could barely take it in.

She kissed him and cried; he laughed and whirled her about until he finally collapsed on the sofa. She landed in a heap across his lap in the face of dark blushing waves.

"Know what I've missed?" He nuzzled her exposed neck as he tucked her bare feet up against his thigh.

"No, what?" She snuggled contentedly.

"You at night," he became all serious and sentimental, "looking what I call 'your most beautiful' in your nightgown and little ruffles."

"My cotton nightgown?" she astonished.

"Wasn't anything to do with clothes, gorgeous; rather you looking like this." His arm reached round and began removing hairpins. When he'd finished and run his fingers through thick hair that hung below her waist, he whispered, "This is how I've remembered you a thousand times, that and your skin and breath against my shoulder, like our first night together when you were so sick, remember?"

At her nod, a deep hunger consumed him, his kiss so passionate they could only cling to one another.

"You know, Joe," she slid into his shoulder for breath, "I don't think we should hide away down here forever. It's a lovely romantic thought, darling, and I want us to have lots of time alone together—including a real honeymoon. And I do want us to have all those children, but your family needs love too. I realize now how essentially wrong I was to retire from your world. We really need to show them how God answered Pastor's prayer. How else will they ever know about God's love…if we don't show them?"

He pondered the misery they had both suffered and made no immediate response. "Alright, dear," he finally soothed, "is that what I'm supposed to say?"

"Well, not exactly like that!" she flustered prettily.

He smiled a contented sigh, reassured he could not lose her over words ever again, that their "roots" were intertwining even as they held each other. The white bedroom's faint candlelight beckoning, he embraced her against his chest, wishing he could hold her and never let her go. "All our tomorrows, sweet Beth," he whispered, "will be lovely with God's help, and we'll promise to meet them one day at a time. But, for the tonight…and many, many days to come, you will be mine and mine alone!"

Bethany slipped off to urge him upward. As they renewed their embrace she stood long moments just holding him. "I shall be yours long after you've a harder time keeping your mind on business, and have more little reasons to come home," she vowed with a twinkle of mischief.

"Promise?" He kissed her eyes first, then hairline at the temple.

Her body thrilled responding, "I promise with all my heart, Joe. Besides, if you'll recall, we have a greater than normal responsibility; after all," she snuggled and offered a low laugh of contentment, "we just might be the most married couple on earth!"

"One lifetime might be far too short to fulfill our vows three times over," he caught on. "But I promise we'll give it our best efforts." It suddenly occurred. "I don't even have a change of clothes. But, no matter, because you're right, tomorrow's going to be a really wonderful, beautiful day!"

He scooped to carry her to *their* "love nest" and again kissed enticing lips. Every tomorrow promised a life of God's blessings, their lives radiating pure hearts and a promise as beautiful as the love shining from the eyes and smile of his enchanting bride!